D0670167

Arlette

Books by
NICOLAS FREELING

Fiction

Love in Amsterdam
Because of the Cats
A Question of Loyalty
Valparaiso
Double Barrel
Criminal Conversation
The King of the Rainy Country
The Dresden Green
Strike Out Where Not Applicable
This Is the Castle
Tsing-Boum
The Lovely Ladies
Auprès de ma Blonde
Dressing of Diamond
What Are the Bugles Blowing For?
Sabine
Gadget
The Night Lords
The Widow
Castang's City
One Damn Thing After Another

Non-Fiction

Kitchen Book
Cook Book

Arlette

Nicolas Freeling

PANTHEON BOOKS, NEW YORK

 Published in the United States by Pantheon Books, a division of Random House, Inc., New York. Originally published in Great Britain by Willmer Brothers Limited.

Grateful acknowledgment is made to the following for permission to reprint previously published material:

The National Trust of Great Britain: Excerpt from Rudyard Kipling's *The Harp Song of the Dane Women*, published by A.P. Watt Ltd.

Library of Congress Cataloging in Publication Data

Freeling, Nicolas.
Arlette.

I. Title.
PR6056.R4A88 1981 823'.914 80-8653
ISBN 0-394-51454-8

Manufactured in the United States of America
FIRST AMERICAN EDITION

1. A Man from Somewhere

Arlette van der Valk was having lunch with a commissaire of police. He addressed her as Madame Davidson, which was the name of her second husband. That is my real name? – she asked herself. Should I say my correct name?

Her first husband had been dead for nine years. And it will soon be ten, she thought, with a small sharp pinch at the heart. She kept his name for professional use: it was what she had printed on business cards. He, too, had been a commissaire of police. Cosy; keeping things in the family, as it were.

Arlette van der Valk, counsellor in personal problems. It was easier to define what she didn't do than what she did. Not legal, financial, or medical problems. And certainly not police problems. Whatever she was, it was not a Private Eye. The Commissaire – there are several in a town of the size and importance of Strasbourg, the capital of a region – was there to ensure that Arlette did not make police business her own. However, there are a lot of things ill-defined by the Penal Code which for excellent reasons do not interest the police. To give her an unofficial and largely spurious standing, she had a card stating that her activities were known to and had the approval of the undersigned Officer of Judicial Police. From the same authority she had a licence to possess a pistol, which she was supposed to carry, but very seldom did, when mixing with dubious company.

All of this was the fruit of a conspiracy fomented by her husband; one Arthur Davidson, sociologist by profession, one of the numerous resident experts revolving in the orbit of the Council of Europe, which has its home in Strasbourg. He disliked the term criminology. Society, exactly like the human body, has its pathological aspect.

These lunches were becoming a ritual: this was the second such. At six-monthly intervals, more or less, the Commissaire, who maintained a bland official disregard of her existence, would invite her out for small-talk about rain and fine weather; in reality, a shrewd little cross-examination into her state of mind. It was the end of August and the town was empty – full that is to say of tourists. Pretext for a phonecall, saying it was a relatively quiet moment for himself also and would lunch be nice? He would have seen that her little advertisement, which she placed three times a week in the local press, announced that she proposed being away on holiday for the coming month.

He was an urbane person with formal manners, who took her to an expensive restaurant with large tables, and space between them; pink tablecloths, and real flowers in imitation-silver vases. They got an adulterous little alcove, with no neighbours hanging their ear out. The food here was elaborate, occasionally eatable. He gave her a good bottle of wine. Probably they gave him a reduction.

With the second glass a slight vivacity crept into the polite kindliness of his questions about her affairs.

"One chooses between idealism, at the peril of sentimentalizing, and a realism that too frequently becomes a mask for cynicism." Very true.

"Well, you've had a year. Only experience can teach you the course to steer, and it is hard-bought."

"Yes, indeed. A woman the other day . . . I'd have been ready to put my hand in the fire for her; I swallowed her whole. Turned out to be a pathological liar, and alcoholic into the bargain – no visible sign at all."

"What on?"

"Cinzano." A smile.

"You'd be less shocked, nowadays, by a few of our professional attitudes."

"Less shocked, yes. More understanding – I certainly hope so. It doesn't always have to make me more tolerant, I believe."

"No . . . no." The bit about government service was left unsaid: he twiddled his glass. "This morning – it's an anecdote – a man was brought to my notice. I know him quite well, which is to say a good deal of him, not much about him. Under different circumstances, it could have been your work; to know about him. Not much you could have done about it. The Prosecutor calls him a nasty piece of work."

"And what do you call him?"

"Oh, I don't call him anything at all. He's a professional assassin – no, that sounds dramatic. He's not a public enemy. He's uninteresting, unobtrusive. Small intelligence, no character. A speciality of violence; menaces, blows and wounds. He has killed people. There exist hired hit men. They rarely go as far as assassination. It happens. They're small squalid people. Sly; there's never been sufficient proof, to put him on trial I mean, for anything of that sort." Arlette wondered where he was leading her.

"Murders, and murderers, don't interest me much. There are so many crimes so much worse, and even more frequent."

"Yes, indeed. I agree . . . no, no pudding for me – do any of these delectable things tempt you at all, Madame? Then coffee, please. And a cigar . . . I don't have a lot of interest in him. So that when I saw him, which was more or less accidental, I said, 'My lad, that gun of yours is sticking out; I don't want to see you any more. In fact, France doesn't want to see you any more. In fact, if I hear of you anywhere at all in my territory I'll make difficulties for you.' " He broke off, chose a cigar, handed it to be clipped, and leaned towards the match.

"As with Basque terrorists," said Arlette. "Go away. Pester somebody else. But they come back. You'd fake something against him, if necessary. Possession of drugs, something like that." He smiled at this female naïveté and obstinacy.

"You still find my behaviour outrageous?" Placid, tasting the cigar.

"Of course I do, personally, but I realize that your work has very little to do with justice. Administration is what concerns you. He's a man from nowhere: you send him back to nowhere."

"Not quite nowhere. His name is Henkie and he's from Holland. He's a cook on a river tug, on the Rhine here."

"Aren't you depriving him, then, of an honest livelihood?"

"I dare say I am. But I dare say the Dutch can afford to give him social-security payments and keep him at home."

A headwaiter came sidling up.

"Forgive me, Monsieur le Commissaire – telephone." He frowned at this, drew on his cigar, drank his coffee leisurely.

"Will you excuse me an instant?" When he came back, he sat silent awhile: he accepted a second cup of coffee.

"Would a short drive tempt you at all? If, that is, you are in no great hurry. It is not of any great interest – as you say – and what's more, it's none of your business. But by one of the coincidences that occur in this trade," drawing at the cigar, "– which aren't coincidences – it becomes, in a sense, your business as well as my own. The identical man has just been found drowned."

"Good heavens."

"As you say. It's the concern of the River Police, really. I could send an understrapper, for liaison and information. It occurs to me now to go myself, and to suggest your accompanying me. If you've finished your meal – shall we?"

"I'd be very glad to." Her instinct had been to refuse. But it was a lesson, plainly, he wished her to learn. Furthermore, it was a privilege. The police dislike amateurs anywhere near scenes of crime. Even languid members of the English upper classes. It always did.

She had no curiosity either, morbid or otherwise. But for Arthur's sake – amusement at this Dickensian situation. He would be much entertained. Mr Mortimer Lightwood, he would say. In a silk top hat. The Man from Nowhere – found drowned . . .

Perhaps, too, the Commissaire saw a professional moment too good to pass up. He might think, being Dickensian too, that a dead moist unpleasant body would be just the thing to cure the sentimentalities of bourgeois ladies.

They went in his personal car, a grey Peugeot two-litre with a diesel motor, so anonymous as to be impersonal; virtually a taxi. Clean, tidy and empty: so unlike her own small Lancia full of shoes and lipsticks, the ashtrays always full of revolting debris from Arthur's pipe.

Lauterbourg is a small town on the Rhine, on the north-eastern skirt of Alsace and at the extreme limit of French territory. An unimportant frontier crossing. Various administrations are found there dealing with technical aspects of the important river traffic, and a post of the River Police. This he explained as he drove, which was the way he spoke; quietly, with prudence, and decision.

The Rhine hereabouts is the frontier between France and Germany. Where there is a bridge, at each end will be a customs and police post. Across open water, well now, your line drawn down the middle is a legal fiction. One cannot speak hereabouts of having a foot in France and the other in the Federal Republic of Germany, can one now? Technically thus, the Rhine is considered as international waters. A nice excuse for everyone to have a good conscience about polluting it.

The River Police comprises mostly German river patrols, since below Lauterbourg both banks are theirs. Up as far as the Swiss frontier at Basel the French maintain patrols. The two forces live in an amicable, collegiate spirit of co-operation.

Arlette received an impression that the man from nowhere had shown bad taste in getting himself drowned upstream of Lauterbourg.

"Suppose something happens which concerns the courts – what then?"

"Unless things happen," approaching a crossroads carefully, "more or less flagrantly," shifting gear, "on the French bank it would concern – in principle – the German courts. Things happen in midstream . . . this waterway is a good deal more dangerous, and a great deal trickier, than people give it credit for." He launched into a voluble anecdote, about a barge convoy and a tug – French tug, and French skipper – which ran over an unlucky, but foolish, boy – German boy – acting the goat in a kayak, and what was worse, in the dark. Tug did its best to stop and search: you can't, you know, stop a barge convoy at all easily. Reported the accident to the River Police and continued on his way. Slightly over-zealous patrol commander pegs the skipper for failure to assist persons-in-danger. Criminal offence, as you know, under the code.

Comes up before the tribunal in Mannheim, or somewhere. Skipper pleads with some indignation that his over-riding responsibility was the safety of his convoy and security of river traffic. Court upholds this argument. Police officer reprimanded.

"And was there any sequel?"

"Sequel?" sounding surprised. "Not unless you count that particular cop living in hopes ever since of catching that particular skipper with a sidelight obscured. It's a highly-skilled affair, navigating on the Rhine. Speed limit, too, strictly enforced – too much wash and you damage the banks, moored vessels, all sorts of things. The Royal Navy got pegged for that the other day, engagingly enough."

"What could it possibly be doing – defending us from the Russians?"

"Oh, courtesy visit. Coastal launch – Air-Sea Rescue or something. Lieutenant was cross; got his head washed when he reached home. But it's quite a serious offence, you see. Bit of wash unexpectedly sets a boat rolling, and somebody might fall overboard. Something of the kind has probably happened here."

They entered a dingy building with a dirty flag and a large number of brass nameplates in need of polish: the usual musty smell and great numbers of files gone brown at the edges, peopled by the sort of official who has nothing whatever to do, and looks at you with indignation should you be unlucky enough to need a rubber stamp on a piece of paper. These were all now fussing slightly, for fear of some court that might be called upon to pronounce about civil damages, or whatever.

Arlette was the subject of curious glances and pinched lips, but nothing was said: she was with a commissaire, and that is a personage.

There was no corpse, to her relief, and the police were not perturbed either. There very often was no corpse. Might turn up several days later and a long way downstream – in Germany.

There was, instead, lots of paper. The Police Judiciaire dealt with this deftly, with authority. Tug pulled in to carry out obligations; quite. Cause of death, accident; quite. Place and time; quite. Tug has now proceeded on its way. To be sure: immobilizing a Rhine convoy costs a thousand marks a minute. Crews have no watch on shore: they are replaced, briskly, the moment their shift ends. A reserve crewman would be driven out and picked up on the hop at Mainz.

Good, let's have these declarations by the crew members. There are four, since a river tug carries five. There were three, since the engineer was below and witnessed nothing. Skipper, helmsman, deckhand.

Cookie came up to empty a bucket of potato-peel. Slight drizzle at the time: the deckplates would be greasy. Visibility was reduced. It is a busy stretch, traffic was heavy, there are a lot of building works, dredging and general frigging about. Everyone had their eyes skinned, but frankly, with more to do than stare at the cookie. There was no untoward movement or disturbance of the boat. The man had been his normal self. He was certainly not drunk, and nowise appearing perturbed or depressed. A quiet personality: a competent and experienced crewman. Suffered, as far as was known (can be verified from company medical records), from no illness or incapacitating condition.

Conclusion by skipper, a highly responsible person, whose declaration no one would query: negligence. Carrying out a routine chore, performed thousands of times – a momentary carelessness. No cry had been heard. It might be possible to stun oneself in falling.

Certificate produced for recent routine technical inspection of boat. Nothing defective in guard-rails or safety mechanisms.

Right, let's have the personal papers and belongings. Dutch citizen; Dutch company – Rijnscheepsvaart-something-unpronounceable to a French mouth. Clothing, and a few oddments. Like a book of crossword puzzles, and a few pornographic magazines. Nothing untoward.

Very well. A death in unexplained circumstances is reported to the PJ – routine. If violence is involved – say, an altercation – equally routine report is made to the Procureur, who can if he sees fit launch a judicial enquiry, an 'instruction'. In conditions that are obscure, the matter comes under the discretion of an officer of judicial police. Every country gendarme is ex-officio a PJ officer. The deceased was known, as the saying goes, to the criminal brigade, and the Commissaire had come to see for himself. But there's nothing here outside the usual administrative enquiry. We'll just countersign these. Copies of your reports to the German and Dutch consular authorities. In the – unlikely – event of any backlash from the Federal Republic or the Kingdom of the Netherlands, advise and inform. There we are then: I'll drive you home, Madame, shall I?

"No comment or criticism?" he asked mildly after five minutes' silence.

"The glance at his belongings – might that have been a bit superficial?"

"I knew him you see. Careful chap. Kept things in his head. Self-censorship you might call it."

"Then with his head gone – the man from nowhere goes somewhere. But wherever; it's out of sight."

"And out of my jurisdiction. The enquiry will leave it open. Suicide or accident – they say accident, for the sake of the next of kin."

"If there are any."

"If, as you say, there are any. Rotterdam will know. And take charge of his possessions. Either he had his gun on him, or the skipper, sensibly, suppressed it."

"You don't want any loose ends."

"It's the trouble with your type of interest; there are always too many loose ends, first, last and foremost. To me, there's a body. When the Germans find it, they have a disposal problem. You find me, I dare say, infernally callous."

"Only," said Arlette, "if you had him pushed."

"There's that," smiling very slightly. "No, chère Madame, reassure yourself. I think, if you wish me to indulge in a thoroughly uncharacteristic indiscretion, that it's not totally to be ruled out that someone jiggled him. But of that there's no evidence."

"Nor ever will be. Well, I've had my lesson: I hope I've learned it."

"If there's a lesson. I suppose there might be. That it's ill meddling with the dead, or with the living, come to that. One thinks carefully, before judging."

"I must thank you, too, for a nice lunch."

2. Widow, and widow-maker

Towards the end of the day they turned off the main road, and were rewarded by the sun setting across Quiberon Bay, the inland sea, melancholy and curlew-haunted. They sat on a sand-dune above the tidemark, propped against an overturned pram dinghy, and looked at the golden burning water; whose hydrocarbon content, said Arthur, one would not wish to analyse. Arlette, all van der Valk personages firmly occulted until return to Strasbourg, a thousand kilometres away on the eastern marches of France, wiggled her toes and said nothing.

They had been for nearly a month on the Atlantic coast. September, with hardly any tourists left, around the pleasant town of La Rochelle and the islands. She had got nicely tanned; the fair and the grey in her hair had bleached to something like blonde. Arthur did not tan: went pink and wore strange hats. A restless soul, he had wished to turn north, across the Loire estuary into Brittany. She did not much like Brittany: too sad. We must, he said, because one more oil spill and it won't be there any more, so that this will be the last time. The old peninsula appealed to his Englishness. The opinion of a hard-headed southern woman was that this was a pack of Celtic twilight and that La Baule was the farthest-flung outpost of civilization.

But she was enjoying herself. Seagulls sat upon decrepit wooden posts and looked at her attentively. More seagulls lolled upon the flat water, looking contemptuous. There was no one to be seen anywhere, and a lovely silence. Until Arthur, who never could leave well alone, began declaiming to the seagulls:

"Ah, what is woman that you forsake her,
And the hearth fire, and the home acre,
To go with the old grey widow-maker?"

Arlette, sufficiently accustomed to these performances, was unmoved.

"Very fine; what is it?"

"The Harp Song of the Dane Women, and plainly wasted on you."

"Yes, well, that'll do for now. There are going to be flies, other nasty beasts, living in all that rotting weed." The nip of chill that at the end of the most perfect day tells you it is late in the year, was beginning: she unwound her body.

Women, thought Arthur, can never leave well alone: they aren't content to sit and look, but must Get their Cardigan.

Dear old Arthur, cross now at my being deflating, and at being English! Well, I loathe being French. Nationalism makes me sick. The nineteenth-century Darwinism, making wars and sending children to be killed in them. Indulging, now, in economic bragging and commercial rivalry.

"Don't appreciate much, either, all these references to Old Grey Widows."

"The prettier you become, the more moronically you behave. It's nearly over: we may as well make a move. Once it goes all red I must have cliffs, and lighthouses, and Tristan's ship black with tattered sails, riding in to Penmarch." They were proposing to spend their last week on the Cornouailles coast, around Concarneau. Suddenly supper was uppermost in Arthur's mind, and there was still that nasty autoroute to follow up past Vannes and Auray. "I want shellfish, and to go to bed looking out on the lights of Belle-Isle."

He had eaten enough shellfish already to give even the Great White Shark an allergy. This, he said, was to vaccinate him against a year in Strasbourg, where there is no fish. He could bend her to his will: a woman born in Toulon is not frightened of fishy things even with huge glaring eyes and a great many red spikes.

She'd do anything to forget Strasbourg a while still. And the Widow, and the Help Bureau, that odd sociological invention of Arthur's. Help indeed – there was so little one could give. Blind leading the lame, most of the time.

A year ago now: in October she'd begun, very frightened and knowing nothing. She'd learned something, and a lot about the ways of bureaucracy, a lot about the trouble one runs into the moment one does not fit the conventional and above all passive role exacted by government, whose great slogan is We'll Do the Thinking.

Individualists, the French? Oh yes, in petty selfishness, in refusal of all self-discipline, in hedonistic indulgence. But since the General went, we get nothing to eat but premasticated babypap. Oh, for a fish again, with bones in it, and a flavour.

She had felt so discouraged towards the end of the year, and weary of the heavy heat of Strasbourg in July and August. Arthur liked the long summer vacation. Gave him time to write his latest book. To which, it was true, her year's work contributed a paragraph or so.

As if it were only the job! Getting remarried aged fifty wasn't a smoothly run-in, easy-riding affair either. No problems with children or pills, no material anxieties, worries about the career or the mortgage. That's what they say. Mature understanding, dear. Two balanced and well-integrated personalities.

Arlette snorted suddenly with laughter. Her children all considered her a profoundly perturbed personality, if not actually a mental case, and after ten years of saying Menopause in tolerant tones, had greeted Arthur with enthusiasm: Interesting and Amusing new Therapy. Emotional Basket case Himself – in short, just the job for Mum.

In fact, we are excellently matched. We love each other very much, need one another very badly, and fight all day. The maturity and experience goes up like smoke. I think that Arthur's intellectual grasp of a problem, his academic approach, is bound to be sterile. To him, naturally, my instinctive moves make as much sense as a dog turning round and round before lying down (Arthur's simile . . .).

They'd had a row on the way up, in one of the yacht-harbour villages. The pub where they were staying was buzzing with gossip. Nothing better than a local scandal to promote good fellowship and stimulate another round of drinks. The verb regale, conjugated in English often in the passive – we were regaled with the tale – and transitive, is in French active and intransitive. We regaled: meaning we lapped it up. Given death as well as sex, a good man behind the bar can double his turnover.

The facts that nobody thought to dispute were in essence as follows: a rich man from the city, who had a cottage in the district and a boat in the harbour, came down for a weekend's sailing, with his pretty – and by all account beloved – young wife crewing for him. It had been a bad weekend; lot of wind, nasty sea. Nobody had gone out, but him. Ex-cel-lent seaman; this emphasized by all. Been sailing here since childhood and nobody knew the water better. Boat – very good sea boat, tiptop order, spic-span condition throughout. Designed for these waters and in perfect harmony with them. If there was anything he loved more than that wife, it was that boat.

He'd come back with neither wife nor boat. Given the volume of gossip, the local gendarmerie had made an enquiry. Had to, mate, couldn't get out of it. But it wasn't saying anything to anybody, mate. Not just tight-lipped: they got very, very irritable indeed if the subject was mentioned. Nix prosecutor, nix judge of instruction. No judicial follow-up: hence no crime, huh?

Arthur, who had indulged in white wine somewhat, nudged her with a greasy elbow.

"The widow would be in her element here, haw haw haw."

She felt her eyes injecting with blood: the expression 'to see red'.

"Rebecca?" guffawing odiously on, "– I *hated* Rebecca!" She managed not to speak in front of the assembled company, but stormed out giving the door an unmerciful slam.

The tide was out and she strode angrily along the beach.

And if the man had indeed murdered his wife – then he had also murdered his boat. These legalistic clichés about attenuating circumstances! Didn't it show the pitch to which he had been screwed? In all men, as in all things, there is a breaking point. If the police kept their mouth shut, then in that, at least, they showed wisdom.

This quack about murder – these antique attitudes. As though there weren't a thousand graver crimes. They say murder is grave because irrevocable, because you can't bring life back. Are the crimes not graver when, and because, life goes on? When the consequences continue to ripple stealthily outward, carrying their venom, distorting and destroying for a hundred years. Any crime, my lords, against a child.

We are afraid of murder, but only because we are so terrified of dying. Life is cheap, and replaceable. The building of a family is as slow and dearly bought as the growth of a tree along the shore here, in the teeth of the salt Tartar wind. If that man killed his wife, it was because someone killed his family. She, or another. My lords, many live who deserve death. And many die, who deserve life.

A dolphin had been washed ashore on this beach, alive, but with its sense of orientation destroyed. A veterinary doctor had fought for the animal, in vain, for four hours: the beast had not wanted to live any longer. It had absorbed too much poison. Crude oil, a virtual certainty, said the marine biologists. The ecological balance of a family is as fragile as anything else in nature. A few chemicals, of oil and of concrete, and a kilometre of Breton or Corsican coastline can be destroyed while you watch.

We make a fuss about murder, since the time the first editor noticed that it helped build circulation figures.

This land of Brittany, said Arthur quoting Mary Renault, has a doomed and holy brightness.

Driving now again along the happy, happy autoroute towards supper, Arlette wondered how many of these families had lost a man to the Widow-maker.

Nowadays to be sure we have roads, which kill for preference women and children. Well, well: Sainte Anne d'Auray, pray for those upon the sea, and for us upon the concrete.

"I can't remember," said Arthur beside her, driving, "what that old fool Tristan was supposed to be doing in Ireland."

"Marrying the king's daughter as I recall vaguely. Wasn't there a second Iseult – les Mains Blanches? Sounds a useless cow, that one. It's a great muddle."

"I incline to think he was the one who got muddled – never was quite sure which was which. Which, at least, he found himself in bed with at any given moment."

"Not, I hope, to be thought of as screamingly funny on this account," said Arlette a little cattily.

"Why is it that adultery is screamingly funny in the theatre? Because it is so singularly the opposite outside? For saying that all the world's a stage, that old bastard Shakespeare has much to answer for. The fact is, that the advice Mr Coward gave Mrs Worthington is sounder than he knew."

3. The last day of the holidays

In the last week, there is always an urge to get back and slop about in bedroom slippers, saying loudly 'Comfort again at last'. This fights with the joys of lingering-by-the-wayside. But with Arthur in a car there were rituals to perform, as well as autoroutes to be avoided, and they took the long way round. The Lancia was urged at a gallop out of Brittany, with cries from Arlette of 'Civilization again at last' upon reaching the marches of Normandy.

But one must climb every step of the Mont Saint Michel: one must tread the holy ground (sadly desecrated) of the Grand Hotel at Cabourg: one must climb the hill at Trouville to look at the four views.

"Even if you had a straw hat, even if you had a gardenia in

your buttonhole, by no stretch of the imagination could you be made to look Proustian."

"No," agreed Arthur readily enough. "But I wish to resemble a famous character in fiction: who can it possibly be?" There was silence for some time before Arlette said, "Mr Tod." He meditated vengeance at length before saying, "Of course – Mrs Tabitha Twitchit."

From the Seine to the Somme: Gothic churches, and Flemish town halls, with Arthur lecturing upon the deplorable provincialism of Betjemanesque tastes in architecture.

Even with a small agile Lancia, one cannot hurry the roads of Champagne and Lorraine, and it was early evening before the sudden frenzy to be home overtook them, and they galloped over the bleak grey plateau, welcoming the red cliffs of the Col de Saverne, and the first Alsatian houses.

"First one to see the cathedral spire gets a choc. No," generous " – two chocs." How absurd to be homesick for a city adopted only a few years ago. How pleasant again to be trundling along the Avenue des Vosges, swept by a chilly shower of rain, looking severely out for any architectural monstrosities that might have sprouted in their absence. For supper they picnicked off stale bread and liverwurst, in the stale-smelling dusty livingroom, instead of the fleshpots of the Moselle valley. After a day this long, one goes on driving the damned car in one's head, and goes to bed instead, thankfully early, with an old James Bond book.

Arlette, freed of hotel bolsters, steely cylinders known as the polochon, plunged in voluptuary, got the giggles at the arrival of her consort, wearing buttercup yellow pyjamas, his reading glasses perched upon his eyebrows to find his way.

"What's that you've got?" he asked severely.

"*Hunting Tower* by John Buchan."

"Ho, yes – well, snigger as you may, ye'll no fickle Tammas Yownie."

"And you?"

"By the same unerring instinct, *Greenmantle*. Not another word, please. Lovely, it's only half past eight."

The ghastly realities of next day: filthy flat, dirty washing strewn everywhere, and shopping to do. Arthur stumped off to the post-office where, nothing having been forwarded, all the month's mail had been kept 'en instance'. No Paris paper since they were home a day early and not yet officially 'back': but a huge depressing pile of sordid threats – what would happen if one didn't do something quick about the television tax, the parking fine, the bank overdraft and several repair bills. Strasbourg, lent enchantment by distance, was hideously actual through the computers of all the service companies.

The Administration, refreshed by repose through July and August, was zealous: right-thinking people do not go away in September. The Council of Europe, in a devious way Arthur's employer or, to put things more politely, milch-cow, was changing all its organigrammes.

As Arthur read through all this rubbish, stage one (the lengthening lip) passed quickly to stage two, exasperated muttering. The measured tearing-up of paper into neat small pieces became ripping across and flinging. The mesh of Arthur's sieve was in fact slightly too large. He would curse later, discovering – in a rage – that in rage at a maze of moronic verbiage, one had thrown away quite a lot of recondite information one might later rather want.

Arlette's pile was smaller, but more mysterious. Most of it she couldn't understand at all. What was this extraordinary tangle her Social Security contributions had got into? Who were these acronyms? – as cherished by the French as by Americans. And people bidding her acidly, please, to make it her business to call upon them at her earliest convenience, since her telephone did not answer. Stuff and nonsense; she'd left it on record with a brief and clear message stating when she would be back.

Her sieve was plainly much too fine in mesh. Apart from appeals to subscribe to the *Reader's Digest*, American Express, *Fortune* magazine and the Encyclopaedia Britannica, there seemed to be nothing she could throw away at all.

Like anonymous letters: she got a lot and over a year had learned prudence, keeping them in a special file, even when plainly mad, illiterate and pornographic. This one was not: neat red ballpoint, in the hand-printed style that several educational systems urge upon schoolchildren, sacrificing character to legibility, so that there is not much to tell about the writer.

German, in language and style. Neat layout, proper paragraphing, good spelling. Cheap paper: that meant nothing, any more than the red ink. Approach, formal and quite polite: if she complied with certain demands (unspecified), it would be much to her advantage. This concerned her family affairs, underlined. But if she did not comply, she would regret it, because the Press, both national and international, would be taking a close interest in her affairs.

Family? – those buried roots down in the south? – and how could that possibly interest anyone, let alone Germans? Piet van der Valk, being a police officer, got many anonymous letters, but he had been dead nearly ten years and could perhaps be allowed to rest in peace.

Of the boys, one was in Spain. Got to know any nice Basque terrorists lately? The other in Norway, when last heard of making improbably large quantities of money. Ruth, her adopted daughter, a medical student right here in Strasbourg; an intense and independent girl, who, after being for many years extremely nasty, had become extremely nice. And not at all inclined to get into scrapes – not that this sounded like that sort of scrape.

The boys she saw little of, and they were notoriously bad letter-writers. Ruth she saw a lot of. One thing all three had in common: if they got into a scrape they would handle it themselves – but they would tell her about it before anyone else did. Her confidence in the children was equalled by theirs in herself. Furthermore, they got on effortlessly well with Arthur.

Arthur? – the blackmail flavour to this . . . Arthur did not lend himself to such things. And let nobody think they could drive a wedge between her and Arthur.

Herself? She tried to think of things in recent months involving Germans. There were several: she shrugged.

Arthur was still over there playing the celebrated scene from 'L'Aiglon' – 'Je déchire'; echoed forty years after by Tommy

Handley's wartime postman, who said it didn't matter what you did as long as you Tore-them-Up, and forty years after that more valid than ever.

She didn't tear it up: she put it in the file. One shrugged, but one looked to see whether anything ever came of it.

Down at the bottom there were more Germans. Letterhead, flaring, gigantic, of the *Graphik*: notorious, not to say thumb in your eye scandal-raking weekly. Signed, this one, with a big splashy felt pen. Woman journalist, anxious forsooth to interview her. Since she had such an interesting-sounding job! And, if possible, also her so-distinguished Herr Doktor Husband – Arthur would be thrilled to find himself in *Graphik* amidst the pornographers and politicians . . . Would she call the local office to fix this up? Polite in a vulgar soapy way.

Perish the thought; she was in no particular need of publicity and certainly not that sort. That one, at least, could be torn up.

Last of all, and saddest, was a van der Valk one, made incoherent by misery. Your phone says you'll be back by suchaday, but I don't know whether that's true. I've lost faith in everything and everyone. I'll try this just in case. If I don't hear, there's nothing for it: I'll kill myself.

Postmarked a week back. What could one do about it? There was no hard and fast rule: were the ones who talked about it less inclined to do it? 'I'll kill myself and then it will be your fault' – a kind of emotional blackmail the immature are given to. Arlette hated talk of this sort. Suicide is murder, just as each and every murder is also a suicide: that, if you like, was indeed a firm rule. No phone number: an address, in Neudorf. A week ago . . . she would try to go. But tomorrow: she was still 'on holiday' damn it, and everything was crowding in already. An awful lot to do and she didn't feel like any of it, and especially not cooking.

Arthur, hearing deep sighs being heaved and much refreshed by his trip on the tear, offered most gallantly to make his super-special shepherd's pie. Excellent idea, after all that fish too.

"The really boring shopping I can do this afternoon."

"Good; I'll go to that dust-laden office, dump all this paper there and pretend I've never seen it. Then have a stern word with the Secretary-General, maybe then kiss his bum a bit; he likes to be thought important now and then." Yes, and she'd better try herself to get some wits and courage into her own lead-laden bum, and sort out these idiot bureaucracies. She brought Arthur's typewriter into the livingroom, was drafting a stern dignified protest to Social Security, when the phone rang. Ruth. Oh, hallo darling . . . I just wondered whether-you-were-back . . . Oh, yes, it was lovely . . . Oh, good, I'll come to supper can I, and hear all about it . . . That'll be lovely: oh, and do you know any Germans? . . . Yes, lots, why? . . .Oh, a silly letter sounding blackmaily, that's all . . . Nobody I know then, okay, see you this evening.

She had just refabricated concentration upon 'Dear Sir, I am astonished' – make that disagreeably astonished – 'at the inability of your computer to understand childishly simple instructions' – cut childishly – when the front door bell went.

Before she could peek through the judas, she heard happy yelps and scratchings. The Davidson dog, towing her Spanish cleaning-woman, who had been looking after it.

"Hallo! – qué tal?"

"Qué tal? – I thought you might – "

"Yes, yes, acabamos de llegar. Hallo, darling, stop bounding about then. Sí, sí, cansados, pero contentos. Googoogoo, oh do shut up. Down, I told you."

"I met Doctor Davidson in the supermarket. All right, I guess; my rheumatism's being troublesome – oh, aren't you glad Mother's back."

"Do stop calling me mother. Delighted to see you: we've an awful lot to do. Get away, you wretched beast."

"Give him a paw; then he'll be happy. Oh, I can't stay today – I just brought old Perro, I knew he'd be so thrilled." No way of quarrelling with this, alas.

"Tomorrow then, as usual, and you can hear all the news. Like all holidays, you know, quien más tiene más quiere." Her Spanish was rudimentary, a degree more so than her German.

"Ah yes," solemnly, and much given to sibylline meaningless aphorisms, "decir y hacer no comen a una mesa." Saying and doing don't eat at the same table: self-pitying remark and meant to convey 'I can't afford expensive holidays on the coast'.

"Sure you can't stay?" hopefully. "I'm rather exhausted."

"Ah, yes, one always comes back tired from holidays. Ir por lana y volver trasquilado." No sympathy forthcoming.

"Tras what? Go for wool and come back – ?"

"Shaved – no, cropped."

"Sheared. Yes, quite. Tomorrow then. He's had breakfast, has he?"

She went into the kitchen and wrote down 'Dogfood'. The beast gambolled about. His name was Dog, generally spoken as Hangdog. Sometimes, as now, Maddog, at others Saddog; when he felt amorous, Gaydog. He was supposed to be a Gun Dog, at which he was useless, though he pointed at things. But he was large enough, and made enough noise, to keep people respectful: as Watch Dog he bristled at every step, including Arlette's. He had been Arthur's idea, after a repulsive person had come up the stairs one day, and smeared blood all over their front door. He was, in fact, perfectly gentle and wouldn't hurt a fly. Wouldn't know how. As Talleyrand said of his wife, wins the first prize for imbecility. He was really like Joe Gargery: what larks, eh, old chap?

"What larks we have, Dog, hey?" Arthur came in and dumped numerous things on the table needful to super-shepherds.

"Ah, yes, I met her in the supermarket. Wouldn't work today of course. Caught sight of me and went Yoohoo, hallo, old chap."

"I'll do the strict minimum," said Arlette, making faces at the kitchen floor.

4. Failures

Seven in the morning, drinking a cup of coffee. Obscurely, she felt a little stale, a little sour. Trying to rationalize this, she brought it home to a puritanical worry at a duty not performed: something of which she had said 'I'll think about that tomorrow'. And now it was tomorrow.

A woman had asked for help and she'd done nothing about it. It had sounded so dreary. There was nothing to do, that was sure. Ninety per cent. Well, a strong probability. She realized that a dialogue was taking place between the fiend and her conscience.

Neudorf – that is no distance. You can be there in a few minutes. Very likely the woman works, and will already have left. Nonsense, it's not even seven-thirty and if she has, you can leave a note in her box.

Angry at being so unwilling, she threw on a jacket, took the car keys. The Lancia coughed and hawked, cleared its throat and spat several times in a bronchial, early-morning bad mood.

Strasbourg south of the river is – as in London – at once a drop in social standing, and the suburbs there, despite resolute efforts now and then to be bright and modern, are depressed and down at heel. Neudorf is the nearest, and the oldest, and least-planned; a hundred streets pell-mell in a heap, named with a thumping lack of originality after Alsace villages, so that it is never possible to recall which is which though they have much character, varying from one minute to the next. Some are rambling and villagey, with old cottages and truncated bits of lichened orchard, where peasant obstinacy has held the speculative builder at bay. Others are slums; lightless alleys smelling of drains, leprous blocks looking like Berlin before they bombed it; worst of all when the sun shines. She lost two minutes looking it up on the streetmap.

A block too big for the ground it occupied; lowering down. Everything in it too small: mean little windows that refuse to open, balconies too small to sit on, tunnel-like entries half underground. Living-space milked far beyond what is permitted, even by the tolerant municipal rules concerning hygiene. The windows, as grimy as the shutters, cut off much of what light there is: the curtains behind eat what is left. A nicely tepid breeding-ground for misery. The people who live here take immense pains over the expense and smartness of their cars.

The two minutes Arlette wasted on the streetmap might as well have been two hours, for before she had found a place to park, she knew she had failed and it was too late. At seven-thirty to eight in the morning, these streets are animated – the only moment they ever are – by people going to work with the thin polish of jauntiness and fellowship upon them, given by the night's sleep. The air is made a scrap less stagnant and sullen by the voices and the car doors slamming. Not today. The women were standing in groups on the pavement like an unmade bed, arms folded in resignation. Men climbed shamed and sick-faced into cars, their expressions saying no-business-of-mine. Children went to school with jerky stumbling walk, white and pinched, hurried on their way with slaps. The fire-brigade's red Peugeot was unneeded: the street stank of failure and bitterness. Their truck was long gone, and the ambulance, too.

On the stairs, Arlette found a reporter she knew slightly. He had already finished his enquiry. What enquiry? Nobody knew the woman; hardly more was known about her. It rated four lines. He was only waiting for the fire-brigade officer, who was checking the gas mains because a jerry-built dump of this sort – bit of subsidence and you got a mains-pipe fracturing. The place was three years old, but cracks everywhere. Did you know anything about her, Madame Davidson, then? – because I've nothing worth printing.

"No. She'd written to me. I'm just back from holiday,"

defensively. "I thought I'd look her up." It should have been done yesterday, died upon her tongue.

"Two kids as well." Same as a road accident. The lump-idiot that caused it has a few bruises. The dead children are in the other car.

The technician with his clipboard was in a hurry now to get away, but stopped for the Press.

"Straightforward. No doubt at all about the suicide. I've no use for these people who choose gas deaths. Couldn't care less about the rest of the building – a spark could do it, like switching on a lamp. Bloody lucky the first man up, around five, was on the same landing and smelt it straight off. She'd made a poor job of blocking the draughts, and the concentration took longer to build up. By good luck, there was a window open on the landing above: weather still warm. In the winter it would have been a bomb. Fellow had the sense to ring us, and warn the tenants. They think of no one but themselves, those people. Why not go do it in the water and cause less trouble?"

"Perhaps," said Arlette, "she thought of the children."

"Huh?" Meaning huh!

"They'd have been asleep at least, and wouldn't suffer. Would you throw children in the water? Or out of a window? Perhaps she thought of that."

"Possible, I suppose," grudgingly.

"Let's give her that much credit," said the journalist, writing.

There was nothing Arlette could do. Sit in the car, say her remorse. Say a prayer that it was so: that the mother had said something kind and tucked them in. 'Things will be better in the morning.' And they were.

It is at these moments that you are aware of being Catholic, and grateful for it. For these moments you light a candle, and say the prayer taught to small children born near the sea, whenever the wind blows. Bonne Mère, look after the sailors. Be by me, when my time comes. And the smooth-worn, sliding words of a formula pattered off by heart, paid out like a line: and may she and all the souls of the faithful departed rest in peace, amen: make a sincere act of contrition dear-child.

She had left a 'back in an hour' word for Arthur, who had pottered off upon lawful occasions. But he'd left somebody – another middle-aged woman – in the 'waiting-room'. "With you in just one moment," said Arlette. She went hastily to drink a cup of stale coffee, recollect herself. A pest, when people turned up without appointments. But she was grateful now. Take her mind off the failure; there'd been too many. Force her to make more effort. Composed now, she recognized another face set to be composed in the face of failure.

"I'm sorry to have kept you waiting. Please come in."

"I don't know whether it's of any use."

"It's always of use. If there's nothing I can do it costs you nothing. But we'll see, shall we?" A woman of the 'working class', of the poor, shabbily dressed, because she has always more important things than her back to spend money on. But a firm, self-reliant face.

And with a filthy story, the kind one doesn't want to hear, but has to: not, perhaps, as frequently nowadays, but still, sadly, often. Some people think the frequency is again increasing. The standards of police recruitment have been terribly low over these past ten years. No more than semi-literate, most of them. The instructor in elementary street duty was wondering why they did so poorly with a map until he tumbled to it – they had trouble with streets named in alphabetical order . . .

Madame Solange Bartholdi. Forty-seven years old, widowed after an accident at work (building site) eight years ago. Two children (sons), now twenty-one and nineteen. (Difficult age-group, just coming to terms with manhood. And – mental arithmetic – thirteen, thus, and eleven, when they lost their father: another difficult agegroup.) Hard work, but she'd brought them up respectable. Address in Neudorf (stone's throw from this morning: the sort of coincidence Arlette had learned to accept). The neighbourhood was 'not too bad'. She did a morning shift as a cleaning-woman, a lunchtime shift as help-cook in a canteen. She didn't complain: rough, certainly, but stable, steady work and not badly paid. She wanted to emphasize she'd never been a woman to bear a grudge against society.

The boys had been her mainstay: affectionate, loyal, steady.

Nothing wonderful at school, but the teachers would bear her out, gave no trouble and asked for none, weren't workshy and had proper manners. Brought up to be polite; she'd always insisted on that. Same when they'd gone to work (apprenticeships in metal-working, and in armoured cement) – the bosses would say a word for her: good boys and no backchat. Of course boys give trouble – Mrs van der Valk would understand. Right, she'd had two herself. And hardship, the being poor, knitted a family together. It made one self-reliant. It was everything. She knew something about the subject; child of the Assistance Publique herself – that was her family. Hardship she had known all her days. Poverty on her bread, and thickly spread. Why complain? It was her lot; that's what one got when the cards were dealt. Don't ever envy anyone.

Her man had family, back in Calabria. She'd not seen much of them, since losing him. Normal: they were poor, too, had their own troubles, enough without hers added. Been a good man. No drinking, no betting, and always jobs done around the house.

Arlette felt a lot better. All right, so much for the background: one had to get that first, you understand? So, now for the story; what had happened?

Told quickly enough, said Madame Bartholdi grimly: the police was what had happened. Banging on the door first thing in the morning. Where were the boys?

The boys worked, and earned, and brought money in. They had the right to some freedom, and to enjoy themselves. They went out with their friends and the odd time, weekends and such, stayed out all night. She didn't ask. They were men now, and entitled to be treated as such. And didn't welcome Mum nosey-parkering, or playing the anxious old hen.

"It's all right," grimly. "I'm not going to break down and cry. But these bloody police, sorry, but I've said it and I'm not about to go back on it, they just rang up and said 'Your son is dead'. Like that. As though it was a dog run over. Can you imagine that?"

"One sec. First they came?"

"That's right. Pascal was in bed, so was I. Saturday, you

know; didn't have to get up that early. Where was Olivier? – did I know, did he know? Neither of us knew anything about it. And they knew, all the time. Roaming around, poking their noses in everything. Hour or so after, bop. Your son is dead – your number came up, you know."

"Pascal is the younger?"

"No, the elder. Olivier was nineteen." And now she could not stop her tears.

"This is abominable," said Arlette.

Solange had thrown her coat on, rushed to the local police post. They said they knew nothing about it, try down town, that's right, the central headquarters. Pushed around there from pillar to post, nobody wants to know, oh yes, finally, here's a fellow willing to tell you.

Arlette who – one way or the other – had a fairly wide experience of the police, could of course see the other side. They'd behaved, alas, with a heavy-handed callousness and brutality that was simply inadmissible, but at the time they made the raid, they hadn't grasped that the boy was dead. It had happened in the country: a message from the gendarmerie in the middle of the night had been misunderstood or garbled. Once the urban police realized the boy was dead, and not wounded or captive, they'd make a clumsy cover-up.

The facts were that a group of boys had broken into a country house they thought empty. But the owner had been there – a weekend cottage. In a panic he had reached for his gun and fired into the night. The boy had been fatally wounded. Naturally, the others fled in terror. The gendarmes called to the scene had found the boy's identity papers and sent the urban police to rope in the rest of the band.

Solange had come to terms with this. It wasn't just stupid, she said bleakly, it was damn dishonest. There he'd asked for trouble, and got it. Excessively, yes. Unfairly, yes, but it was her experience that life was that way. She blamed herself more than him. She'd let the reins drop too soon. It was a crime, all right.

She took, in fact, a much more severe view than Arlette did. But there, it wasn't Arlette's son.

Her own two sons, aged seventeen and fifteen, had been run in for what the Amsterdam police called street hooliganism. Piet van der Valk, at that time a Chief Inspector, had been called round to the station: the boys were being let go after a talking-to. Intensely humiliated, he had lost his cool. He'd hit them both in the face, baff baff, in front of the station sergeant. It had taken a long time, for all concerned, to get over this episode.

The police had called the elder son down to headquarters and questioned him roughly. They hadn't perhaps beaten him up, but Arlette could guess that they'd roared and slapped him about. They simply didn't believe his tale (which he stuck to) that he knew nothing about his brother's friends, or their activities, or movements. She didn't think she believed it herself. It was loyalty, solidarity. Bastardly cops. They'd clapped him in the cell, kept him three weeks. The judge of instruction let him go then, for lack of evidence. Without apologies.

Sure, bastardly cops. Everybody knew, Arlette knew. Pack of fascists. This, though, was just a little simple-minded. A bad performance, but the result of their exasperation at these weekend-cottage break-ins. There were too many of them. The police had a lot of work and trouble, and when they caught the authors, the effing tribunal let them go again. This police viewpoint was rather simplistic also, but equally it was understandable. If the population and the police are both boiling with frustration (said Arthur Davidson) and a government riddled with hypocrisy does nothing, you are going to have trouble on both sides. Explaining this to Madame Solange Bartholdi would be a lame performance, and useless. Telling her, abruptly, that Madame van der Valk did not wish to get involved in police matters was no help either. Evasiveness, no denying it, prompted her to point out that there were aspects of all this not as yet touched upon. What had happened to the man who shot the boy?

This was the heart of it. Honest with everyone, and herself, Solange could not accept this. It had been a fearful blow that her boy had been carried along in a set that thought it funny to break into weekend houses (boredom more than vengeance, but let that pass). The boy had paid with his life, but she was not vindictive. The police were swine. These were facts of life. But that man, who had killed her son for no more than a broken shutter. Wasn't that a crime? He had got clean away with it.

The gendarmerie had arrested him. He'd been held for thirty-six hours. The judge of instruction had released him. No, not on bail. Unconditional. She'd found out. Legitimate defence had been claimed and accepted. No prosecution, let alone a trial. The automatic formal charge brought, of manslaughter, had simply been dropped.

Arlette frowned.

"Not quite good enough, that."

"I said I'd get that fellow. But what can I do? I went down and I said, I said I lay a charge against that man, for killing my son. They said you can't, not a criminal charge you can't, that's been dropped, they said. No going back on that. You can lay a civil charge for damages they said, you'll have to get a lawyer. I went to one. He hemmed a lot, said yes, that's possible, I can do that, I have to have five thousand francs as a guarantee against costs, for taking it up. Five thousand francs! He might as well have asked me for the moon."

"You can get legal aid."

"Those pro deo chaps," Frenchly and shrewdly, "their heart's not in it. Nothing for nothing and not much for sixpence. I thought – I thought I'd try and see if you could help me."

"It's what I'm here for. I'll ask you fifty, for the hour. Another hundred and fifty for whatever I can do, provisional. There might not be an awful lot I can do. Police business I can't touch; I haven't the right. Legal – I'm not qualified and can't infringe on those who are. I can find out exactly what happened, and if anything has been concealed or kept back. I can find you an advocate, and a good one, who'll advise you and without it costing you a fifth of that extortionate sum you quoted. That, you see, was to get rid of you, because this is a troublesome affair. For now – let me work on it and get in touch with you. It'll take me a day or two. Is that any good?"

"It sure to God is," said Madame Bartholdi.

Arlette made a face, a lot less sanguine than her words. She knew the snag that made Johnny Sly ask five thousand. Nobody was anxious to plead against a legitimate-defence claim, not without some element giving leverage. The bourgeois feeling, so widespread as to be near universal, was that violence, in defence of property, was quite permissible. What! One is terrorized systematically. Bands of hooligans roam about unimpeded, and not a cop in sight. A man – one of us – shoots one? Best of luck, say we all. Teach the ruffians they can't always get away with it.

One such bandit, who'd been booby-trapped breaking in, even had the infernal cheek to bring a civil suit. Unlawful injuries, so please you. Think of it! A damned left-wing pink of an advocate had pleaded that. Judges, with no more backbone nowadays than a pack of shrinking pansies, had retained a few scraps of sense, just barely enough to throw this preposterous nonsense out of court.

Cultivate the bourgeois, said Arthur nastily, and that's what you get as dinner-table conversation: Bring Back The Cat. Poor old France hasn't got a cat. Never mind; a good fifteen-year-stretch at hard labour: Bring Back Devil's Island. An offence against property will always be punished far more heavily than an offence against the person.

Doing something for Madame Bartholdi isn't going to be easy, thought Arlette unhappily. It rather looks, my girl, as though you've another failure on your hands.

5. Sergeant Subleyras

A restless impulse sent Arlette into the kitchen, where the cleaning woman was, as usual, placidly drinking coffee. One or two Spanish platitudes were exchanged, and she worked a while on the midday meal. Another jerky caprice – she was trying to think, found it difficult, and was, as she realized, putting it off – sent her feet in the direction of the livingroom, where she found a mess of Arthur's. The cleaning woman, strictly forbidden to touch 'work', had dusted pointedly around an island of toast-crumbs, tobacco-flakes and a dirty piece of paper pinned down by the marmalade pot. Arlette left this disgusting object-lesson in male piggery where it was, but read the paper.

'Mental Intoxication . . . An everyday example is modishness or fashion. A man and I were studying together a new car, of unparalleled hideousness in design & colour, & cf. Lurie's appellation "The Jar of Peanut Butter". Knowing nothing, & caring less about its engineering capacities, I remarked mildly that its vile aspect sufficed to condemn. The man looked at me in total consternation and said, "But it's this year's model!" Nothing I could say shook his conviction that this was a criterion of excellence.'

For this one could forgive Arthur's rooted refusal to keep his beastly breakfast on the kitchen table.

She could not remember whether she had left the phone on direct ring or on record, and went back to her workroom to find out. It was on record, meaning a taped instruction to leave a message, and there was a message on the tape; a male voice, quiet and agreeably unaggressive, saying, 'Sergeant Subleyras, Crime Squad, don't ring me, I'll ring again in an hour's time' and wasted no further time. More or less without thinking, Arlette switched the phone to direct and it rang almost at once, and the same voice, still wasting no time, said, "Good morning, Madame, Subleyras, Urban Police. Have you any free time this morning?"

"What's it about?" searching her mind for any possible recent transgressions: despite experience, she still felt guilty when the police called.

"I'd rather not discuss it on the phone: I'd prefer a confidential interview." Surprise. Try to be businesslike. Her watch said nine forty-eight; heavens, it's still early.

"Now, if you like. Ten o'clock?"

"That'll do nicely," with no beating about the bush at all.

"Be with you in a few minutes." Tolerably startled, she hung up and wondered what on earth the cops . . . surely Madame Bartholdi hadn't . . . no, impossible. Well, she'd see shortly. And hear. Time for a pee and repair one's lipstick. The ring at the doorbell was brisk but not intimidating, and she was ready with the right degree of smile.

"Please come in." A rapid enveloping look round the little 'waitingroom', part of the entrance corridor really, partitioned off and pine-panelled, hung with flower prints in clean water-colour. He said nothing but "Subleyras", holding his hand out.

"Arlette Davidson. Van der Valk was my former name which I use professionally."

"I know."

"Well, then – sit down, do – where have I gone off the path of virtue?"

"Nowhere to my knowledge. In fact, there's nothing professional about this call. My profession, that is." And for the first time he hesitated, as though searching for words. "I rehearsed this," he said smiling, "but not, it seems, very well." The Strasbourg police force mostly follows the pattern of the Strasbourgeois; thick and short in morphology, running rapidly to flesh through the addiction to beer, tomato sauce, noodles and pork sausage; short, likewise, and thick in manner, voice and lifestyle. This man was not very tall and solidly boned, ribbed up with muscle; a broad face and plenty of jaw, but there was all the difference in the world. He was finely proportioned and amazingly light on his feet.

"I've had nothing to do with you but over this last year, one way or another, I've heard quite a lot about you." For a professional, and a cop at that, and a harmonious, assured man, he was ill at ease. He took a cigarette to give himself a countenance. "I announced myself with a rank – force of habit – but I'm off duty and this is in fact unofficial; personal if you will." The only thing that really said 'Police' was the steady unwinking gaze. Cops and children stare: every sociologist has noticed it, and they weren't the first. The eyes took a quick flick, from one side to the other of Arlette's table. She was still totally in the dark, but decided to help him.

"You're wondering just how confidential this is? If I couldn't respect secrecy, I wouldn't be here; I wouldn't have lasted a week. I give some of my files to my husband for study, but with all personal data effaced, and everything withheld at request. There is a tape-recorder, but it's not on. I don't believe in tricks, and use none. Your own experience will have to be the judge." He looked to be about thirty-five. A rugby player, Piet would have said, a number seven, a wing forward with fast reactions. The face a woman, and a man too, would call handsome, but had taken other people's shoulders head-on a few times. A few scars; the nose unbroken, but the front upper teeth were false.

"You're right, a cop is going to be suspicious, he can't help it. I made up my mind I wouldn't do it that way. It would have been easy to come with a phony story, try you out, see how you reacted. That would be a cop method. But it would take away the whole point. It's true though – I get this far and I'm stalled. I don't like what I'm going to say: it's contrary to too many of my instincts."

"What I generally do," said Arlette, opening her day book and picking up a pen, "is get the background first. The personal data mentioned. If you'd rather not, we'll leave it at that. Or you can think it over and come again if you decide to. Either way, the story – whatever it is – can wait: there's no hurry for it." For it was another dirty story, that much was plain, and for a cop to come to her with it meant it must be something they didn't want to touch, and even if the whole damn police department was ready to cover up for her, she still wouldn't want to know, but she couldn't refuse to listen.

"Subleyras, Charles, and generally called Charley. Not born hereabouts – bit further south."

"That's right, there's just a touch of the accent. I have it myself."

"Nîmes. It's of no importance. Thirty-three years old. Married. Three little girls. And that's the whole point really."

"Ah. I begin to get a glimmer. This really is a personal thing. Sorry – go on."

"Profession, cop. Never had any other. Not an officer – no baccalaureate."

"Can you give me your definition of the word 'profession'?"

"For me, Madame, it's something one works at professionally, meaning you put your back into it and your brains: if the job isn't well done, it isn't professional."

"Revealing answer." Subleyras had a grin; tight without being pinched, crooked without being false. Not Sunny Jim, thank God, but far from a cold fish. He lit a cigarette from the butt of the last and shook one loose for her.

"I didn't come here to fence with you," he said. "There isn't any story. The background is the story. I've done this job for fifteen years. Well, or less well, but professionally. I've come to a point where I'm no longer able, or allowed maybe, to do this work the way I see it. I'm not talking about justice. There's more rough than smooth to this job and that's a fact. I accept that – if you don't, you don't last one year, let alone ten. I've no fancy philosophies; don't pretend to be an educated man. I'm talking about common sense."

"I don't have anything written on the door," said Arlette, choosing her words slowly. "Those adverts I put in the paper say Counsel. Are you asking my advice, or my opinion? Have you really made your own mind up, but you're sticking a bit over the decision, and perhaps you're looking for something to push you into it? I wouldn't have the nerve, you know, to go advising a man like you what he should do with his life."

"All right," he said placidly. "I'll say only that I haven't altogether made my mind up, and all the light I can get, I can use."

"So you come to a perfect stranger," said Arlette, "to push the pendulum one way or the other."

"I can go on splitting hairs. When you talk about common sense – give me a concrete example."

He threw away the cigarette, crossed his arms and looked at Arlette.

"One that seems unimportant, but – illustrates?"

"Symptomatic?"

"Right. I'm off duty, near midnight, the ring boulevard,

couple of hundred metres past the station, not many people about. I'm in plain clothes, my own car, alone, at a red light. I see a girl walking – not loitering. A few paces behind her, a black man. I'm not sure I recognize him – not much light – but I don't care for the look of him. Cop instinct, if you like. Sidling up on her. I stop the car, cross the street, show my card, ask for his papers. He gives me lip in a loud voice, the girl stops and turns round, asks what I think I'm doing, pretty aggressive. I say I don't like the way he's marking her steps. He goes on backchatting, she calls me a fucking fascist. I'm a wee bit irritated, I pin him and say Up against the wall, boy."

"With a gun?"

"Off duty I don't carry one; I'm bigger," bleakly, "than I look."

"Sorry I interrupted."

"He doesn't resist. I tap his pockets, come up with a blade fifteen centimetres long. Ask what he's doing with that, he says it's for cleaning his nails with. I show it to the girl and say, See that? She just looks, shrugs her shoulders, says to me, quite indifferent, 'Stick it in your tripes,' like that, turns round, walks off. As dry and as cool as yesterday's pizza. So? I tell Billyboy he made no attack, so I press no charge against him: he's carrying a prohibited weapon, sure, but in view of the young woman's attitude, I'll confiscate the blade and leave it at that. I go back to my car and leave him there laughing. He'll have bought a nice new blade," reflectively, "next morning."

"You'd have arrested him and so what? Tribunal would have let him go."

"I see you know your penal code. That's right: there wasn't what the law calls commencement of execution. Loitering with intent is only a misdemeanour anyhow. I should have waited till he put the knife in her ribs. I wanted to spare her that – and got thanked for it. I don't know why I bothered to tell you. Any cop can tell ten better stories. I'd call this just average. People who say a cop's work should be preventive wouldn't believe me. Might say, like that woman did, I was being provocative. With a black – that much more so."

"Except that my husband collects these stories. What does your wife say?"

"She doesn't," smile getting narrower. "She's too fair to say choose between the job and me. She'd sure as hell like to. If your husband says to you he's telling them to take the job and stick it – what's your reaction?"

"A marriage comes first," said Arlette, "up to a borderline and where is it? I think perhaps it's the difference between a job and a vocation. A profession is something you do: a vocation is what one's got to do. That's an opinion, for what it's worth. I wouldn't want to make it subjective – either to you or to me. I see what you mean – about it making no sense . . . Tell me – you're crime-squad? – on another subject altogether, does the name Bartholdi mean anything to you?"

Sergeant Subleyras drew his brows together.

"Seems to me that it does, but I'm not sure offhand what. Cue me."

"A boy who got shot out in the country, breaking into a cottage."

"I'm with you now."

"His brother was kept some weeks in the jug on suspicion." A slow dark flush was climbing up a face pale from too much desk work.

"I'm aware of the case. Officially, I'd have no comment about that. If we're off the record still . . . ?"

"As we've been throughout."

"Then it was lamentable. Can I, without seeming to be excusing myself, say that it was not my work?"

"Naturally. To be straight with you, I know nothing about it. Madame Bartholdi, the boys' mother, came to see me, in considerable distress. I said I'd do what I could – you know, I think, that I don't interfere in anything touching police work?" Nod.

"So, I'm wondering why you bring the subject up. It's another example, certainly, of what I've been talking about. There are plenty more."

"I'll tell you why. You come to your own decisions, and if I can contribute any light I'll be glad, because I'll feel rewarded.

So we don't owe one another anything. This much – if you decide for reasons of your own to leave the department, and if at that moment you think it right, communicate any information you have on that subject to me, and you'd be helping that woman, maybe. She's not happy, you see, that the charges against the man who shot her boy got dropped. As things stand, no one feels much enthusiasm about going to bat for her."

"I'll bear what you tell me in mind. I'd rather pay you a consultancy fee, your usual way, than promise you a service I might not be able to make good. Okay?"

"Of course. Fifty francs, and no misunderstandings."

"Because if anybody gives me a margin to be straight in," writing neatly and carefully in a chequebook, "I try, and I don't mean acting like I was John Wayne."

"This cheque," said Arlette, "isn't signed John Wayne, not that I'd frame it if it was. And I don't see any drawing of an arrow either. We'll manage, Monsieur Subleyras, to trust one another."

"I've been reaching the same conclusion," standing up, "so I won't say goodbye and thanks, Madame, but I'll say I'll be in touch. And I'll look up that file," not smilingly.

"Thanks to you – for coming. Or is that sentimental?"

"If it is I'm not quarrelling with it. Don't get up; I can find my way."

6. Xavier

She hadn't finished writing her notes up when the bell went again, and the telephone with it. Bonne Mère, grumbled Arlette, pressing buttons, scarcely even home and a day like this . . .

"Yes; this is Arlette van der Valk."

A clipped, high woman's voice resonated haughtily.

"This is Madame Hervé Laboisserie. I've been wondering whether you'd care to call round, and we could discuss a matter, don't you know. This afternoon, preferably." There were times when Arlette responded to this kind of remark by 'Come to my office and we'll see', but the holiday had been expensive and house-calls not to be sneezed at.

"Very well; two-thirty," which sounded either over-eager or over-scornful, but she didn't care that badly.

"Oh. Well, yes, I think that will be satisfactory."

"What's the address?"

"Oh. Rue Ravel, number twenty-one. The Orangerie end." Surprised that anybody needed telling. Why can't people carry essential information in their head? The voice showed symptoms of complaining about this.

"Excuse me will you? – I've somebody waiting." She hated having people waiting, but if they would come without appointments . . . Making them wait on purpose was a puffy trick running counter to all she tried to live by. Nothing is more boring than the very-busy-clerk making believe that he is Managing something. She had begun her career by apologizing to people kept waiting. She then discovered that this made them more suspicious, as though there were a catch somewhere.

All she said now to the person studying the flower-prints with a little more attention than they merited was, "Will you come in?"

"Good those," turning round with a connoisseur's air, "early nineteenth century." Since this expertise was fairly easily acquired by anyone not suffering from myopia – the date was as usual printed at the bottom with the artist's and engraver's names – there was not much to say but, "They're supposed to make a wait less boring."

A gentleman of forty. Soigné about the hair and fingernails, and aftershaved with elegant-smelling toiletries. An executive suit, a shimmering tie, fine, fragile Italian shoes, the air of his time being worth a great deal. Briefcase – all very Via dei Condotti. He snapped it shut, held out a card between his fingertips.

"Xavier Marchand." Slight formal bow, assured easy manner. Impressive. Since she was fifty-two years old and experienced, she resolved to watch him on the way out, make sure a print didn't get slid in the briefcase. They were worth some money, if not much. Now he was busy inspecting her big marine landscape.

"Please sit down."

"Sorry – splendid thing, that."

"Forgive me just a moment." To put the phone back to 'record' since she loathed being interrupted by it, to write '14.30 Twenty-one, Rue Ravel. Mme Hervé Laboisserie'. Was that spelt right? – bourgeoisie! Out of the corner of her eye, she caught this bourgeois fiddling with a cigarette case and matching lighter. There are the lacquer ones from Dupont, the florentine ones from Cartier – part of the panoply, she thought with some irritation. She preferred Sergeant Subleyras. So turn a patient-bland, boiled eye upon the present interlocutor.

She was taken aback. He was staring out of the window with haggard concentration upon twigs and a patch of sky, oblivious to what she said or did. All the elaborate veneer had cracked across from side to side like the Lady of Shalott's looking-glass. She had been mistaken. It was understandable, because she did sometimes get the fast-paced, high-priced executives. Generally, they were trying to get out from under an adultery rap or cover some such turpitude that would make the pyramid more slippery still. Blackmail always in their minds, they were sensitive about the tape-recorder and hated anything in writing. This was not the same. She regretted her toffee-nosed reaction.

"Monsieur Marchand," she said gently.

"I'm sorry. You're waiting for me to tell you what it's all about. I had a spiel prepared. Now I find there's no use for it. To the point – it's all said in one sentence really. My wife has left me." The monosyllables held nothing but plain blank misery.

She took one of his cigarettes. He was there at once with the electronic thing: she preferred her pale-green plastic Cricket, but this was necessary.

"I'd better hear why, in your view."

"Simple, I'm afraid. I was no longer good enough for her."
"With someone else?"
"No – or I don't think so. Maybe. Not yet, perhaps."
Simplest, and most difficult of all, the man who has to spit it out. He will spit it on a park bench, for he asks nothing but to be allowed to talk. To face Arlette he had screwed himself up: hence the façade.

The moment he realized he could talk and that she would listen, it flowed without a prompt. Business training kept him from rambling much: all to the point.

He'd lost his job out of the blue. Secure job, in which he felt content and competent; the right man. So he was, and well-thought-of by his company, which was large, prosperous, established. He was not given any sack. The thing was being streamlined and the job no longer existed. From no more than loyalty – you'd think – they'd find you another. Error. If the job no longer exists, from head office's standpoint, neither do you. Arlette, who had heard such tales before, was unsurprised at the heartlessness of it: a heart is a muscle, to be preserved from accidents or even twinges. These fates are the other face of the coin.

On this side is the high salary and the plummy perks; aeroplanes and restaurants, careful servility from juniors and golf-club familiarity from seniors; a slice of secrets and strategies, a promise of power. One day, though, a seed lodges in a vice-president's mind: on its label is written some euphemism about Structures. Something to do with Next Year's Model.

You have done nothing wrong, and are surprised. Your immediate superior, who has known you some years and in whose heart, it might be thought, is more than greed, fear, and effrontery, prevaricates at length, until you realize – at length – that it was his neck or yours. So, it's yours. No hard feelings about that, of course.

You'll say it to nobody else but yourself – this is upsetting. But you're unworried. You have a proven record of success, eminent titles to esteem, numerous valuable connections, and know all the ropes. You belong, and you're in.

You don't ekshally, and you aren't, but it takes some months to find this out. By then your past, which was yesterday, has suddenly become remote. Let's see, old chap, your record was on last year's model: we're talking about this year's: you aren't really in on that, are you now? Next year's? Somehow the company has a new policy, which is not to hire anyone new over the age of thirty-five. We're stretching that of course, since it's for you. You're on the short list.

Quite gradually it becomes we're-keeping-you-in-mind, old chap, and do give my regards to your lovely wife. Your lovely wife has by this time found out.

You hadn't wanted to upset her, so you hadn't said anything about it. She is accustomed to reticence in matters of business. Some wives do gossip, and there have been leaks known. But now six months have gone by. You are living in more expensive fashion than before, because things the company paid for . . . there was not much saved and gratuities melt with horrid speed. You must keep up your subscriptions, buy new suits. Nobody must be allowed to perceive the smallest ripple in your customary ways, business manners, or leisure pursuits. Nothing in the community is so deadly as a loss of face. Let it once place you in the Russian sector – meaning in a low income bracket – and you're finished.

Xavier put it all well, thought Arlette. Quietly, without inflated language and with little self-pity. He had been struck by the plague; it is endemic in the community and nobody is ever quite immune. It was when he spoke of his wife that he became unbalanced and bitterness rose, a thick black smoke, to choke him.

The failure is in a lack of imagination? Businessmen are not paid to have imagination, and it is unfair to blame them for failure to escape from this world of rigid shibboleths and slogans in which they must believe in order to survive, into which they lock themselves.

Can they even be blamed for the male failure towards the woman, an even more glaring failure to imagine what it is like for her? In the business world all values are childish and only vanity can reign. Does one need more evidence than the toys and gadgets upon which they so rely? In this world the woman is trapped. She too has to put out more flags. They come uncommon high in price for him; for her still higher. She must acquire a thicker defensive plating of boastfulness and arrogance, and women are not good at this. They become crude and shrill and hateful. The giver of life has been forced into a world to which she is not in the least suited. She hates her own hardness, and revenges herself upon the men. Her resentment is bitterer still when she does not perceive why she must degrade all within her and around her.

Why, wondered Arlette, does he come to me? Thinking that I would soften the conduct of this woman towards him, with understanding and explanations? He will have told his tale to men, who will have bought drinks, nodded wisely, shrugged helplessly, muttered 'Women . . . just shows you, though . . .'

Useless to point out that when economies began to bite, the wife's expenses, which he found extravagances, were the first to be curbed. The very bent he had encouraged and fomented; an elegant wife being needful to standing. In Arthur-Davidson language, he it was who 'nursed the pinion that impelled the steel'.

"Did she write to you?"

"A word. Telling me not to pursue her, or try to find her. Advising me 'to forget all that' – 'not to think of it any more'! Twenty years of marriage. I loved her. To lose one's job, already . . . and then that . . . As though the moment I no longer brought in the pile of loot, I no longer existed. Don't talk to me of loyalty. One thing, thank God for it – there are no children."

If allowed to go on talking, he would provide answers to a good many unspoken questions. Mm; 'twenty years' was certainly a rhetorical exaggeration. One could begin digging out explanations. But nobody wanted them.

"Where are you living?"

"In a room. Where was the point in trying to hang on to the flat? Even if it had been possible – what sense would it make? This is where it has all hit hardest – a whole life gone. What am I now? – nothing. Once you're poor, nobody has any use for you." She didn't need to ask why he had come: he'd come to be pitied.

"There's nothing in view?"

"Nothing. Why bother, now? The advantage of a great misery is that you forget, at least, about the small ones." A sad little smile. He tapped the briefcase. "All this is still intact, or just. Rub cream into the leatherwork: keep things polished, brushed, pressed. Good quality stuff, wears well. But a few more months and even that . . . little signs. They show up when people look for them, and in business the eyes are pretty sharp. A suit begins to look a bit dated . . ." The shoes look mended, the tie begins to fray; imperceptibly a dingy, shabby air hangs about things. "I'm dressing for dinner in the jungle." It was flooding him now, and she had to put a stop to it.

"All right," said Arlette. "You're still fleeing. There comes a moment when you stop fleeing. Touching bottom, as the platitude has it, there's no place to go but up. But you're still looking backwards."

Arthur, who had a phrase for most things, would have said Ichabod. Fair Ichabod ol' man; there's no going back to things like that. Mr Polly said it first. The woman had been right in that at least. "I'm not saying she was right – far from it. But having done as she did, she was right to warn you not to try to follow her. Where do you live?"

He did not hesitate.

"Round the corner – in the Rue de Flandre," the smile brittle.

And, she guessed, with no telephone.

"Yes, you hadn't far to come. Handy – I haven't far to go. I'll come and see you. One has to drain the abscess, you know. And here – this is too formal. I mean, I'm in my office, behind the desk, and you are very stiff and tight. I'll come and see you – say, tomorrow afternoon. You come to see me, that's fine, breaks the ice. So, tomorrow, we'll talk about it."

"Money," bleakly.

"Tomorrow," said Arlette.

7. Watch the cat out of the tree

Arthur, coming home for lunch, found lunch ready, which was very agreeable. No sweaty wife panicking about in the kitchen trying to race against time, with a lot of nasty things spilt on the stove top which, against all justice, he would later have to clean up. Arthur's notion of justice was that hating the dishwasher, a thing that went rumble-belly interminably and was both extravagant and inefficient, he washed the dishes. Women's view of things is that the dish-washer cleans the stove: men's view isn't.

Instead, he found his wife standing stock-still in the middle of the livingroom, which meant she was staring at nothing and thinking. He stopped in the doorway to admire this vision. Female in office skirt and navy-blue jumper. Looking her years but wearing well; good bones and good carriage. Tallish, thinnish; a cinders-blonde with big brown eyes that go green without green eyeshadow. High-bridged Phoenician nose. Looks good sitting down and better still walking. A really good walk is very rare in women. He was pleased by what he saw.

"You forgot to empty the mailbox."

"So I did. I've had quite a busy morning, and I've three different sorts of oddball, and my mind wasn't really on the mailbox."

"Who are all these people writing to you from Germany?" She frowned: she'd seen that neat small printing in red ball-point before. Inside the envelope was a half-sheet of paper.

'It's silly, you know, shutting your eyes to things and hoping they'll just go away.' She showed this to Arthur, who looked blank.

"Means nothing to me. Mildly deranged in the sense that

quite a sensible commonplace remark becomes dotty when put in a dotty context."

"I've another, full of vague hints and warnings. Since it means nothing to me either there's nothing one could do even if I wanted, which I don't. Piet used to have a good phrase, typically Dutch, about waiting for the cat to come out of the tree. Down to earth, you know. Let's have dinner: the pot's in the oven."

During dinner the telephone rang. This was Arthur's telephone, but since he refused to answer phones at meals, she got up patiently. Arthur was one of those people anyhow who chew each mouthful thirty times, was indistinct and elliptical at the best of times: even if he did answer nobody would understand what he said. The woman just swallows and says "Yes, this is Mrs Davidson."

"Ah," said a man's voice, cheerful and ingratiating, "you got our letter, then?"

"Who is 'our'?"

"You're still pretending, you see."

"If you're the anonymous author, I can't congratulate you. It's meaningless."

"Ach, you don't want it to be made public: that's understandable. We don't want to make things difficult for you. We'll be right around, now you're at home."

"Give me your name, please." A chuckle.

"One doesn't forget a name that easily. Be with you in a few minutes."

"You aren't going to be let in, you know." But the phone had been put down. Arlette walked heavily back to the table, where Arthur, having taken another mouthful, said nothing. People who insist on believing that you're staying in the tree and playing cute, while the plain truth is that you haven't the remotest what they're talking about, are tiresome.

Outside the livingroom window was another Dutch invention. Known as a 'spionnetje' and one saw them on all the old Amsterdam houses. Simply a mirror on a flexible bracket: a rear-viewer from a car will do. All the old biddies had one fixed to the windowframe, so as to see what is happening in the street without getting up from your chair and your knitting. Not only cheaper than closed-circuit television; much more efficient.

When the doorbell went, Arthur strolled over with his hands in his pockets.

"Youngish man, considerably overweight, with a large bushy beard – not a success in the circumstances. Youngish, thin woman, nervous, abrupt movements. Faded middle-aged woman, leather raincoat, knitted woolly hat. This is weird. Further observation discloses grey Mercedes car, rather dirty, looking fairly old. German numberplate, but even with my glasses I can't read it." He wasn't worried about them getting in. Since last year, when an unpleasant person had got in, all the tenants in the house were on the qui-vive.

"Tactical withdrawal to the car, for consultations." He lost interest and walked away. If Arlette wasn't worried, and plainly her mind was on other things, he certainly wasn't.

When Arthur went back to work, which he did on foot, or by bicycle since it was only a question of crossing the boulevard and crossing the university 'campus', Arlette heard sounds of altercation, but by the time she reached the window the adversary, it would appear, had been put to flight. His public persona was mild and indeed diffident, but he had an English talent for shockingly direct speech in a loud voice: invective rather than insult. She observed his walk down to the end of the street; rather fast and a bit pigeon-toed; one arm swinging broadly and the other carried still by his side, with the shoulder tucked in as though afflicted by a slight paralysis; every few steps a small, but perceptible, toss of the head. This walk, much imitated by facetious students, bespoke a passage of arms with 'some jackanapes'. Victory was apparently complete, since while she watched, the grey Mercedes trundled off, turning up towards the town centre. Assembly of loose screws in disarray? – or simply going off to get something to eat?

Mm, she had herself an errand. Rue Ravel. One of the most elegant of the 'Musicians' quarter', which is considered, broadly, the most desirable place in Strasbourg to live. Much of it is in large ponderous blocks of the late nineteenth century, built during the German occupation and of Kaiser-Wilhelm weight and majesty, and absence of any aesthetic sense whatever. There are also large – and small – villas standing in gardens. Wherever a speculator has got his paws on one of these, he has instantly knocked it down and built an apartment-block designed to milk the space to the last square millimetre.

It wasn't at all far. She could walk, as she often did when feeling ruffled. The weather was afternoon-autumnal, and delicious. What had the silly woman said? 'The Orangerie end'. Since the Rue Ravel runs parallel to Strasbourg's prettiest public garden, it wasn't a helpful direction.

One of the new ones: everything bijou. The wretched fellow called in to 'landscape the garden' which is the size of a pint pot, employs the little horrors sold by nurserymen to this end; a dwarf cypress, a dwarf weeping ash, and one of those stunted bushes with gold and silver foliage. The entrance is a corkscrew of crazy paving between shelves of artificial stone inadequately clothed with miniature alpines. There is no room for plaster gnomes; they must live in the house, getting their beards caught in all the burglar alarms.

The interior arrangements show the same inadequacy: there seems no provision for anything but drinking, fornicating, and being-in-the-bathroom; activities catered for with a lavishness amounting to frenzy. There are a very few unreadable books, several hideous daubs purporting to be pictures and many of those ugly things florists insist are flowers.

The furniture, generally a mix of oriental, modern and bogus-Louis, is dwarf-size and gossamer-fragile. The slightest rip or chip in the leather or lacquer and you must throw it all away. The owners do not mind. Whatever their pretended profession, they have a great deal of money. One need not feel sorry for them, nor for the cramped and squalid discomfort of their pastures in Passy or Neuilly: they like it this way.

The woman who let Arlette in was called Madame Estelle Laboisserie. There was also a daughter of late teen age, spotty and supercilious, with neither brains, looks, nor character, named Ghislaine. Mama was thin, with a beige face, and a body like the furniture, of kindling wood swathed in beige suède with gold accessories. On her spindly legs were high boots of glove-leather, coloured violet.

This all sounds, Arlette was later to remark, exceedingly improbable. I swear, she said, it's all true. I did have such a strong sense of unreality I could hardly concentrate upon what the woman said. And she had one of those voices thought in Passy to be Parisian, that swoops upward upon high at every punctuation mark. Government ministers, those expletive-deleted counter-tenors, adopt this voice in television interviews when taxed therein with peculation.

The one thing real is the story. It comes out very slowly, with a multiplicity of evasions and euphemisms. But this woman is not a plaster dwarf after all. Was once a human being, and produced a baby from between her legs. Has still occasionally remnants of human emotion. Is terribly ashamed of them, but they're there. It is a shameful story, and pitiful.

Monsieur Hervé Laboisserie is a consul. The French Foreign Service, still known as the Quai d'Orsay, exactly the way M. de Norpois spoke of Saint-James's and the Ballplatz, is as snobbish as it is useless, and despises consuls terribly.

> 'Le service consulaire
> C'est une belle carrière,
> Je ne dis pas le contraire:
> Mais, moi, je suis Ministre.'

Monsieur, and Madame, suffered terribly from this. However, he had grown to become a very grand consul. In one of those extremely large oriental cities thought to be strategic and important. Singapore, or Shanghai? Or perhaps Hong Kong? Well, I'm sorry, but they're somehow all Hong Kong to me. Anyway the mixture of climate, airconditioning, and natives, doesn't suit Madame's health, and the children are a great bother, and anyway they've got to be sent back to Paris because you can only get educated at the Collège Stanislas or the Lycée Louis le Grand, I don't recall which. Yes, there's a boy as well, year or two older than the girl, his name is Gilles. Of course I've got it all down exactly, but my notes are in the office.

The boy produces, as was very much to be expected, a fairly massive revolution against both Shanghai and Victor Hugo, and goes native in the Rue Monsieur-le-Prince or thereabouts. Works selling life insurance, throws that up because of its extreme dishonesty, acquires a girlfriend called Caroline and traffics in heroin. He is caught in possession of a ludicrous quantity, sixteen grammes or something. To him, this simply represents a sum of x francs upon which he can live for x months. He gets clapped in the Santé for x months instead: x plus y, probably. She, Caroline that is, is heaved into the Petite Roquette or whatever the modern version is. This breaks the boy up utterly because she kills herself there, the poor silly wretch. End of story.

"How, end of story?" asked Arthur.

"The father doesn't want to know. A consular career is quite difficult enough without children, and of course he does worse things daily than ever the boy did. The mother is blackened totally by the shame of it all, it seems the old aunts in Passy made some very disapproving sounds, and has retired to this dusty provincial corner where she has relatives of sorts until she can live it down."

"What are you supposed to do?"

"Find the boy: he did a bunk the moment he was released."

"Is it known where he bunked to?"

"Yes, it is."

"Then it's a cop problem and not a widow problem, no?"

"That's what I thought, until I got told it was Buenos Aires."

"You can't go there!"

"No," said Arlette. "No, I suppose not. I've in any case at the present moment a great deal too much to think about."

Very close by the Rue Ravel lived a friend of hers, an advocate called Paul Friedmann. She possessed after a year's practice a few handy contacts, lawyers and doctors, and so forth, spoken of vaguely as 'tame'. Paul was anything but tame, but as well as being close by was bright. He wasn't at home, reportedly was not pleading at the Palace of Justice, was, reportedly, in his office in the Rue de Verdun, and there with difficulty was routed out.

"Come on round," he said on the phone.

"I'm on foot."

"I'll drive you home."

From this exchange Arlette concluded that Maître Friedmann would welcome a pretext for putting an end to a boring day. It was pleasant to see her: she found it pleasant to see him. It was nice having a sprightly chat: likewise. He was plainly making lots of money, which showed in the furniture – nothing like that she had been looking at – and was indeed boringly lecturing at some length about Chippendale pattern-books, and being learned about mahogany. But he wasn't very helpful about Madame Bartholdi. Ready enough to have her as a client, but couldn't see what it all had to do with actions-at-law.

"You were nodding a bit there, weren't you? Any criminal action is extinguished. Remains a civil action, consisting of efforts to put a price upon a boy's life. Not up my street, not, if I've understood, up hers, and in the circumstances a weary row to hoe. She feels like pulling all this fellow's teeth out one by one and we can sympathize in that laudable aim, but court-wise it's a Pyrrhic victory and largely symbolic damages. Think about it some more. I'm strongly averse to litigation."

She avoided the subject of Argentina: not a place, she thought, likely to interest Paul Friedmann much. She said nothing either about peculiar Germans outside the door. They were there again, hovering at no great distance when Paul dropped her and said no, he wouldn't come in for a drink but love to Arthur. They made no attempt to accost her. She felt obscurely grateful for his unwitting protection.

This though was absurd. These Germans weren't a threat. She should go perhaps and have it out with them.

There was nothing on her phone tape, but while she was checking it the phone rang in the livingroom.

"Brigitte Buckenburg here from *Graphik*." She'd forgotten about this but wouldn't you know it . . . The combination of

The Press, and the type of German womanhood that would work for this kind of press . . .

"Yes, well, my German isn't too brilliant. I got your proposal. Very kind of you and thanks, but no, thanks. I mean, I don't much want to be interviewed."

"Really – why?"

"Now ja – I don't feel obliged to give reasons, you know."

"But do, though."

"Let's say that I see no need for it."

"But of course there is need for it. Very valuable for you. And most interesting to us, and our readership."

"Doubtless: I've simply decided against it."

"Oh, I seeee," knowingly. "I don't believe you really mean that. I'm sure you'll change your mind."

"Better not count on that. And good day," ringing off firmly. Let those people once get their teeth into you! . . . And the tone had been patronizing, as of 'Oh yes, the old hard-to-get act; we're used to that'. Why could people never accept simple truths?

And those people outside . . . but that must be sheer coincidence. *Graphik* probably was capable of anything, but wouldn't use so roundabout an approach, and people seeming unbalanced: that was not their style. The dog started making a noise, keys clattered in the hallway; that was Arthur.

"I was just thinking of taking the dog out, and seeing once and for all what these stupid people want."

"Wait a moment," said Arthur. "It's not going to be quite so easy. When I went out this afternoon they started bawling after me."

"Yes, I heard that, and I'm not putting up with it."

"It was all about Jacky Karstens. So I stopped, and said I knew all about him, and wasn't in the least interested. They kept on yelling about the SS, so I got a bit cross and told them to shove off, sharpish, and went upon my way."

"I'll have them cleared off by the police. Let me handle this."

"When I came back just now, they started waving in a pally way and shouting Hallo, Karstens, hallo, old chap." This was a little ambiguous since he was going hallo-old-chap at Dog, but she got it disentangled.

"Oh dear," she said. But at least the cat, in the tree, had shown what colour it was.

8. A putative father

Karstens had been the name of Arthur's first wife. A woman she viewed – whose memory she viewed – with small sympathy, indeed none at all. After leading him a fearful dance, including divorcing him, thinking better of it, proposing to come back, and abandoning him again – among numerous other engaging tricks – the woman had killed herself in the end, which should have been the end, save that for years she had managed to persuade Arthur that this was somehow his fault. He had, hoped Arlette, forgotten as well as forgiven Nathalie Karstens, but she had left a lot of scar tissue.

Flemish. Arlette had plenty of friends in both Belgium and Holland, but in this case had seen the point of Jacques Brel's embittered line, 'Catholic between wars – and Nazi when they're on.' And here came the woman cropping up again. Ripping open scars.

"You're going to let me handle this," said Arlette.

"I can't say either yes or no to that yet – we'll see how it turns out."

"You've seen none of these people before?"

"No, I can't place any of them."

"Germans, too; not Dutch or Belgian. And why on earth call you Karstens?"

"An oblique way, I suppose, of indicating that my unlamented ex has thought up some new trick from behind the unsilent tomb." He was unhappier than he'd admit.

"I'm going to drain this abscess." So that when the street-door bell went, Arlette pressed the catch and opened her own front door. The young woman was there, with a winning smile.

"Hallo, Mum," was her joyful greeting.

"Wrong floor. Doctor Rauschenberg is the psychiatrist – one down."

"Well, stepmother then. Only being friendly. Why keep the pretence up?"

"Sorry, my German and my patience are running out rapidly. The elaborate mystification is offensive; pester me no further." She could see two pairs of feet on the stairway up, listening. "I don't like that, either. This is a private house and I consider my neighbours."

"Oh yes, of course, the neighbours" – the female understood but went on talking German. "Well, you've only to let me in."

"When you behave like that?" shutting the door, knowing the bell would ring again directly.

"Come off it," said the girl with vulgar familiarity. "You speak Dutch, too. No use saying you don't know Jacky Karstens. Formerly an officer in the Waffen SS."

"I've heard of him, and so what? Is it supposed to be news? I'm not interested, so please leave." An effort at blackmail, just as she had guessed. A poor effort, and cheap. Nathalie's brother had been in the Charlemagne Division. And something of a warrior–hero by some accounts. Much decorated in Russia. Arthur had not met him often, since in those days they weren't all that popular in central Europe. Lived in Spain, in, one presumed, franquist circles. Said to be an amusing fellow – engaging.

"All is now clear," she said accepting a drink. "Since you once had an SS brother-in-law, they imagine you'd be embarrassed. Since you have an official position in the Council, the Secretary-General is presumably the target."

"The whole administration is stuffed with ex-party members, and the old boy will be profoundly unmoved. Still, I don't want these loonies bothering him."

"They've tried this act on several Dutch politicians recently."

The phone went. This time the fat man, but conciliatory, with a soft voice and an effort at tact.

"Sorry, I don't speak French. I know my wife was a bit over-emphatic, but why don't you let me in, and we can speak quietly."

"And have you a passport, or identity-card to show me?"

"No need, no need."

"Then I shall tell you that I have your car registration, and shall not hesitate to complain to the police if you give me further cause."

"Do, do," appearing to find this funny. "Why not the press while we're at it?"

"Don't ring again."

There must be more behind this. Inspired by *Graphik*? But it was so thin. Nobody nowadays could think that Arthur, a consultant sociologist on criminal and penal questions, could seriously be embarrassed. The fellow had been in a fighting unit, not any shitty camp guard.

Before supper she took Dog on the lead, for a pee in the Observatory bushes. The Mercedes was still standing guard. She frowned, and went fairly ostentatiously as far as the police station, which was at the end of the street, Avenue de la Forêt Noire.

"You want to make an official complaint?" asked a bored policewoman, with small zeal for an official form with five carbons.

"I don't think so – unless it persists. I bring to your attention a state of affairs. Harassment, and invasion of privacy."

"I'll make a note in the daybook, then. If you make it formal, we can send someone, and sort them out."

"I'll see tomorrow morning. Dotty Germans after all . . . stories about Nazis . . ." In Strasbourg, it is small change.

The grey Mercedes was gone when she got back, but what did that mean? Did it mean anything? How infinitely more restful the world of John Buchan, a childhood world in which one obliterated a horrible day by drawing the curtains on the autumn evening, and wallowing on one's bed with a box of chocolates and a really nice book from the 'for older girls' shelf.

A world in which Arthur made supper; as simple as could be, an artichoke with mayonnaise. The self-indulgent massacre of one's own digestion, by eating too much mayonnaise, which had a little too much garlic in it – disgusting, delicious – counteracting this with a glass of grappa and Act Two of splendid, robust barrel-organ Verdi. And still having chocolates as well as romance to look forward to. Doctor Davidson, whose name for all this was 'Working up a good fug', understood what was needed. Arlette Sauve, primitive Mediterranean woman, was good at squirrelling away things in obscure places, to be resurrected at moments when famine stalked the land. Virtuous ant. Arthur, lean and improvident northern cicada, bit a small corner of praliné 'to make it last longer'. Strasbourg, northern city much given to chill fog on autumn nights, went about its business on the other side of the curtains. Dralon velvet is one of the more satisfying inventions of recent times.

"I've been giving this matter thought," said Arthur at breakfast. "Doorbells rung by agitated locals are your province, but," gazing out of the window, "this, flatly, is mine. I recognize the spirit which moves you, but any further ghosts out of my past will be exorcized by me. Aha, there are reinforcements this morning. A newish Renault with Paris plates – the good Mr Hertz or the unrare Mr Avis. A deputation is going to call, I fancy. I shan't go to work – this has to be settled."

"Very well," said Arlette clearing away breakfast things: it wasn't a 'Spanish day'. "I'll just go listen to my tape." There was nothing on it, but the doorbell burred while she was resetting it.

"Suiting the action to the word," said Arthur going to answer it. She made herself still in a corner of the livingroom, with the mending-basket and her sewing box.

He came back with a young woman not previously seen, soberly dressed and restrained in manner, but plainly in the grip of strong emotion. She looked extremely tired, and bit her mouth to keep from tears and shrillness.

"My wife," said Arthur politely. "And this is Frau Hartung. She has shown me her passport. Please sit down."

Immobile, as near as might be invisible in her corner, Arlette watched a moving-picture. In her own office she had the habit of detachment, but she had to speak, make notes, work upon the scenario. Here she had only to bite her thread and knot it. It was her job that Arthur was doing. She had never seen him at work before, and this in itself was strange. She was often forced to realize that she herself was only a semi-amateur still. And Arthur was after all a professional. His weakness, of seeing human beings as paragraphs of written case-histories, was less of a handicap than she had thought, which reproved her vanity.

All the stories brought to her were alike: this was no exception. Take a simple, everyday emotion. Play on it a few years until it becomes a neurosis. Complicate it by a stupid misunderstanding. Result, melodrama. One tried to stop them falling over the edge, into murders, policemen, trials.

Such a banal story. In Germany alone, there must be many thousands such.

The woman was making a huge effort. And she was doing it in English. Arlette, who had sometimes had to search the bottom of her soul in a language not her own, knew what it must cost her.

There was a man whom she loved, who was everything to her. This man had suffered and was suffering, and she bore this, but she had become afraid. He had been fathered during the war, by a soldier. The soldier had gone away at the end of the war. While it continued he had come back, and stayed what time leave, and wounds, had allowed, but since the war's end had never more been seen. He had not been killed, or imprisoned – he had simply gone away.

Is it so much to ask? To want to know one's father? She . . . They wished him no harm, they had no resentment. They did not want money. But to know . . . why. Not even that – to be accepted. To have one's bare existence acknowledged. To put, to put, to put things right, at last.

Frau Hartung was sorry, for her incoherence and her poor self-control. She apologized, she had been travelling all night; in the train; she hadn't slept. She did not wish to be an embarrassment, an annoyance, a pest. The man she loved could not come himself, could not bring himself to face this moment. She had come for him. Herself, she had no importance.

What was her work? asked Arthur quietly.

She was a nurse, in a children's hospital, in northern Germany. But forget that: forget her.

Certainly not, said Arthur. But he had one question. However stupid it must appear to her. Why come to him?

Her tension was mounting in a way painful to see, but she kept hold of herself.

But he knew, very well. Wasn't that true?

Yes, he thought he did. She was talking, he thought, about Jacky Karstens. Whom he knew, though not well. Who lived in Spain. He would help her, as far as he could, which was not much. But why these phone calls, these anonymous letters? These presences, amounting to a threat, outside the door? Aggressive behaviour – one got nowhere that way.

She was sorry. That had not been her way of doing things.

Her way, undoubtedly, was better. Very well. This much he could do – an address, in Spain. Because there was undoubtedly a responsibility there, that Mr Karstens must understand, and accept. But – a word of warning. He had a wife there, a family. If he might offer some advice, to go bursting in there, making scenes outside the door, was not at all clever. One must save people's face. He was sure she would agree.

The young woman sat still, looking at him with steady pale eyes.

"I think you can do better than that," she said.

Arthur smiled, but without condescension.

"How do you reach such a conclusion?"

She gathered herself for the last effort.

"Jacky Karstens is here. I am speaking with him."

Arlette, forgotten in her corner, sat stiller yet.

9. The power of the press

It was funny, if ever this could be called funny. Arthur, for once, was fair flabbergasted: he would have said it himself, if able to find a word at all, a splendid word.

Doctor Davidson's self-control, so conspicuously absent when, for example, he had mislaid his reading glasses, was quite unimpaired.

"You are convinced of that?" he asked gently.

"Totally." She was free of it now: her voice had an altogether different timbre. "Beyond any possibility of error."

"I see," musing. "You, of course, have never seen Mr Karstens."

"There is no need."

"I suppose," said Arthur, half-voice, "that we do have about the same height and build. No facial resemblance; mm, features become effaced in the memory. He's some seven-eight years older – after thirty-five years, good God, that doesn't have much bearing. But a voice, surely, one doesn't . . . Tell me," in his speaking voice, "is there among the people outside, anyone who has ever seen Mr Karstens?" He could not avoid giving the 'has' a slight sarcastic emphasis, without any wish to be cruel. The cruelty was not of his making . . .

"Of course," she said with perfect calm.

Arlette got up and slipped quietly out of the room. They stood on the pavement in a group talking; the young woman with fierce emphatic arm movements, the old woman passive, the man calm. Nothing irrational in his bearing, at least.

"I think," said Arlette smiling politely, "there's a good chance of getting this unravelled. If everyone can manage to stay unexcited, why don't you all come in?" They all trooped soberly up the stairs. She stole a glance at that placid elderly soul, who was the key to all this. A vaguely expectant look: one would say of mild curiosity. Yet she saw him – on the pavement, close up – heard his voice – saw him walk. Wasn't that, surely, the moment the bell would ring?

Arthur was standing, with no undue show of dignity, and had lit a cigar; with no need to give himself a countenance. It had occurred to him that he would enjoy one.

"Do you mind introducing yourselves?" in a very British accent.

The girl stood a few paces away, eyes devouring, tense as a cat before the pounce. Pretty girl, if rather too tuned-in.

"I'm your daughter, Angelika. This is my husband, Ernest. My mother – Magda – needs, I think, no introduction." Self-possessed, and polite, he did not laugh. Arlette could see that this Lady-Bracknell situation was afflicting him with a sense of farce. He gave a small formal bow. She's not that old, thought Arlette suddenly. Faded, certainly. But only a few years older than me.

"Now let's see," said Doctor Davidson clinically. "Is there any unmistakeable sign – you might perhaps know, Madame – by which Jacky Karstens could be recognized? Even at this date?"

There was a silence. Then Ernest said, "Yes; there is."

"You see – we don't want any possibility of error."

"Quite so. You," emphatic; it was the clincher, "have a strongly incised scar on your thigh. You were hit by a shell splinter and roughly stitched in a field hospital. There are three small circular marks in a line on your abdomen; entry wounds from machine-gun bullets. And, of course, a tattoo-mark." Arthur beamed, delighted.

"I seem to have a distinguished record."

"After the first action a cross, second-class. After the second, a Knight's Cross." Unsmiling.

"I am delighted to find you so well documented. You, my dear sir, are going to step with me into the next room. By removing my trousers I can rapidly overturn your convictions."

"Cosmetic surgery," said the girl fiercely.

"Not possible," said Ernest shaking his head, with a soothing hand movement. "I'll accept that."

Arthur, now plainly enjoying himself, put the cigar back in his mouth at a Humphrey Bogart angle (facially altered by the plastic surgeon) and stalked out.

Four women and none of them said anything. The Hartung girl sat with downcast eyes and her hands in her lap. Magda, plainly a good soul but a bit bypassed by events – and always had been, by the look of things – sat and looked dazed. Angelika went on standing in the centre of the room, looking at everything, all around, with naked hunger. Arlette felt ashamed of her own comfort. She went and got glasses, and a bottle of perk-Scotch (Council-of-Europe, duty-free) and Perrier water. Mucking about with all this gave Arthur time to reappear blithe as a bird, and Ernest behind him with a long face.

"We're mistaken, I'm afraid," he said bleakly.

"No," Angelika contradicted flatly. "We are not. I know, in my bones."

"A drink all round," said Arlette.

The goddam doorbell rang.

The circulation figures of *Graphik* are as sensational as its style: European society is fascinated by its own pathology. Every week the cripples and monsters are brought into the circus-ring, stripped naked, and paraded with a brass band. They need little prodding; most seem proud of their spectacular deformations. Fat Woman, Two-Headed Child, Girl-sodomized-by-Donkey beam placidly. Even above the smell of sweat, said Arthur Davidson, you smell cant. And cancer. If the metaphor seems too literary or the language too florid, consult any cop or fireman. A traffic accident on any scale above trivial will collect the circus audience from a hundred kilometres off. Showpieces should include ninety per cent third-degree burns, and with luck a good juicy decapitation. Public executions, in our little sea-girt European peninsula, having fallen into disrepute.

Arlette was interested in the acolytes of the ritual. The brass band glances at the acts with indifference; just enough to get their timing right: like cops. But the discoverers, and promoters, of novelties may be expected to show interest in their protégés.

The door opening disclosed a female, normal-looking, but Arlette knew at once who it was. Thirtyish, modest manner, winning smile. This year's fashion; disparate motley of floating chiffons, leather boots, large bag as designed by female Kikuyu for gathering mealie-cobs. Mouth large and spongy; oversize sunglasses failed to mask a trained eye.

"Brigitte Buckenburg."

"To be sure. I knew you were behind this somewhere."

"And I got to thinking that if I came and explained . . ."

"I do think it a good idea. So come in. Things aren't turning out quite as you expected."

Behind her stood a young man, a pleasant face and indifference written all over it. Cop eyes. Trombone-player.

"Oh sorry, I forgot. Herr Schumacher, our photographer," unnecessarily.

"No pictures, I'm afraid." He just nodded. During the next hour she lost sight of him often, for he had the gift of invisibility. She was sure he never uttered the slightest word. Took a drink when given one, with a nod of thanks.

Across what was rapidly becoming a crowded room, Arlette caught a comic look of consternation. What! – more of my putative family?

"From *Graphik*, Arthur." His face cleared in a delightful grin; an interesting phenomenon had come into the sociologist's ken.

"Very nice," he said. "For a moment I thought it was another of my daughters." Arthur needed no help with *Graphik*.

Angelika was crying noisily, being comforted, and having her nose blown by her husband, whom one was warming to. The other young woman was sitting quietly, controlling pain. A nurse in a children's hospital; she knew how to do it. Strangely apart and silent sat Magda, a stiff, half-silly expression on the used, worn face.

"Do you think," said Arlette smiling, "that you could give me a hand making coffee for all these people?" She agreed with alacrity. And a quick, neat-fingered help she was, needing no telling where to find things, nor where things went. A sensible, experienced housewife.

"I'm so sorry," she said. "I didn't want to cause you any trouble. I only wanted to see the children happy . . . I'll just rinse these spoons, shall I?"

It became quite like a party. The young women, repaired and organized by withdrawal to powder their noses, became quite animated. The charming Brigitte and the worthy Ernest explained the comic misunderstanding to one another at some length. The photographer, retired in a corner, made common cause with Hangdog, who loathed people. Arthur got into serious talk with his former daughter, and daughter-in – well, common-law, Arlette supposed it would be called. Magda, having emptied, washed, and polished all the ashtrays, was all set to begin again. The expression on her face said she was itching for a tin of furniture polish in her hand. Arthur, suddenly getting sick of all this, gathered them up with the clear intention of throwing the tribe out.

"You do see, I hope," he was saying to Buckenburg, "that there's nothing to print."

"Oh no. It's dead. I'll be phoning my editor straightaway. What a pity though – would have made a great, great story."

"I'm glad to hear it. A sad story, about simple and honest people." His voice was sinking as his mouth approached her ear: Arlette got closer, to hear.

"Of course, of course; no, dead."

"Because if you printed anything, I should come after you in the middle of the black night, grab a great handful of your pubic hair and give the most unmerciful twist." Great trill or perhaps peal of girlish laughter, eyes blinking very fast behind the huge glasses.

"Scouts Honour," she said.

"Libel wouldn't stop them; it never does," sticking a pipe between his teeth. "I could sue them of course and get damages. They'd risk that happily, if they saw a killing."

"Getting damages is to make a meal of ashes," in a paraphrase of Paul Friedmann's advice to poor Solange Bartholdi. She gave herself some whisky. There weren't even coffee-cups to wash up; Magda had done them all. "I don't really grasp how those people came to make such a foolish error in the first place, and having made it, to persist in it so rigidly." He drew hard on the pipe to get it going.

"They did a bit of bad detective work that connected me with the family Karstens and jumped to a conclusion. The boy – interesting that he couldn't bring himself to face me – was at the bottom of it." The pipe refused to draw and he tapped it out. "In days when I was still interested in such things, I wrote a piece once about soldiery, and the mentality of the Waffen SS. Illustrated by some first-hand details I actually got from Jacky Karstens, one night when we had a few drinks together. This somehow reached the boy's eye. From thread to needle, as you say, the conclusion was jumped at because he wanted to jump at it. For the rest, they were worked up by that infernal press cow. She didn't deny it. Showed me her file. The boy put a silly insert in the agony column of a national newspaper, saying Daddy – should I call you Jacky Karstens or should I say Doctor Arthur Davidson? *Graphik* have a very keen eye for things like that. Said Davidson, within a narrow field, is not an unheard-of person. He's working in Strasbourg; oho, rope the bloodhounds in, let them loose outside his door. Sit back, and watch mischief working. It would, as she said so wistfully, have made a great story.

"A thing, though, I have not grasped. The girl saw her father last when she was two; the boy can never have seen him at all. But that woman – for several periods of up to months at a time I was supposed to share her life. I'd been to bed with her, she'd borne me two children. She knows me, dammit. In her head is a whole fictitious 'me'. Now when she arrives here, the fiction has to be superposed upon a reality, and the two don't fit."

"As you remark, people believe what they want to believe. Rather glib, perhaps, to say Especially Germans of the wartime generation. But it was wartime. It was very long ago. She was very young."

"Dazzle? Rosy haze?"

"I'm not a shrink, you know," said Arlette a little wearily. "I think the capacities of young girls for getting into a rosy haze are exaggerated by legend." She shrugged. "After he left, perhaps she explained things to herself, and her premises weren't very accurate. She had to construct a picture of him, and of what happened, that would allow her to keep her self-respect. Over the years it's been polished and retouched, until it doesn't resemble the original much any more. Like a few old-master pictures . . . It's a good thing, no doubt, that those children get to know their father. But it would probably be a very bad thing if she were ever to meet him again."

"She brought those two children up. Say the girl is aggressive and the boy a bit paralysed, she still didn't do too badly."

"She did a normal thing; there's no need to sentimentalize," said Arlette a little tartly. "Sorry, I'm rather tired." Yawning. "You'll get a soft-boiled egg."

"What was Jacky Karstens like?" she asked, tapping her egg.

"What you'd expect," indistinctly through a mouthful of toast. "Handsome in a florid way, funny, good company, excellent raconteur. Quite intelligent, plenty of gifts, but of no real interest; there was a basic piece lacking, in the character. His great principle in life was never to get involved; then you never get stung. Learned that, perhaps, as a young hero on the Russian front. Boring, because a bit too like a real-life Basil Seal. He would find this episode hilarious. The thought of me having to take my pants off to prove I wasn't him would put him in stitches laughing."

"It's funny for about thirty seconds, and you're the only person entitled to laugh." Arlette had admired the simplicity with which he had solved the problem. Few people have simplicity. They tend to be too vain.

Arthur scraped his eggshell out and looked inside it accusingly. Why was it empty? A fraud there somewhere.

10. Tea and small sympathy

The pavement seemed oddly empty. No Germans. They had gone home, or they had gone into the town for a massive pot of sauerkraut, which is the Strasbourg cure to most ailments, and nearly all frustrations.

She had almost no distance to go. Two minutes' walk, to the corner of the Boulevard de la Victoire. The University is all around one here, and a week or so before the start of an academic year, there were students everywhere. Looking thoughtful: well they might.

Turn left; less than a minute to the busy crossroad of the Boulevard de la Marne, and the Esplanade. The 'real' world, the 'true' world of commerce, haste, greed. Cars streamed past glued to each other's tails, all in a hell of a hurry from where, towards where. When the lights changed she ran across quickly, knowing from experience one had better. People in cars don't like people afoot. What business has anyone being afoot? Such folk are layabouts, parasites, and whatever they're doing, they're up to no good. Another minute, along the peaceful backwater of the Rue Vauban, only leading to the Anvers bridge, and the Port du Rhin quarter; which one would prefer to avoid, on the whole.

There are two or three side-streets. It is an out-of-the-way corner of Strasbourg, and a dingy one. Most of the houses seem to be let in rooms to students, probably because nobody else would want to live there. And here lived, or rather perched, Xavier, whom she had promised to Think About, and she wondered what she was going to say to him. But . . .

Arlette was having an obscure, but surprisingly strong, feeling of being watched. She'd had it all the way. She was being followed. Not at all far; true. Still, at every corner a compulsion to turn around and look carefully about her. All passers-by seemed to be pottering upon banal and innocent pursuits. Was this alarmingly sharp sensation thus irrational? It would appear so. In Arlette-logic, it should be given weight accordingly: she had learned to distrust reason and pay close heed to instinct.

Certainly reason was no help at all, because who the hell could have any use for following her? No Germans or press people. She reviewed in her mind all the people she'd met recently. The only person she could find that seemed remotely likely was Sergeant Subleyras, and that likelihood, based on the supposition that the police did sometimes follow people, and perhaps skilfully enough sometimes not to be clumsy and obvious, was surely precious remote. She had, though, learned a lot over the past year of how devious people can be. The world, which is as simple as $E=mc^2$, is as complicated as Henry James could make it. A great pest, said Arthur, but this is what gives us a living.

The house was very dark, and the minuting of electricity so nicely adjusted that you were plunged into pitchy blackness as you opened the lift door, whereupon the light in the lift went out too, leaving you liable to be mugged, raped, and left in a huddled heap. Arlette searched crossly in her bag for a lighter. Since her bag as usual was stuffed with treasures which men – ha ha – called rubbish, and since a lighter, like a key, a pen, or anything else one wants in a hurry, is adept at hiding, she stayed in the dark long enough to get frightened. Suppose the follower were creeping soft-soled up the fire stairs . . . She cursed this idiotic performance, found the lighter; the lighter found her the electricity switch for the passage; the current lasted just long enough for her to find the number of Xavier's door and went out. It was that kind of building. She found the bell-push with her finger, and pressed it. Xavier opened the door, shed light on everything, and was confused at finding her looking put-out. His profuse apologies put her much further out: she swallowed her malcontent.

The 'studio' was fairly large, which meant old: they have

shrunk steadily in size as the years have gone by. Light, because the window was large, even though the street was both dingy and narrow. Neat, although there was too much furniture; consequence of having had a much larger flat. Clean, because Xavier had made a special effort. He had learned, and doubtless painfully, the arts of living alone in a studio flat, and how very difficult it is to get fresh vegetables, after once eating cabbage three days running and still having to throw half away. He'd never had a broom in his hand, or known what eau-de-javel is used for. There is nothing more helpless than the bourgeois male deprived of that necessary adjunct, the bourgeois female, who is so much tougher than he is.

It was what Arlette had come to see. She felt heartened; Xavier had had that much resource. He was very stiff and pompous, and pathetically glad to see her.

She wanted to finish with him quickly. This was not only from unworthy motives of feeling unable to charge him anything: self-respect would make him insist on paying her for her time. Collecting lame ducks wasn't the thing: had she needed the lesson her years doing physiotherapy had taught her. She wasn't a psychiatrist; nor was she a soup-kitchen. In order to be helped, people must help themselves. He mustn't depend upon her: he'd be falling in love with her or something, which would be most unsuitable.

So drinking coffee, and not about to jump-up-to-help with cups and stuff, she did her best to be pithy.

"What did you say?" asked Arthur at suppertime that evening.

"If I'd been talking to you – English bourgeois man of literary leanings – I'd have said go read *Little Dorrit* – all about society."

"Shaw said that after reading it, one could be nothing but a socialist; which is perfectly true."

"He's in the same position as Arthur Clennam."

"And if he doesn't meet a little Dorrit, who are after all sadly rare."

"But he's likelier to meet the man who is so skilful with his hands, but knows nothing of business or formfilling or administration – they're not so rare."

"Daniel Doyce – well, you give him good advice. Will he be able to follow it? Flexible enough, enough sap in him? Will he bend, or break?"

"He's a classic, isn't he, and they're often a wet mess, and one can't tell. I suppose he's likely to remain a wet mess whatever happens and whatever I say. One has known so many like that. Monasteries are always full of them; they incline to religion. Or Alcoholics Anonymous."

"There should be a Businessmen Anonymous. I think in Paris at least there is, existing to help bewildered ex-executives exist. To coin a phrase."

"I've a nasty feeling I haven't heard the end of him. One should get them to go and read Carlos Castaneda – Don Juan has such very good advice for them. Too dangerous though; they're far too fatally inclined as it is to topple over into Transcendental Meditation." She had cooked a large and successful supper, to make up for the soft-boiled egg at lunch, to make up for the cup of coffee Xavier had given her, and the rather small sympathy she'd given him. She felt a good deal better.

She had come home, in fact, much depressed. Luckily Arthur had felt that a half day's work was not better than none at all; was in fact rather worse; had come home early too; had done some shopping; was in a cookery mood. Why don't we both do it? – something nice and long and complex? Now while we're at it, why don't you tell about all these mysterious errands you've been upon?

"Such a boring story," wailed Mrs Davidson. "Or rather, about ten boring stories. All those failures."

"Now come on. You're supposed to be building up. Motivating yourself. Winding your spring. Whatever they call it."

"I'm getting more and more frustrated. All these people and nothing whatever I can do about it. There was the little man who disappeared in the Rhine. That man over on the coast who did away with Rebecca – you were drunkenly facetious and I was very greatly vexed. Since we've been home, barely two days: that poor wretch I was too late to stop killing herself. The woman whose son was killed. These silly Germans and that poor limp boy telling himself stories about his heroic father. This drink of water, Xavier."

"Come on; you're not doing yourself justice. The girl who, the woman who, the drink-of-water who, you're talking as though they were all dead. Like actors one hears complaining about those awful fish faces in the front row: without them, they wouldn't be functioning at all; they wouldn't even be alive. Same with you. Without all these people, you wouldn't be getting anywhere with Xavier. You told him to act like a man for once in his life and that's excellent advice. Been plenty of times in my own life when I stood gravely in need of it. This is a lot of grit, no doubt, but you're like a hen's digestion, you don't work properly without grit. If you're going to be any use to Madame Bartholdi or Xavier, or Subleyras, you've got to accept a high percentage of failure."

"Subleyras – marvellous man I thought then – beset by doubts, now."

"If you weren't beset by doubt, you'd be another self-satisfied prick like our President."

"I do realize," still in a tearful tone, "but, it's all one thing after another."

"Odtaa," said Arthur comfortably, "good old English expression that. Title likewise of delightful book to which I am much attached – I wonder whether that would find a reader, now. Have a drink – those wretched Germans tired you."

"I had much too much, already this morning."

"Then have some more," said Arthur sensibly, and went down to the cellar for a bottle of bulls' blood. One was in need of a transfusion, he said.

Arlette was looking desolately at the television. There was some governmental propaganda going on about Industrial Accidents. We must have Fewer: illustrated by white-faced woman being told that her man has just had an unhappy meeting with an overhead crane in the factory. She turned this off.

"Sociologically speaking, they should be asking for more, not less. Help get their unemployment figures down. There'll be the President, shortly. Ask him about – oh, take Vietnamese drowning by the boatload. Again sociologically, you'd point out that it's perhaps less painful and certainly quicker than dying in heaps by starvation, which is the fate of a great many more. But what he'll say is Waw, we must sawtainly have a committee about this next month. He'll deliver a peroration abawt this pawblem. And with any luck at all, they'll all be dead by then."

Arlette was brightening, whether at the Davidson patter or the bulls' blood didn't matter much.

He had bought, most extravagantly, a saddle of lamb. As he remarked, very Forsytean. They didn't know how to cook it nor how to cut it, but doubtless it was a pretext for a lot of excellent claret. He did know how to cook it and how to cut it, but was no claret-lover. What did this prove?

He continued in this vein until she was herself again.

The washing-up was done. Peace reigned. Or a sort of comfortable content, which served the same purpose. Arthur installed himself with pomp in his chair, and started to clean a pipe, with a nice book – *The History of Anti-Semitism* by Monsieur Poliakoff, a majestic affair – to hand. Arlette read her Spanish newspaper, being a believer in Mr Maugham's dictum that this is the way to learn foreign languages. There was a sotto voce mutter when she did this. The French mouth does not adapt easily to other pronunciations. It wasn't that bothersome jota since many, many years ago she had had to learn Dutch, and the notorious Dutch g is just the same, but saying Baja de Vizcaya rapidly to oneself creates, thought Arthur, a comfortable small noise something between a cat and an open fire. The doorbell rang. Truedog barked in a purple indignation. Arlette did not look up, but consoled him with her free hand until the noise subsided into someone saying Baja de Vizcaya in a loud angry manner.

"Who on earth can that be this time of night?" said Arthur experimentally. Arlette still didn't look up. He shuffled off like a burdened donkey. He explained, afterwards, his shameful weakness by the double handicap of an empty pipe found in his hand, which he'd stuck in his mouth to get rid of it; and having one sock on and one slipper: the other slipper having got stuck somehow under the chair. The reality was that Miss Buckenburg, disclosed being charming on the doorstep, was under his guard in a flash.

"A peace offering," she said in her nicest voice. "Because I pestered you." She was carrying a large expensive bunch of flowers and a bottle of expensive malt whisky in a box with coats of arms and repoussé silver lettering in cute Celtic script. What was I supposed to do? asked Arthur plaintively. Tear it out of her tenacious little paws and slam the door in her face? This was indeed odtaa . . .

"You don't give up easily, do you?" said Arlette, kicking truedog in the ribs. Dog hated Miss Buckenburg, if possible even more than she did.

"Well, I thought, you see, that to make up for all this stupidity we could do you a really nice little interview." From her bananabag she produced a little pocket recorder, all ready. Arlette looked at the flowers, which were really very pretty. At the whisky, which Arthur was eyeing appreciatively with a face exactly like Captain Haddock. No beard, admitted, but tiny shiny eyes. She sighed deeply.

"Go ahead, then." The press, being utterly brazen, always did get its way in the end.

The American Beauty Rose went blahblahblah professionally into her mike, checked the thing swiftly for voice level, assumed the interviewer's tone and asked, "How actually do you see the job you're doing? Can you define it?"

Arlette thought; the little wheels turned; Arthur uncorked the bottle with a soft plop; what did it amount to, really? A tape.

"Things happen. To us all; today's no exception. Unexpected, disconcerting, perhaps tragic. Who is there, that might help, at the best do something, at the worst listen?

"One doesn't help them much. People have to help themselves." There was a glass under her nose.

"I got a lesson today from my husband. You can't use that. But by being unafraid of humiliation or embarrassment he got rid of a thing that had been a thorn in their eye for years: it's worth the effort.

"People go to the police who say they can't intervene, to lawyers who do nothing, to doctors who give them a pill, or priests with consolations, another pill. They run to these Encounter places and end with a partner for the night; likewise a pill.

"Offices in general have the same handicap: rigidity. They run on fixed tramway lines. They may be interested and they may be experienced and they do good, but they see one facet, and most things are a heap of facets. A woman needs the Social Worker, the Housing Inspector, the Cruelty to Children man, the Battered Wives shelter, the Family Allowance office, the Employment bureau, the Rents Tribunal, and what about an abortion to be going on with. They're swamped. They're up to here with confusion, discouragement, frustration. And most people, as you know, aren't very articulate," pausing for breath and a solid pull at the glass: what a day this had been.

"Often it's a matter of knowing which string to pull. Nobody tells them; I often can. Mr Thing, office two-o-three, phone extension four-o-seven; he's your man. All that's needed, often, is someone to give them the confidence to begin."

"There's a living, in this?"

"I can spend a day, frigging about. Frustration all round. Nothing useful I can do and no payment I can ask. But a quarter of an hour can make a difference. A phonecall, a little good will, a small scrap of effort. A quarter of an hour first, just listening. A specialist consultation like any other. What would you give fifty francs for – say twenty-five marks? – and think it well spent?"

"Since we agree not to use today's episode, can you find a concrete example?"

"A simple one, and very difficult. From just before the holidays. And a German one.

"A house with four or five apartments. One of the tenants is a drunk, a psychopath. Unemployable. Pays no rent; never has. He's noisy, he pesters everyone, flashes a knife. Skilful mix of blackmail and bullying. He has a girl too, Jugoslav, a poor wretch, only seventeen. Illiterate, eight months pregnant, no job, no parents.

"Tenant came to me. Gentle, quiet person, young schoolteacher. What can we do? My wife's in terror; it's very bad for our small child. The owner does nothing, the police will do nothing, the prosecutor, the mayor, nobody. The fellow's antisocial, but there's no legal hold on him. Nobody will touch the problem, they sheer off it. A mixture of violence and cunning, and he has everybody by the balls."

"What do you suggest?" asked Miss Buckenburg, grinning.

"Quite," said Arlette tartly. "These people, like most young Germans, are pacifist and believe in non-violence. So do I. Nothing is ever gained by violence. But after looking at this problem, I could see cowardice everywhere. What do you do when you've exhausted non-violent means, or there just aren't any? Reason is useless. Sociopathic people, the line between reason and nonreason is indistinct. You have to find something they will understand. Which can only be violence. And there you are, on the horns of the dilemma. I found a way of putting him in fear and putting him to flight. I'm not saying how, because I'm not proud of it. I'm not proud of the result, either."

"You put him to flight, and he turns up some place else."

"Intact. More violent than ever. And the problem of the girl not touched. So I didn't do it. I did nothing. And I'm not proud of that either."

"So what happens?"

"Nothing. They learn to live with the problem. Maybe it'll quieten down, maybe the girl and the child will lend him some stability. Not a chance in a hundred, to my mind. Sooner or later a drunk who plays with knives meets someone quicker with a knife than he is. The local police, conspicuous for apathy as well as cowardice, will then have bread on their plate. Somebody will go to jail for a week or so. And then the social-care services will say oh yes, there's a minor in peril, and a child in jeopardy. Until then, nothing." She drank the glass of whisky off, and pushed it across the table for more.

"Short and sweet," said Miss Buckenburg.

"Twenty-five marks please."

"That'll make a very nice piece," with profound insincerity as she switched the recorder off.

"You don't have to bother about them using a single word of that," remarked Doctor Davidson after Miss Buckenburg had finally removed herself. "That one was strictly of no interest to the readership."

"It was whisky talking, too," said Arlette sadly.

"Mr Chamberlain acquired much odium for his behaviour at Munich. Conveniently forgotten is the praise he received at the time. Do you know that there was a member of the Commons who suggested there should be a statue to the preserver of world peace? It strikes you as fulsome? We have here a number of German men, including those in uniform, who when faced with this loud personage yelling that he'll see the colour of their stripes, hasten to offer sympathy and cups of tea. This I find poignant."

"I just found it typical. Everyone pushed the odium on to someone else."

"What, by the way, was the solution you discreetly censored?"

"Oh, that they should get together, take hold of the fellow and tip him in the canal. They weren't up to that, naturally. Then I found a Pole, in the village. Ex-foreign-legion type. You can imagine the kind of barbarian that is."

"Yes, indeed," laughing heartily.

"He saw no problem at all. 'I wait outside pub. I say, you, Nazi pig, take yourself bloody quick out everybody's sight. Otherwise I break quart beerbottle over ugly skull, shove splinters in your nasty face.' I had great difficulty stopping him."

"It would have worked too."

"That's right: you wouldn't have seen his heels for dust. These irrational people, they're ever so rational and ever so sensitive, when they smell smoke. But I—well, would you?"

"No," said Arthur. "Cups of tea, rational and sympathetic consideration is my strength. Who am I, to go kicking Neville Chamberlain?"

"And it was such a lovely war. I'm utterly drained, let's go to bed."

11. Alarms too loud, and excursions too numerous

Day dawned, neither good nor bad. The sun did not shine, but it wasn't raining either. Arthur, the coffee-maker, made coffee. Discussion at breakfast was desultory.

"What was all that about Argentina?" asked Arthur, turning the pages of the local paper with languid distaste. "I know the subject was raised, but I must admit I wasn't listening very attentively."

"People seemed to think I'd be thrilled at the prospect. As though it were next door, Frankfurt or somewhere. As though I could do the faintest good if I did go. Wave a magic wand or something. What am I supposed to do – walk in to see the general? Tell him sorry, I've lost a boy, d'you mind rounding him up for me? Weird thing about this sort of folk; take it for granted that any caprice they get in their head will be law to me."

"Only wanted to clear my mind," alarmed at all this tirade.

"Set it at rest."

After listening to her tape – there was nothing on it – she put her coat on and was painting her face in the hallway, when Arthur stumped through on his way to work.

"Try and have a quiet day, mm?"

"I'm only slipping over to Neudorf. Nobody battering the door down, for once."

"What good d'you think you'll do there?"

"None, probably. I said I would, that's all. Be back to look after the dinner."

The purlieues of Solange's flat smelt, as expected, of drains, dustbins and neglect: to wit, poverty. The flat, also as expected, was spotless and smelt like it: her windows put Arlette to shame.

Solange beamed at seeing her, and offered all the hospitality of poor people; embarrassing because there is so much of it. Coffee, and I'll just-whip-out-to-the-baker: saying no, no, please don't bother, sounds both high-hat and ungrateful. It isn't a bother to them. You've given away that it would be a bother, if you had to do it.

"I've nothing much to bring you." She wasn't going to mention Sergeant Subleyras. "There's a faint chance of digging up the police file, but I don't hold much hope out. If there were any irregularities in it, they'd be that much more determined to keep them covered up. There are legal means of getting it, but the advocate I've consulted doesn't like them. It's not that he's frightened – on the contrary, he's strongly left wing – but he doesn't like the grounds on which he'd have to plead. They lead rather towards that grudging award of the symbolic franc, don't you know. You could give the man a bad time in court, saddle him with high costs, but he doesn't see much point in being vindictive just to satisfy rancour, and I felt able to tell him that it wasn't the way I read your intentions either."

"Two wrongs wouldn't make a right."

"And they'd see to giving you as nasty a time as possible in court, and the costs – very likely no award, and however hard we try to keep them down, they're bound to be high."

"I can't see any use in it."

"Remains a human sort of approach to this man – would you let me try that?"

"I wrote him a letter. Never got any answer, of course. Was stupid of me; let off steam, 'n I must have sounded pretty spiteful."

"All the same I can try."

"Thibault, William Thibault. I wouldn't mind – but the world's full of it. How many more are there?" It wasn't too clearly put, but Arlette understood. "We're this whatsername, advanced society, they keep telling us. Liberal, and social justice for all, and we're supposed to feel so grateful. We're not in Africa being massacred by a cannibal general, being starved to death like the Gambodges. Who're they all trying to kid? When everybody knows it isn't so. I know I'm ignorant and stupid and I'll always be poor because I don't deserve any better. So fair enough. I don't need that slimy bastard on the television in his beautiful suit and his big armchair telling me. Used always to be, there's good times just around the corner. We know that song. Now he keeps saying everything's lovely already. For the rich it is, sure. I'm not voting neither for that communist bastard laughing all the time at his own cleverness. Big a bullshitter as the other, don't care a fuck about the poor, wanting to get their own muzzle in the trough is all."

And could Mrs Davidson put it any more succinctly? Could she see any further into the glorious rosy dawn? Did she feel any more satisfied with all those smiling well-fed faces?

"I have to trust you," said Solange. "If there's no way out of this – tell me so straight."

"I will; I promise."

It was not market-day in the Boulevard de la Marne: she stopped in the Esplanade for one or two things, since she was 'out anyway'. In the kitchen she thought a while about dinner, got a rather sluggish Spanish response to a request that the windows be cleaner; it was an hour before she got back to the office to think about Mr William Thibault.

On her tape were grunts and clicks indicative of people who'd got wrong numbers, or cold feet: quite a lot of people didn't like leaving recorded messages; it was as though they were afraid of giving themselves away. She could sympathize. Talking to somebody you could not see was bad enough; talking to recorders, computers, and such cattle was preferably left to the Japanese. Timed some way back was a message from Arthur saying "Arlette, ring me back, would you," that sounded brusque.

"Doctor there?" Originally a joke, then a cliché, it had become campus-wide: even pompous professors from the Law Faculty rang up these days asking for Doctor.

"Oh, he flew out. Said if you rang it wasn't to worry about and see you at lunch." All right then. She had heaved the directory up on the table and was fluttering it when the thing rang in her ear.

"Van der Valk," she said in a manner bespeaking irritation.

There was a pause, and a voice said, "Recorders, hey?"

"No, this is a direct line."

"You mean, this is the lady speaking?"

"That's right; you can speak freely."

"That's good." Funny voice; soft and a little hoarse, and with a giggle or chuckle in it as though something were highly entertaining. "This is a message from a friend, good friend, of someone you got into trouble. So he'd like to know some trouble came back to you. Be a satisfaction to him, y'know. Juss for starters. The soup."

"What is?" enunciating clearly and crossly.

"Oh you don't know yet? Take a look, then, in the Rue Vauban."

"Quatsch," said Arlette in vulgar German and banged the phone down. More idiot mystifications. That voice, though, had not been German. French, but an accent she could not quite bring home. And what was interesting about the Rue Vauban?

She jumped up. Arthur? She ran downstairs.

The car was pointing the wrong way – but the wrong way, while longer, was as quick. All right turns instead of left . . . she flew down to the avenue, over the crossing of the Boulevard de la Marne, turned right at the Rue de Flandre – and felt a surge of relief. There was Arthur, looking quite normal and in earnest conversation with somebody on the pavement. She braked to a stop and jumped out. Arthur looked startled.

"Where do you spring from?"

"Never mind that: what's happened?"

"Something rather nasty. This is the police, by the way." Meaning be prudent, and keep your mouth shut? Or only . . .

"That poor man who lives here . . ."

"Whom you know, Madame, do you?" struck in the cop, staring at her with a boiled police eye.

She realized that she had to get a grip upon herself. But Arthur was all right.

"Whom I know very slightly; he's a client of mine."

"Got himself mugged," said the cop succinctly, staring for signs of reaction.

"The ambulance just left," said Arthur, pointing down the road towards the Esplanade. "He's not too badly hurt, they hope. I was going to see him, and more or less stumbled over him."

Thoughts chased one another very rapidly. Why on earth would Arthur want to go and see Xavier? Good God, that horrible dark passage. She'd been frightened herself. And just before, she'd had the weirdest sensation of hostile eyes . . . And all this, but definitely, she wasn't going to blab out on the pavement. Not only because of cops, but those hostile eyes were there this minute somewhere here, looking, and laughing silently, heartily, at her disarray.

"He had business troubles about which he consulted me – I'm an advice bureau."

"Madame van der Valk, is that right? But you're the wife of this gentleman here? Professional name, I understand. All right, I'm waiting for the van here, so we can look about a bit. There's no point in your sticking around, but I'll ask you to come down to the station this afternoon, both of you, for a statement, okay? Make it soon after lunch, what it looks like I won't get. Bon appétit tout de même," without any wish to be nasty, just cop-blunt.

"You get in the car," said Arthur. "I'll drive."

"But Arthur – what . . . ?"

"Wait till we're home."

It was not difficult to piece together. The voice with the chuckle – Arthur couldn't bring the accent home either – had phoned him this morning at the office, while Arlette was in Neudorf. Look mister, this is a kind word from a friend, something you ought to know, and that is your wife's cheating on you. Going along with this generous thought, meaning without laughing, Arthur asked for more, to be told that yesterday she was up there screwing with this guy. He had thanked the kind friend politely, thought of ringing her, hadn't got her, recalled afterthought that she'd said there in the Rue Vauban, and – seeing it was no distance – decided that since the kind-friend would very likely attempt to tap the wealthy-looking Monsieur Thing for a small loan until his ship came in, it was a good idea to pass by and put him wise. Since Arlette still wasn't home – oh, she'd been to the supermarket, of course that was it – he'd broken all the rules, gone in her office and peeked at her day-book, but did she agree, it seemed justified on the whole. The kind-friend sounded like trouble, and he didn't want any spilling over on her.

Absolutely. K-f had tried to ring her, found the recorder on, didn't fancy a record of his voice, or presumably his message, got her much later after she'd been in the kitchen – let's eat now or it'll spoil – and been put out at her not going off pop, so had told her to see for herself. She'd been alarmed for Him. Bouh, that horrible dark passage, she'd had premonitions about it.

"I simply haven't a clue about this: it makes no sense at all."

"Yes, I feel like the man who went to the play by Shakespeare and when asked what he thought of it said the alarums were too loud and the excursions too numerous."

"Indeed. Or like President Hindenburg being taken to a gala performance of *The Magic Flute*: he said afterwards that if he'd known what it was all about maybe he'd have enjoyed it better."

"Our trouble is now that the cops are mixed up in all this."

"Yes. The poor man – was he much hurt?"

"I couldn't see too well in that dark passage. Nobody answered the bell, and I was just thinking it would keep, after all, when I noticed the door was open a crack, and in a building like that where the main door's open half the time – found it open myself – that's bad news. So I gave it a push, and there was the resistance that gives a little, and I realized he was there behind the door. I worked in, and there was a nasty amount of blood. He'd been bashed around the head. I didn't look further, ran like crazy I don't mind saying, rang the police at once. Ambulance man said concussion certainly, and facial injuries, and they'd have to hope nothing internal: he was semi-conscious, but couldn't talk. Cops took a look and said the place was turned upside down and stuff stolen."

"Poor Xavier. He had so little left. It might be good to get rid of all the old pattern: let's hope that will be so. He was rather an albatross round my neck; be still more of one now, poor devil."

"But why does the kind-friend pursue this fantasy of you going for a screw?"

"And where does he get these imaginative flights from?" added Arlette a bit dry. "Xavier was hardly the person to – mm, perhaps to get such fantasies, but to boast of them . . . No, this is all from somewhere outside. What on earth are we to tell the police?"

12. Up to here in cops

"What I must do, I think, is get hold of Sergeant Subleyras."

" 'Everybody tries to get into the act'," suggested Arthur.

"I don't think so," said Arlette. "Not just a banal break-in; blows and wounds, that's for the Crime Squad. I think it as well to have an ally. Or not so much of an ally, as someone one knows to be both intelligent and conscientious, and to have notions of tact. All rather rare qualities in these circles." Looking it up: dialling.

"Sergeant Subleyras, please: I don't know the extension."

"Putting you through . . . Sohn here, Crime Squad. Wanted Subleyras, did you? Well, he's not available for the moment. Get him to ring you back, or can I help you?"

"Tell him Madame Davidson, if you would."

"Okay." She hadn't said 'Van der Valk' and Subleyras would have the intelligence to put two and two together.

"We'll hold on a bit," suggested Arlette, "before going down to act the wide-eyed innocent. Just in case there's something we ought to know. Murky waters. First, nobody I can think of has any grievances against me. Second, even if they had, why slash at Xavier who's perfectly inoffensive? And if it's somebody with a grievance against Xavier, then why me?" The phone rang.

"Subleyras here," said a quiet even voice. "Yes, Madame Davidson, what is there for your service?" It is a formal French phrase whose pomposity is given an ironic inflection, generally used to distance the speaker a little, and whose meaning is not far off 'What are you bothering me about?'

"There was a man mugged this morning in the Rue Vauban, and rather badly injured I'm afraid. He was a client of mine, but I hardly know him. I'll have to go down to the commissariat to make a statement about it. Before I do, I wondered whether anything had come to light that would provide any explanation. Because I don't understand it in the least. I got an anonymous phonecall, seeming to hold some veiled menace to myself."

"I see. The conduct of this affair is not in my hands. I suggest that you come down and ask to see the officer in charge of the matter you refer to. That's the best advice I can give you." And the ringing off couldn't be more icy.

"Jesus," said Arlette much disconcerted.

"Well, I'd be a wide-eyed innocent," said Arthur.

"Very good then. When in doubt, tell the truth. I've no intention of getting into trouble with the constabulary."

"Trouble with peelers is that they can never bring themselves to believe that anyone would tell them the truth, any old where."

So, sadly, it proved. What an unlikely tale, said the face of the plainclothes man behind the typewriter, at the commissariat, gunbelt hung on the back of his chair, in a forbidding little office with all the windows shut. The knowing look. If that's what you say, we'll write it down. When, as is very likely, the instructing magistrate has questions to ask, for this is a serious-bodily-harm rap, you will have different things to say, and I shan't be surprised because you look dodgy to me.

The cops like things simple. So it was a fellow there breaking and entering, and when caught he used violence. Or it was a vice thing. This – what was his name . . . hunting in the file – Marchand. A homosexual, no doubt?

Madame Davidson didn't know him that well. Thought it unlikely; had no worthwhile opinion, one way or another.

Right. So he consulted you. And then you went to see him?

Correct. I always do when I can. What people say, and how they behave, in the office is one thing. At home is another. One learns more.

Quite so. Now when you hardly knew him – despite going to see him – it's funny someone rings you up about it, to tell you he's been clonked. Verdad?

Si, verdad, very funny. Like to know why myself. Hope the police will be able to tell me.

And what does Mr Davidson have to say about that?

He doesn't. Got a funny phonecall, as his secretary will confirm. Blackmail or malice directed at whom, and why, no idea. Mischief-making is obvious, and to cut it off at the root is desirable. One goes round to see Mr Marchand, is the obvious reaction, to see what, if anything, he knows about this.

This? Meaning the phonecall, or meaning sleeping with your wife?

Please take the trouble, Mister, not to be offensive.

No insult intended: no need to be touchy. Was there now? You are touchy, very touchy; at the suggestion. Aren't you now?

Anybody can insinuate anything, anonymously. As this shows. It doesn't help if a responsible official does the same. In other words, if you have a hypothesis to suppose, suppose it.

Could be a workable hypothesis, couldn't it though. Nothing implausible, nothing improbable. Common form. Mr X has a certain doubt as to whether the relations between Mrs X and Mr Y are altogether free from shadow. To relieve his mind, Mr X pays a visit to Mr Y. Who doesn't like the insinuation, or maybe again he does. He might enjoy shoving it up Mr X and twisting it. Self-control snaps, and X reaches for the nearest blunt instrument. Call this the corniest scenario known to mankind and you won't make it the less frequent or less real. The good old triangle, right? Crime of passion, right? Hardly a crime at all to some people's thinking. Stuff that a jury scarcely bothered to retire for. Hell, the fellow wasn't even dead. Handsome home-wrecker. Put him in court and he doesn't have a leg to stand on. Look, one has only to play ball and the sympathy and support of everyone right up to the president of the tribunal is assured. Automatically. As night follows day.

"If you've finished typing out my deposition," said Arthur, "I'll have pleasure in signing it."

"You've nothing further to add?"

"If you insist. You can put it on the record and welcome. Since you have insulted my wife here present in a singularly dirty way, any lapse of self-control on my part would lead to the blunt instrument flying your way, I'm afraid. Which would lead to a charge of violence against duly constituted authority. That would be deplorable. If you find me offensive, I'm sorry for it. Shall we agree to leave it all unsaid? Finish at the point where the ascertainable facts came to a stop?"

"You take responsibility for your attitude, Mr Davidson," unrolling the forms and pushing them across to sign.

"So does Mrs Davidson," colourlessly.

"Mrs Davidson," said Arlette, "has no comment at all of any kind to add to that last remark."

"Have we earned a drink?"

"We have indeed. Does it occur to you that we may have discovered the motivation for the whole thing?" asked Arthur. "I mean that it appeared meaningless, which puzzled us. But if somebody wished to plunge us both into a barrel of shit. Suppose my fingerprints were on the blood-spattered marble paperweight. I could have lost my job and you, your career."

"I don't think so. The mechanics of it don't stand up. Even if you receive a highly needling and exasperating set of hints, nobody can guarantee your reaction. The hint wasn't that if you popped round sharpish you'd catch the guilty pair in bed. Or was it?"

"No, the trend was more I should go pin a black eye on you."

"Give it all no further thought," said Arlette. "Malice is

ever-present. If a dimension can be added to it by the crass imbecility of Dogberries, that's putting whipped cream on it. Nobody can drive a wedge into our solidarity and malice is defeated."

"Irrational belief is a strange thing," pronounced Arthur. "I mean how hard it can be to shake. Look at my daughter, Angelika. If I'd once caught my tummy on a barbed-wire fence we'd now be a headline in *Graphik*. That would add a dimension, wouldn't it!" Arlette, laughing, moved to stop the telephone ringing.

"Yes, this is Madame Davidson," in an extraordinary high hawing soprano.

"Subleyras," said a voice also much changed from the last time she had heard it.

"Well, well, fancy hearing from you. My favourite flic."

"Yes, perhaps it calls for some clarification, as the PR people say. I was going to ask whether a drink would find favour, after office hours. On neutral ground like. But judging by your voice, you're good and mad at me."

"As far as I'm concerned, office hours are over right now. I've been having the loveliest time with cops all afternoon. I could say one more wouldn't make any difference, and I could say one more was the drop that made the cup flow over."

"Want to find out? I'm out of the office myself."

"Then the pub is the place," said Arlette. "The Elephant on the boulevard."

"A quarter of an hour, to allow for traffic?"

"And be glad I'm a forgiving person." Ringing off.

"Boozy we are, these last days," said Arthur.

"God, yes, putting on pounds and pounds. Go on the wagon tomorrow or none of my poppers will fasten. You want to meet one of my prospective lovers?"

"The prospect, as you put it, is attractive. In general, I think I'd better stay out of your affairs. And what I'm thinking of, you know, is a visit to the hospital. The wounded one. Two on one day might be a bit much."

"He might not want to see me. But if he does, I'll go this evening."

"Will you be back before supper?" A way of asking whether she was going to make the supper.

"If I'm not," said Arlette, "raise the alarm."

"A cup of coffee, please, and a small Vittel water."

"And a pastis," added Subleyras. He was dressed as she had last seen him, and looked no different. But was different.

"To clear up whatever left a bad smell," he said, "I've handed my cards in. The authorities took a dim view. Whether or not they're sorry to lose me is beside the point: they decided I'd regret this decision and I could start regretting it right now. It was suggested to me that any pretence of going through the motions – I asked, you see, for a private interview with the old man this morning – was sort of superfluous to requirements. When I said to you that the affair didn't concern me, I was telling the truth strict and exact: I was asked to concern myself no longer with any current affairs, and hand my files over. Also, there were ears flapping in that office, because the grapevine in that building functions better than most electronics and not much slower."

"I see perfectly."

"Now I have some administrative demobbing to do, while they see how much of any gratuities and suchlike they can screw me out of. But as of now, my medal is dead. I better, you know, keep a corner of my eye well screwed on the Official Secrets Act. But my brains are my own." Reaching into his pocket, producing a cigar, lighting it and blowing a smoke ring. "So I don't know much about what happened to you. Still, if you give me an outline, I might be able to fill in gaps." He listened, peacefully. He looked serious, then he grinned.

"First, you've nothing to worry about. If there was any idea afoot of discrediting you or putting a spoke in your professional wheel, I'd know. Remember that before I came down to see you, I looked you up fairly thoroughly. You've a clean slate, and a couple of good friends. The boss over at the PJ, who took sort of a fancy to you, and you might say started you off, is being transferred. Up, not down. That will be official in a day or so or a week. There isn't a formal review of all his little arrangements. There might be, if he were being sent sideways, but he isn't. He's getting Versailles, and that's close to the ears and eyes up at the top. So nobody's going to stab you. The new one's been here before, in a less exalted role, but he knows all the ropes. So no boats get rocked. Don't get lodged in his eye for a few months. As a man, incidentally, he bears a far resemblance to a human being. More than that I either can't say, or couldn't.

"Second, the fellow who took your statement, I know him of course, he's just a misbegotten oaf, but he has no importance. Reading it with my eye, I'd say he'd got told you were all right, and of course your husband is all right, and he just thought he'd throw a bit of bullshit up against the fan to keep you from getting uppity. You'll never hear any more about this, but of course if they peg anybody, which I've no idea about at all because they know nothing, that's clear, then you'll just have the usual witnessing to do with whatever judge is on the job.

"Third, just remember that anybody who's like your husband and has friends in the European set-up is a sensitive subject among cops. Recall those Danes who had a turnup in a nightclub. Recall the Austrian Foreign Minister being mugged. Need say no more, I think."

"Correct my reading – if we did something blatant we'd get pegged loudly and with much self-righteous virtue, but they'd really make sure first they weren't in any way vulnerable."

"A little crude, but it'll pass. You have to bear in mind that they're trying to push Strasbourg as the seat of European government, and that's not by any means a foregone conclusion. Why not Brussels, where everyone, and not just cops, is housetrained and breaks no china?"

"And is this going to be the seat of whatnot?"

"Don't ask me; I'm not the mayor. What's more, I don't care. All I know is things will fumble on a while, a longish while, neither one thing nor another, because when did you ever know a government, any government, that made its mind up about anything ticklish and having done so, said so? Do nothing, is their motto. The money's coming in, right?"

"Which, finally, is why you've decided to stop doing nothing, make your mind up, and say so."

"The dignity of my office," said Subleyras sounding exactly like Mr Ziegler of the good old Nixon days, "forbids my making the slightest comment on any insinuation that low. Anything I said would only give the scandal-rags an importance they don't deserve."

"No comment is needed. Two cops got jugged yesterday for fifteen years, for raping a thirteen-year-old Arab."

"Which nearly," now quite serious, "stopped me this morning. There's good, you see, as well as bad. But finally, it's like priests. Fewer means better, because you really got to make your mind up that this is what your life is for. But it's got to be clearly defined. What are priests for? And what are cops for? A few priests become bishops, and a few cops become commissaires, and they better by God be good."

"So, celibate cops from now on," getting unworthy giggles at the splendid thought. Ex-sergeant Subleyras had perhaps a sense of humour as well as of wit; it is a quality not so many policemen, perhaps, have, or, she reasoned, they would not be cops.

"I would have had fewer problems," he grinned, "in a celibate state."

"Or if you'd had a doormat wife." The police when off duty tends to be disciplinarian and to make a big thing of domestic authority, not to say tyranny. Arlette had even known a police wife marked downright battered. Marked was the word; shown her 'here in this room', back and thighs flogged with a leather belt. She suspected there were a lot more. But she wasn't 'here in this room': she was in the pub, pleasantly off-duty, and didn't want to get wound up in Subleyras' cases of conscience. He seemed to have solved them, without any intervention from her, and that was as it should be.

"One thing." He was feeling in his pockets, fished a piece of paper. "I pulled that file you asked me to look up. I'm not breaking any confidences, nor any frigging official secrets neither. Don't even have to worry about loyalties to ex-colleagues, because there was nothing hairy about it. The procedure of the gendarmerie brigade, out in the country, is perfectly correct. Scrupulous, I'd say, even. No skeletons in cupboards there. The older brother, here in the town – I read through the transcripts. There's nothing untoward. You could say clumsy, you could say heavy-handed I'm not employing police euphemisms, okay? I'm not hinting he was knocked about because he wasn't. I'm saying verbal brutality, grossness, couldn't-care-lessness. To think of that as anything but common form would be a mistake. Say alas, yes, but keep your sense of realities. Boy is marked as sullen, insolent and hostile. No reason to disbelieve that, you know. It'll take a lot to change these attitudes – on both sides.

"Regarding the judicial end – the boy was harshly treated, seeing there was no evidence against him. Again, not unduly so. On both angles you might disagree with me over the definition of the phrase 'unduly harsh'. Can't help that, but it's an honest opinion I'm giving you.

"Oh yes, and the complainant, who benefited by a nolle prosequi over the unlawful use of weapons . . . Pretty moot point that. There was a shutter broken, which constitutes a felony. It's robbery with violence all right. Not to bother with legalisms, he's a Monsieur William Thibault. No marks against him in the office: I don't mean a 'record', but there seems nothing fishy about him. Or not that I could find, at – how to call this? – level of information normally available to my sort of rank. He could have gone to school with somebody, done military service with somebody. Best I could do; okay?"

"On the contrary, I'm really grateful." Arlette was wondering whether this afternoon could be classed as verbal brutality, grossness, in a Subleyras sense. Probably, but it was common-form all right.

"What are you going to do, or haven't you made up your mind yet?"

"I'm a pretty fair metalworker, and I've other talents, like picking locks and such," grinning on one side of his mouth; "it remains to be seen if this'll be enough. It had better."

She'd suddenly had enough of cops, and even ex-cops. Been

up to her neck in them, it felt like longer than all day. She looked at her watch and stood up.

"Got to cook supper for the man."

"Common ailment that, among wives."

"I'd like to meet yours."

"Be mutual I think. She doesn't get out much." He took out his wallet, fished a card, crossed out one phone number, and wrote in another, and an address under, in neat schoolmaster's writing. "Here."

"Thanks. And shall I say – hope to be seeing you?"

"Around and about," he returned, loose and comfortable.

13. The gaudy coral dawn

On her tape was a girl, sounding like a fairly frequent kind of girl, wanting an abortion, or thinking she wanted one. Arlette didn't do anything about the first kind. With the second kind she made an effort, though too often it was the sort of effort judges – junior judges – are legally bound to make in divorce cases; the interview in chambers known as the Attempt at Reconciliation: as a general rule a pretty forlorn effort. Sometimes the girls decided they didn't want an abortion after all. Not that that was automatically good news either. Arlette felt strongly on the subject, but had learned that the tone of voice known as a good talking-to produced backlash.

She had her apron on when the bell rang. On her doorstep was another girl, at first glance another in the abortion-category, or the run-away-from-home category equally frequent, but at second glance was that girl she had glanced at superficially, judged not very sympathetic: the daughter of the Consul's Wife – and presumably of the Consul . . . Sister of that rather ruinous-sounding boy who'd been caught in a heroin fiddle and hammered, and disappeared to Buenos Aires: good luck one rather felt if not good riddance, because what could one do, but say bonjour? Ghislaine was it? – Arlette looked pointedly at her watch, and pointed at her apron while she was at it.

"I don't work this late you know – I'm a housewife at this time of day."

"Only a minute – please."

"A minute . . ." shrugging. "Look, I'll give you five; but That is All. Come in then." She didn't take her apron off, sat on the edge of her table, picked a cigarette off the table, offered it, lit both, pointed to them meaning 'that length of time' and said, "I can't really add much, to what I told your mother."

"You didn't like my mother, did you much? Or me?"

"Even if that were the case, it would be irrelevant. That's not what brought you."

"You turned us down. Not that I blame you."

"But you're forcing me to repeat myself. What could I do? It's a police problem."

"Argentinian police?"

"I take your point. But that, forgive me if I'm being ingenuous, is what consuls are for, no?"

"What consuls are for no, repeat no."

"Oh, I realize – they get hundreds of these missing-person things and don't at all like that Rescue the Girl role. But again, this one is in the huh, consular family, surely?"

"Yes in one sense, no in the one that counts. My father won't – can't" – hurriedly – "work that way."

"That's for him to decide. I don't follow. If you mean prodigal son attitudes, darken my door no more, I wash my hands of you, then I sympathize with both sides, but I am thoroughly shy of any intervention even where that is possible."

"I want to ask you please to reconsider."

"But my dear girl – sorry, don't want to sound patronizing – what grounds do I have?"

"None I suppose. I ask – I beg."

"Look, I'm sensitive to that, but I ask myself seriously what I could possibly do, and find nothing."

"You hate us. Everybody hates us. I understand more than

my mother. She only sees her little clique, on what's called the right social level. Our kind of people, what. Everybody terribly gushing and sympathetic. In reality they're all delighted. If you're on the way up everything is fine. The smallest little crack and they're eyeing you askance, and ready to put a distance." Yes; it was much like Xavier talking about 'the plague victim'.

"My – my brother walked out on it. I thought he was stupid, and I hated him for being so, well, obvious and noisy about it. And now – it sounds so silly, but I want him back. My mother puts on that exaggerated social act, and I could see you hated that. Lot of snobs, you were thinking. She's – just not able to put it into words. Neither am I, I suppose. One gets frozen up. I've been, well, call it in a wider circle. I know how they hate us." Air of sophistication, at nineteen. Which was touching. And despite the whining, self-pitying voice there would be much that was good, no doubt. And of course that terrible little Foreign Office clique was pathetic, and when a crack appeared in the protective varnish it was painful for them. But what on earth could she do? Xavier was a wet, and this lot was much more wet, and she was tired, and she'd had enough of it all, and in general Oh, Knickers, as Arthur said when exasperated. She stabbed her cigarette out with a notion of wanting, on the whole, to be ruthless about pinching this off.

"I can't, I'm afraid, see my way to changing my mind." Stood up. Got a concentrated look of cold hatred.

"You're obtuse, and you're no goddammed good to anybody, and I'm just sorry I came." At the door she turned round again. "I'm sorry I said that." The look had melted from the desolate eyes.

"I deserve it, often. But do I now? Ask yourself objectively – what in cold reality could I usefully do? Not now: sleep on it, ask yourself then."

Arlette slept on it and a lot more, restlessly, woke early. Got up, made herself a cup of coffee. Went for a shower, made it hot, very hot, turned it very cold, a frightful James Bond act she had steeled herself to over the years. Good for the morale, the skin, the bloodstream. Take a whack at middle-aged cellulitis. Good for tit into the bargain. She wasn't too disappointed in hers, at well over fifty: they weren't that bolstercase known as a Bosom, and they weren't too sad and flabby either. Not subject to rude jokes by Arthur about Silicone-Seekers.

She buttoned her bra in the swift movement that delights the male pig, at once ridiculous and marvellously skilful, like a clown falling down. Drawing the curtains, she was struck by a phenomenon of light.

Day was dawning in a murky sky of a nasty purplish black. One could not see what mixture of haze, cloud or smog this was, nor how it simultaneously masked, reflected and diffused the sunrise, visible only as a lurid and sinister red spreading from the east. The effect was horrid and frightening, strongly suggestive of apocalypse-imminent. Arlette stood rooted while it got redder and took on fireball incandescence.

Arthur, the pedantic etymologist, would have said that the word 'ominous' merely announces an omen. Why does the adjective connote bad and alarming omens? Renouncing superstition she went for more coffee.

"Arthur, get up; coffee's ready."

"Muh."

"Arthur, get up, there's an extraordinary sky."

"Meuh."

Looking again she was thunderstruck. The risen sun was flooding the whole sky with a brilliant colour neither pink nor red, not to be called scarlet.

"Arthur, come quick. Such a gaudy dawn – coral."

"It sounds," grumbled the gentleman scratching his pyjama jacket, "like a bad Travis McGee book . . . Woo," taken back short.

"What does the shepherd say to that?"

"Such sights," standing on the balcony reckless of what the neighbour's wife said or thought, "belong in the lonely immensity of the Pacific, sailing towards the Marquesas, on a schooner" – afterthought – "Gorblimey."

"What's it an omen of?"

"That the whole of Bayer Leverkusen has gone up in smoke. That the Russians are coming."

The first, thought Arlette, was desirable but improbable. The second, perhaps slightly more probable, was somewhat less desirable, and both were on the whole unsatisfactory. Surely it means that something extraordinary is going to happen.

The poetry of the phenomenon lasted only a very few minutes, and by the time she had poured out two cups of coffee, it was again an ordinary autumnal day beginning over Strasbourg in brightish steely-grey tints, neither startling nor objectionable.

Weekend, and market day, and no cleaning woman, nor Spanish lessons, but domestic preoccupations, the weekend supplement to *Monde* and Arthur hanging about in a dressing-gown reading it instead of washing.

On the tape, more outpourings from the young woman, as yet unaborted, of the day before. Arlette rang up and explained at some length that today was market-day and another day would have to do, besides making no great difference to the problem in hand, which was still within legal limits.

Coming back from the market, she picked up the mail. Printed matter, and a letter asking for advice and help in dealing with an insurance company. Reading this in the kitchen she could see two quick solutions: do nothing, or put a heavy charge of plastic explosive under the insurance company. She left it on her table to think about on Monday. This wasn't, surely, what was meant by an omen.

Getting on for lunchtime appeared Xavier, in fair repair but his face looking like Joseph's coat of many colours; apologetic, talkative, much bewildered, full of questions and speculations. She didn't know any answers; gave him a drink and got rid of him. Seeing him reminded her, not very pleasantly, of that strong and nasty feeling of being watched, of that nastily-loony telephone call. She hoped this had nothing to do with the omen: it was something else that she didn't want to think about before Monday. The car very badly needed cleaning, tidying, and in general 'uitmesten'; a good Dutch word meaning literally muck out with the dungfork, highly applicable to car after the holidays, mud-masked without and pigsty within.

No use counting on Arthur to do this. Where was Arthur? – she hadn't seen him for a long time and dinner was ready. She had a small drink, and looked through the printed-matter.

Arthur appeared, dirty, surrounded by a huge unmistakeable halo of virtue, carrying a bag of discarded clothing, tatty maps and sunhats. He had cleaned the car. She made many loud and heartfelt exclamations of gratitude. He was rather short, in dire need of a drink and dinner, in quick time.

Was this the omen? That the husband can be tiresome all week long, but a quiet piece of unselfishness more than makes up for it?

Halfway through dinner the phone rang in characteristic imbecile fashion and Arthur took it, still being nice because usually he refused utterly.

"Davidson . . . Mrs van der Valk? . . . Well, I'll tell you what you can do. She's not available at the moment, but rebook it in half an hour: she'll be there then. Yes, this number will do." Her eyebrows were up very high.

"The operator," returning to the table with heavy plod. "With a long, involved tale about finding your office phone on record and doing a great deal of detective work before ringing this one. Interminable and tedious."

"Why can't they say what they want on the tape? What the hell do they think the recorder's for?"

"She says, she says, that she has a long-distance person to person call for you. Mustard, please."

"What can that be? One of the boys, presumably – no; they wouldn't ring the office phone."

"California, offering you a movie contract," closing his mouth upon a large forkful and refusing to say more. Arlette ruminated, but could think of nothing but that it was too early in the day for California. Anyhow, she knew nobody in California. But she could not stop herself getting wound up with suspense. Perhaps this was what the gaudy coral dawn had come to announce.

14. GO-O-O-o-o-ooooal, goal por AR-gen-TI-na

"Yes, this is Madame van der Valk. All right, put him on."

An oddly clear line: something to do with sunspots, or satellites, or both. A highly polished clear voice. Directly she heard, "Consulat de France," she had understood. Not eight in the morning in California, but nine at night in the Far East. And a great pest either way. No movie contract, either.

Arthur, thoughtfully, provided an ashtray and a lighted cigarette.

"I have, however, refused this, twice. Why do you think I would reverse my decision now? There are other people: there must be people on the spot."

"I am not trying to be overbearing. This is not a tactic for bringing pressure. It is a personal appeal. I understand your refusal. I grasp at least some of your motives for it. I supplicate you nonetheless to reverse it. To answer your second question, you are there ideally placed, if you will agree, to be put in possession of the facts."

"I don't feel convinced, I'm sorry to say."

"You will, though, listen to me? You're not going to cut me off."

"It's your call . . ."

"This, Madame, is an attempt at a rescue. That of a young man, and possibly his health. It is not too far-fetched to say possibly even his life. An attempt, furthermore, to rescue a family, a marriage, and may I say even, in the simplest words, a man's own self-respect. A question of conscience." Wasn't it in those words, or something very like them, that she had interpreted the decisions of Sergeant Subleyras?

"But if I may interrupt, surely you are much better placed than I am."

"If I say that my wife, that various family relations, that even those close friends I could feel I count upon, that all are excluded for urgent and overriding personal reasons, would you be inclined to believe me?"

"I take your word, naturally. But you yourself . . ."

"That I hold, you mean, an official position of some importance. That by virtue of this there are pressures I can bring to bear, relations I could use, even certain manipulations or manoeuvres within my powers?"

"Well . . . more or less."

"You must take my word for it, most solemnly given, that for professional as well as personal reasons any such course of action is formally excluded."

"I'm very sorry naturally to hear it, but – "

"May I, in my turn, interrupt you? Such information as I hold about you, and all that I am led to believe of you, tells me that the human, and, if I may use the word, ethical values I was speaking of just now are foremost in your considerations. You confirm that?"

"Well, I should hope I'm not going to deny it."

"Then why do you hold back, in face of the appeal made to you by both the mother and the father of this young man? And as I even understand, his sister?"

She was a bit bereft of speech, hereabouts.

"Have you yourself overriding personal reasons for a refusal to visit Argentina? Or, if I may use the phrase, ethical scruples?"

"No."

"There are material considerations? I am formally proposing to you that your expenses, whatever they are, will be totally covered, that your time be remunerated at the rate you think fit, that a proper proportion of your estimate, fifty per cent or whatever, be made over to you in advance. I do not know whether you are recording this conversation."

"No."

"I guarantee my personal and family resources and will confirm that in writing."

What was she to say?

"You could, no doubt, arrange your professional obligations so as to free yourself for a certain number of days? Speaking conditionally, that could be done at seven days' notice?"

"Possibly, but I ask you not to be over-confident."

"Confident of your acceptance? I do not believe that you would knowingly refuse your aid to those in need. Of your competence, I have no doubt. Of your ability to do as I ask? The future holds no certainties, but faced with the variations upon what is possible, I seek to place the probabilities upon my side."

"What exactly is it that you are asking of me?"

"That you agree to aid my family to the limits of your capacity. The problem in human terms cannot be measured. It can be defined within certain parameters."

"One of which is being in full possession of the facts."

"My wife, I will promise you, will give you her entire confidence, in full detail, of every relevant factor. Nothing will be held back."

"I must think this over."

"Madame, forgive my insistence, but the arguments for refusal haven't a leg to stand on."

"Except that I may have considerations too, which may be like yours – personal; family."

"Madame, je vous en conjure."

"I don't say yes or no on the telephone, and that's flat. I think it over during the weekend, and get in touch with your wife on Monday."

"But you don't say no."

"Of course I don't say no. I'll do what I can."

"That's all I ask, Madame, and you have my profound thanks."

Would one say yes to the movie contract from California? What one did was not say no.

The drawback to telephones – among others – is that people ring up from California and are extremely pressing, and full of cajolements. The moment you don't say no, in their view you've said yes.

Arthur, plus post-prandial cigar, was looking out of the window with his hands in his pockets, his whole attitude saying that this was all exceedingly odtaa.

Arlette sat foolishly and said nothing. After a little while she tried "Suppose we went out to the country for the weekend," timidly.

"Come," he said, "that's the best idea you've had for a long time."

They got in the car, and nobody seemed to be watching them.

Arlette drove. Arthur appeared blind to all around him. Lengthily, much handicapped by safety belts and the vast number of pockets in a man's clothes, he searched for and at last found a pair of nail scissors. Having at last found them, he started using them to clean his pipe. In this way twenty-five kilometres passed without anybody speaking, through fairly dense traffic imposing concentration upon the driver. The westerly road from Strasbourg towards the Vosges, following the valley of the Bruche, is at all times much encumbered: on a Saturday afternoon, saturated. They were past Molsheim before Arthur at length spoke.

"As dear Dona Silvia is so fond of saying, Hombre propone, pero Dios dispone, which is crushingly unanswerable."

This being so, she did not attempt an answer.

A long way further, when they were nearly there, he broke again the silence.

"The game of futbol is insufferably boring. Long arid deserts of time during which the ball goes backward and sideways in futile effort to gain advantage. One must not say an unparallelled tedium, since telephone conversations upon business proposals are exactly the same."

Arthur's monologues could be equally tortuous, but this was not the moment to say so.

"Except, of course, when Argentinians play it, when it becomes funny. Indeed diabolically inventive and subtle. Even at cheating, which all other teams do with a laborious want of imagination, they have a splendid theatricality and a high sense of comedy."

They had left the main road and were climbing the last switchbacks to the village.

"Hm, old Borges says that upon the Argentinian character sits a curse of futility, and maybe so, Como no? Being best at futbol is like Czechs making the best beer; it simply twists the knife in the wound." People in villages always look up when a car passes. Seeing someone they knew they nodded. One is and always will be a stranger, and the nods are both reluctant and sour.

"Likewise the commentators, who like me sit in idleness and observe; like me supplying pretentious and superfluous comment in jargon, ever seeking elegant variation upon platitude. In this atmosphere of hyper-excitability about nothing, when at last somebody scores it's an anti-climax. Except in Buenos Aires, of course."

Arthur had timed it well. As Arlette turned the car off the track and put the brake on, he got out, clasped his hands over his head, and let out a wolf's howl. "Goooo-ooaal por Ar-gen-ti-na."

15. Indian summer of a sociologist

"An unmannerly piece of needless exhibitionism," said Arlette.

"Not needless. Got rid of a great deal of frustration." She put the key in the door. A key hand-forged and beautiful, twenty centimetres long and weighing a kilo. The lovely start, Piet had called it. The overture to Figaro, she agreed, when they came first.

It was a van der Valk house. He had stayed here. Never lived here, but now he was buried here, which was what he would have wished. The soil of his childhood in Amsterdam had gradually grown unrecognizable even to him, and he had moved his heart, before dying. He had bought it to retire to, over a dubious Arlette's head. She needed people around her, she said. He had always had a perverse streak of romanticism. But she'd accepted it, and been glad of it. She had spent the first year of her widowhood here, leaving because her daughter Ruth, too, needed people as well as a proper school. And because she herself had realized that this, for her, was not the end.

But she had kept it, and unchanged. For some years she had done no more than come conscientiously, three or four times a year, to air and turn out on fine days, and make coffee, and sit a while. Everything had tumbled into neglect: the grass grew up long and rank, and the trees were covered in lichen. But the house was sturdy, and resisted.

It was little more than a cottage; was indeed a solid little house with two storeys and an attic, and a cellar, squarish, of a Georgian simplicity and a good proportion, built of local stone in 1827, in the country style of fifty years before. Arlette, looking at a picture of Chawton Cottage, where Jane Austen had once lived, noticed with delight a remarkably close resemblance. Behind it was a clearing in the woods; rough meadow full in spring of cowslips and wood anemone. In front was the valley of a turbulent hill stream, and what had once been garden. Piet had not had time to make it again garden, although he had been full of projects. During the few years they had spent all their available holidays here, driving down from Holland, Piet working the Volkswagen to its limit over the hilly wooded roads, keenly anticipating his great treat. He had recalled that his father had been a cabinet-maker, and had built rough, plain country furniture, recklessly buying thick slabs of wood; oak and beech and elm that would cost a ransom now. All this she had left as it was. The only thing she had taken to the city was her big working table, now in her office.

Rather naturally, Arthur had been shy of this house. He had never tried to possess her, nor to assimilate her past. There was no rivalry between himself and a dead man. Nor had he wanted to disturb ghosts. Arlette had asked him to come: he had come with no great enthusiasm, although grateful to her. She was knocking down strong, ancient barriers.

She was grateful to him; he had come with simplicity, and no show of wariness. They had both been happy to find the house uncomplicated and welcoming: it had been a simple and happy house: it remained so. Delighted with Piet's bookshelves, with the panelling, with the big, built-in clock and its soft, eighteenth-century note, he had decreed a risorgimento, and set lovingly to work at by now much-needed repair. They came often now. The thick oak shutters had been burned off and repainted, the dampstains effaced, the house made tight . . . In the coarse Dutch mockery that was an essential strand of van-der-Valk-humour Piet had called it 'Het Chaletje', the Little Hut. It had a name now. 'Amers' which means 'Seamarks'. Piet had come from Amsterdam, Arlette from near Toulon; Arthur himself from the south coast of England. For these navigators, seamarks were a fact of life. Coasting, with primitive equipment and few aids, they had all come a good way. Landfall had sometimes to be made in fog and by storm, through the short and sudden, steep and hollow seas of these coasts, whose shipwrecks have deforested the whole of Europe of its oak trees.

Being an orderly fellow, with a conscientious housewife, Arthur left the stove always with its ashes raked, and with a pile of kindling ready, and he had the house warm in no time at all, while she was opening shutters. Dust lay thick, but it was not city dust, being mostly soil and woodash; organic stuff, and doesn't smell bad. Ritual dictated the drinking of white wine, a principle laid down by Piet, and the cleaning of all lamps and candlesticks. Arthur, whose digestion white-Alsace did not agree with, had only substituted Rioja, Burgundy being too expensive for anything but anniversaries. Perhaps this was an anniversary? He went down to the cellar and found something suitable. If his wife wished to go to South America, he wasn't going to try and stop her. Knowing her anyhow, trying would be a forlorn effort, and would at best be a quick way to a very disagreeable week of it.

Indian summer lasts long in this part of the world. Spring comes late and grudgingly, a fitful affair of sunshine thin and acid, like bad white wine. In summer it can be unbearably hot, and it can pour with icy rain for weeks. Winter is snowbound, and sometimes quite splendid.

Autumn is the supreme joy. Ah, visitors from the North American continent say sometimes – like New England. A bit like Vermont yes, on a miniature scale since Alsace, one of the smallest provinces of France, is only two hundred kilometres long and fifty wide. There are stupider gardeners than those of municipal Strasbourg, who have an altogether consequent fondness for maple trees. But the especial charm and delight of Alsace is its division into three parts, like Caesar's Gaul, each with a distinct character; longitudinally, like a tricolour ribbon.

The plain is that of the Rhine valley; fertile, watery, and encased between the twin ranges of the Vosges on the French side, and the Black Forest of present-day Germany. The Vosges, whose summits mark the frontier with neighbouring Lorraine, form a chain of hills rather than mountains. They do not run over two thousand metres, they are gently rounded and much eroded, of a soft rust-colour sandstone that makes a most attractive building material, and wooded to the top. The woods are mostly spruce. Forest of pine, forest of boredom, and the close, stiff, scratchy texture of the spruce gives the Black Forest its forbidding name. The happiness of the Vosges is that pine and beech woods intermingle.

The third division is the foothill country, a narrow streak of sunny orchard land that nourishes the vines. These two have the gaiety and charm of variety: pinots, rieslings and traminers interwoven with local oddities, from patch to patch bearing anything from fine, and even distinguished, grapes to acid rubbish, good only to put in a pot with sour cabbage. The orchards are cherry and plum, pretty trees, streaked with resins, fragrant, fruitful; and everywhere walnuts with grave and lovely foliage. Ah, if we had a house in the foothills, said Arthur wistfully. If one was able to afford it, returned his wife tartly, and you need not regret it: noisy, tourist-ridden, far too many neighbours.

The upper valleys are glens, steep and narrow, full of the noise of water; too cold for vines, too abrupt for tractors. The gardens must be terraced, with drystone walls, and care lest the precious topsoil be washed away.

Arthur sprawled lordly upon the flagged terrace, in a cane chair from Holland: art of rattan learned in the Indies. He poured himself a glass of wine, took off his shirt, and concentrated on becoming a ripe apricot: lank, bony, pinkish English object. Why had stupid Piet not planted maples? He had made efforts, it was true; he had been moving in the right direction. There was a scarlet American oak, a sweet gum, a tulip tree that one hoped one would live to see in flower. One or two semi-failures, like the catalpa that would always look frail and shivery; and this was no landscape for cypresses. One or two abject failures like that horrid copper beech – bourgeois tree – and the Weymouth pine that had died: capricious things they were.

He would plant maples. He had no children – not even silly Angelika – and wouldn't, ever. He would plant maples for children he did not know, a harsher joy, but of higher worth, philosophically.

"Have you poured none for me?" said Arlette's voice. She had put bedclothes out at all windows, hung rugs on everything vertical. Sun struck deeply into the house, eating up gloom and the damp that foxed the pages of Arthur's novelists – only here, he said, could one successfully read *The Heart of Midlothian*, or *The Master of Ballantrae*, or *Chance*. "I intend," she said, "not to think at all for twenty-four hours." The sun had already sapped him of power to do anything but grunt, so he grunted. By Quiberon Bay they had sat, so, in an idle but no way impoverished contemplation. Busy, scuttling world of ants . . . The climate of the temperate zone of Europe, from the northern limit of the olive to the northern limit of the grape, has been, no doubt, the most fertile for thought and art, but makes people too busy to listen for the grass growing. We need Moors too, from the south, and hobgoblins too from Scotland. Under the palms of Samoa, Stevenson wrote beautifully of the rain-curtain weaving magic over the windy streets of Edinburgh. In the Marquesas, Jacques Brel with cancer's cold clutch around the heart wrote poems to the heavy-jointed but vital rhythms of Flanders. Freedom of all the seas of the Pacific can only bring one in the end to the fogs and drains and stinks of the Scheldt-Escaut estuaries. Strasbourg, foggy all morning, stinks all afternoon of industrial effluent so that one longs for the wet westerly wind to come blustering back and shake the sodden leaves down. But up here, beyond the vineline, the air smells of linden and acacia honey, of resin and dry sherry. The sun will sink to a smell of woodsmoke, damptrapped and hanging in the clearing. And will rise in dew and moss and blackberries. No shampoo-salesman, no pederast perfumer can put these essences ignobly into little bottles. The aviation of the French Government, may the foul fiend fly away in, with, and upon same, scars the sky but its disgusting exhalations may, who knows, embellish a sunset for somebody. Alongside the discarded contraceptive, grows the mushroom: oh dear, these lyrical flowers wax ever ranker.

Never mind. Indian summer for the sociologist.

"I would like another glass," said Arlette a little crossly. "I've asked you twice already but you were rapt in the arms of Proserpina or whatever she's called."

Why not suggest to him to stay up here? – assuming, that is to say (she added hastily) that she agreed to go at all. Take the best part of a day to get there. And back; jet lag and whatnot. She could hardly be away less than five, six days – poof, it might as well be five minutes for all the good it would do. Anyway, I'm only going to think about this tomorrow. Correction; day after tomorrow.

Arlette woke up from a sleep so deep; a country sleep, a sea-sleep; that she did not know where she was. She sat bolt upright: the bed was empty beside her, and in it had been Arthur and not Piet. The room faced east and south. Morning sunlight dappled things. The wallpaper Piet had hung had got stained and loose over the years of neglect: Arthur had pulled it all off and whitewashed everywhere. The bed was the same; a country piece in pitchpine, the capitals of the four posts carved into stylized pineapples. She lay down again.

What had woken her was the country sound by definition, even more than logs being split; a scythe being sharpened. The sociologist, clumsy with his hands, did not take kindly to tools, even simple ones of the hobbit variety, and regarded Piet's woodworking chisels and gouges with misgiving. But he had made himself learn elementary skills. Wasn't that, too, social science? What good, finally, were these pale and paperbound folk who got no nearer to a manual task than tables of statistics? Learning to drill a hole in the wall, put a dowel in it, and sink a screw – straight – in, that had given Scholar-Gipsy Davidson the confidence and the courage to go out with a billhook. He scythed, now, with intense pleasure. The garden had all gone wild, and they were not here often enough to look after flowers or vegetables. But he dug, and he weeded. A man needs this: to put his feet in the soil. As needful was something to look forward to, and he constructed fantasies around goats, or geese. What would they do when they were on a pension?

"It's a very old settlement, this." What is sociology after all? Everything. Archaeological, too. Everywhere you go, you look, you wonder what is under the ground.

"Piet said the same. We never turned anything up. The garden was made long before us. The woods are full of queer things, if one knew where to look." One came across traces of foundations, buildings of who knew now what purpose. The ground had been mined for many years; there were forgotten shafts and tunnels of a buried, faintly sinister, Nibelung sort. Here in living memory had been the German front line in 1914. A little higher, along the crests, were the French trenches. In this terrain both positions had been impregnable. At the beginning, here and there, both sides had been ambitious and had a go: lost so many men that here, at least, they'd had the sense to sit it out. Under the dead leaves and the little landslips that occurred whenever a tree fell, tearing out the roots that held the fragile soil together, was the metal that had equipped those ghost armies; an unquiet grave. It didn't do to scratch about in the soil there.

Arlette knew more about it than she would say. She, herself one night, had gone out with pick and spade to dig a grave in the horrible silent owl-haunted wood. In it she had buried the van der Valk armoury. Those souvenirs she hadn't wanted: the submachinegun that had killed Ruth's natural mother, the hunting rifle that had chewed a hunk out of the man's hip bone – the Luger pistol that had killed him, wry-mouthed presentation from a Dutch police officer. Go back and join all your brothers under this hill that so many boys have bled into.

She'd thought of it all – the adverb she supposed was 'sardonically' – when Arthur had insisted, with police connivance, that she possess and, if necessary, carry a revolver, ugly thing, American, efficient, and very frightening. Short barrel and heavy calibre, the sort of thing that at beyond ten metres missed you altogether but at less blew a hole in you one could drive a truck through: she had no wish to experiment either way. She recognized the point, which was that it impressed, mightily, anybody looking at the business end. It had been a temptation on seeing it first to say 'I can do better than that'.

She never brought her pistol out here. Guns didn't do, here. One might, like Monsieur Thibault, be tempted to use them. As bad, if anybody broke in, they would be found – Piet had kept them brazenly in the bottom drawer of the big chest. It had been full of contradictions living with a cop, married to him, bearing him children.

Arthur, after a further transfusion of coffee and cooling the sweat upon the manly brow, went back to his turf where she had clumps of jonquils hidden; yellow daffodils and white narcissi. She was still sitting in her nightie. On the terrace the sun was hot. She went back in to wash and dress. The pump was still out in front, and the smooth-lipped stone watering trough, but she hadn't carried romantic primitivism that far. Even Piet, who let loose, here, all the sentimentalism the job forbade, had had a proper bathroom put in straight away, and borrowed the money moreover, to pay for it.

Hum, as a young woman, very determined to be French

and hard-headed, she'd caught him out once or twice. Being romantic over 'innocent young girls': if she'd ever laid hands on them she'd have wrung them out, the sluts. That damned Lucienne he'd gone soppy over – she'd wrung him out too. He'd had a gritty Dutch bottom that saved him from the worse foolishnesses but . . .

A few years ago she'd have been prepared to agree . . . no, no, she'd never admitted, would never have admitted . . . that to some extent he'd lived, even died, a failure. It was the ghost that had always haunted him, catching him always by the elbow. Most of his equals, nearly all his superiors, treated him with a sort of contempt. That this hid envy she had always known: the man had gifts that they hadn't. But it was only after meeting Arthur that she had learned really, and truly understood, what in the van der Valk days she had only dimly perceived: that the world cannot be understood or handled by merely being 'rational'. Instinct, and emotion, and even sentiment played a greater role than she had ever allowed herself to admit. Davidson taught her. 'It's a well-known philosophic axiom, that he who gives, dominates. Your Piet was a giver, and that's why he won his little wars. You are one too.'

All those years of being married to a cop . . . She'd understood more upon meeting Sergeant Subleyras.

They'd got on together like a house-on-fire. A silly phrase this, and what did it mean? That fire and dry wood got on together? No, they got on together like brother and sister, who haven't seen each other in ten years, who have been indifferent to one another; who realize, only upon meeting afresh, how much they shared that they had forgotten.

A simple problem, that of Subleyras. One that men have: the neuters don't have it. There's this job. You have done it for a long time: you are, even, good at it. But it makes you sick. What are you going to do about that?

Inspector, gradually Chief-Inspector, eventually even Commissaire van der Valk had had protections. 'Educated man'. An officer. A law degree, a bundle of diplomas. An acquired authority and expertise, in the field of juveniles, in forensic criminology. He'd even sat, and exercised humour, upon a committee, God-help-us, a committee on penal reform, and criminal law, and hadn't been ridiculous. But even a young officer is not going to be sacked, short of grave misdemeanours. You have somebody in the department who can handle the dread 'marginals', the weirdos, the artists. So his superiors reasoned. A fellow who can patter a bit of French and Spanish too, handy sometimes. The fellow of whom the Procureur-General remarked dryly one day, 'It's not a bad thing to have one person in the department with a few flashes of imagination.'

In short, he'd been perpetually in the shit, but had always got out again. He'd come skin-thickness near to resigning a score of times, but had never done it. Humour, a rarity in Holland, as well as cynicism, had helped him sit very loose to the job, loose in his skin. For a man like Subleyras, and Only-a-Sergeant into the bargain, it was much harder.

The General, in his exalted way and familiar mystical style, had a phrase about mountains. The slope is steeper up there, the going harder. But the air is better, and there are fewer Peepul. What there are, too, are men and not neuters. The sheep huddle down there at the foot, looking about afeared.

An English chap, in more pragmatic vein, said the same. When you have one of these frightful choices, always take the way that sounds the nastiest, the one you least want: it will invariably be the right one.

Cops, thought Arlette settling to The Dinner, see people at their worst, know far too much of the nastiest human behaviour, get it on their clothes and hands. In their first years they cultivate sick humour. As a trainee, paired with an experienced man, Piet had found a hanged man. I'll get the van, said his mentor, you stay by the corpse. 'Why?' asked Piet, 'will it walk away?'

The next stage is humourless. You're in this job; that's the way it is. Don't bring it home with you. You'll start losing sleep, and the end of that road is the bin: clinic, between two men in white coats. There is a high suicide rate, during this stage.

Many do not arrive at police maturity. The less good turn

into bad cops. Some are crooked. Others morally corrupt. A great many simply become insensitive. They can be brutes; they can also be sheets of toilet-paper. They are no longer men.

Some of the best become like Beckett's Winnie. Buried up to the neck, they are still showing a toughness of humour and of courage that is impressive. But what you cannot see has been eaten away by despair.

Arthur entered, gay, sweaty, very happy.

"Hungry hungry hungry," he said.

"Lay the table then," said Arlette patiently, "and keep your hands off my bottom; this pot is hot."

16. Les nantis

She stopped on the way home on Sunday night, in the village of Grendelbruch.

"I've heard of Grendel's cave," grumbled Arthur, "but what's his bruch?"

"I won't be but five minutes," she promised. He looked pointedly at his watch, let the back of the seat down, and composed himself for slumber.

It is one of the hilltop villages, prettily situated, with a wonderful view and almost an Alpine feel, with fretwork wooden balconies and cows with bells round their necks. Arlette found what she was looking for quickly enough: a gate in a high bank, and steps going up. Once her eyes grew accustomed to the light, she could see well enough for her purposes. She kept in the shadow, and kept a cautious distance. The house was dark, but people had got caught that way before. She did not think it likely that anyone would let off guns at her, but had no wish to be put to ignominious flight by a peremptory challenge. It was only curiosity that had brought her. Could be called effrontery and she would not complain. Creeping about spying, yes? Well; yes.

Bulldozers had been at work here: it was all a little too good to be true. The steep approach to the rounded hillock gave the house a commanding view down to the road and over the unseen valley beyond: all at the exactly wrong angle for a sunset, but eminently eligible. On the far side it was artificially levelled, and a nicely gravelled track swung wide around the contour and back down to the car entrance. Little trees and bushes were dotted about: a landscape gardener had been at work. The house itself was built high, with a massive rounded buttress and a terrace above that. No modernistic angularities, nor anything in the least imaginative, but suburban villa architecture of the most conventional kind. All the lower windows were protected by wrought-iron grilles of atrociously rococo ropework in potbellied curves. Hm, the boys must have made quite a daring escalade. Which, of course, in itself, is a criminal offence. Pebbledash alternated with facings of dressed stonework; stuff that comes two centimetres thick but exceedingly dear, in a gaudily variegated sandstone that sets the teeth on edge. It was not a new house – it might have been ten years old. There were coy, cottagey features. She could swear she knew every detail of the interior.

Arthur was pretending to be asleep.

"You haven't been five minutes," he said. "You've been fifteen."

The road from Grendelbruch winds steeply down into a valley and climbs again to a plateau, before the more deliberate descent to the little foothill towns of the wine country: Rosheim, Obernai and Barr, picturesque places with little medieval gateways and toy-soldier ramparts. It is all real enough, despite nineteenth-century romanticism. All these villages were fortified. They were refuges, against the inrush of the Barbarian across the Rhine; forlorn hopes against the blood-boltered, baby-crunching Swedes of the Thirty Years' War. The holocaust's brighter ideas, such as herding peasants into a wooden church and then setting fire to it, are really nothing very new around here.

The foothills are soft and gentle, in spring placidly bosomy with apple and cherry blossom, and the tender green tendrils of vineshoots. But immediately behind is the scarp of the Hohwald, and the road is in hairpins. Narrow gorges are overhung by perpendicular cliffs, rising to commanding heights, round which one must twist and thread a way over the Vosges passes. By night, the black wings of Dracula fold all about one, but even by day the pinewoods are sombre, in stiff serried ridges like the teeth of a comb.

Wherever there is a pass, the curious eye discerns, upon the height, fingers pointing upward; ruined cliffs and chimneys of stonework that is not natural but built, perched with much daring and greater pain upon narrow ledges of rock. These are the castles of Alsace, a hundred odd, the mountain eyries of the robber barons; built, and improved upon, between the ninth and thirteenth centuries, caring little for bishop or duke, less still for the Holy Roman Emperor. Virtually inaccessible and impregnable, yet often managing to change hands by violence, and more often still by treachery. They are all in ruin, but in nearly all can be traced the skull of a keep, the jagged teeth of portcullis.

Kaiser Wilhelm, arriving in his lovely new province of Alsace in 1870, rather fancied one of these. They had built him a hideous house in Strasbourg, but now they set to and built a really splendid huge baronial hall on the top of a hill. It is called the Haut Koenigsberg; it is all still there, complete and untouched and in perfect order, central heating and elks' antlers: Balmoral is nothing to it.

Discredited minor nobility, younger sons gone bad, poor as rats, climbed up here, screwed themselves in, swooped down to pillage monk, pilgrim, with luck a fatter commercial type, with a purse, dreaming of snatching a bishop or some rich count's daughter that would cough up a ransom. Much, we may suppose, like the mosstrooping Elliots and Liddells of the Scotch Border and like them a hardy crowd, freezing up there in draughty stone hovels, nothing to eat but abominably tough venison, barley bread like granite; plentiful swigs of firewater.

Driving from Grendelbruch down to Strasbourg, Arlette

passed three or four, unseen but there. They make nice picnic grounds on a fine day. Nobody will be up there – too steep a climb for the comfort-loving bourgeois: they'd rather sit in the car with the radio on.

There are still robber-barons, and they still build themselves castles on hill-summits in the Vosges. Fat little affairs like tame rabbits, but their owners steal on a scale far beyond the wildest dreams of the twelfth century.

She turned on to the main road down in the plain, driving cautiously because of late-night drunks. She was thinking of the Chateau de Joux, which guards the horrid gorge from Pontarlier across to Switzerland, and is more terrifying than anything in Alsace. There are in it two things at which the imagination really does boggle. One is a well, some seven-eight metres wide, driven down a hundred and thirty metres through the naked, living rock. The other is that the Seigneur de Joux came back one day unexpectedly from the day's pastime of having people pulled apart by four horses, or whatever, and caught his pretty young wife, Berthe, in a bit of casual adultery with a cavalier. Berthe was put in a cell, two metres by one and a half in the thickness of the wall, and there left for fifteen years. Once a day they brought her out for edification, to look upon her lover's remains displayed in the courtyard. After the fifteen years Monsieur de Joux was kind, or perhaps bored, enough to permit Berthe to retire, aged thirty-three, to a convent for the remainder of her days. Now a robber-baron nowadays, thought Arlette, has to find other pastimes. Do they differ all that much?

Arthur, if he had not been asleep, could have told her about the bourgeois gentleman who decided to sell his house. A prospective buyer, intrigued like Bluebeard's wife by a locked room and what seemed over-elaborate evasions, told people. The gendarmerie arrived. In the room, just her and a mattress, they found the gentleman's mentally-handicapped daughter, who'd been there for more than fifteen years. It was to avoid embarrassment, the gentleman explained.

Arthur was snoring when they reached the Rue de l'Observatoire, and needed a good hard nudge, and woke cross.

Arlette had concluded from a glance at the Weekend Cottage that Mr Thibault would be unlikely to listen with much sympathy to any suggestion of Madame Bartholdi's having had a rough deal. Since any vindictiveness he had felt towards the burglars was presumably stilled, it might have been lack of imagination, or even an understandable diffidence about going to the mother of the boy you have killed and saying Sorry about that, rather. She had thought of a person perhaps narrow, dense, self-righteous, obstinately entrenched in puritan virtue, unable even to hint to himself that perhaps he might have been in the wrong. Someone perhaps who would have liked to mumble Well, what about a hundred quid or something, to think no more about it, but capable, dimly, of realizing that this was not quite good enough.

She had been prepared for a frightened little bourgeois meanness, like that German insurance company. Man lost his wife? Our client is legally responsible? Well, considering the man's age and everything (fairly advanced, mercifully) we suggest a compensation of six hundred marks a month. That's plenty, plenty. Generous. Why, the woman didn't even work: it's not as if he were deprived of INCOME.

She no longer thought all this. The hilltop castle gave her a different picture. Maybe she was wrong, and it had to be verified, but what she saw was Cutpurse. To impress his neighbours, and his family, and those he calls his friends, he spends much money on his rustic retreat. He calls in architects, builders, fitters, landscapists, choosing carefully people he thinks owe him a favour, or will be glad to buy themselves into his graces. Get this big job done, costs a lot, must be had at cut price.

The result is visible, though not to him. However much he spends, and vulgarity will always demand that it be a great deal; The Best; it will always look like a cutprice job for Cutpurse.

There's something to be said for him; at least he's a leopard. Those spots he has, that he can't change, that spell out Look after Number One, they can be all sorts of beasts, right down to things like colorado beetles. There are things much worse.

"As long as it's a person," said Arthur, consulted at breakfast. "Whatever sort of animal it is, there's an individual. As long as it's not an institution, what sociology calls a Blessed Trinity. Merck, Sharp and Dohme, Freeman, Hardy and Willis, Smith, French and Kline. Try to fit them to faces. You might come up with a picture of something grim of jaw, steely-eyed and slickum-haired, you know, looking something like Robert MacNamara, but you're quite wrong. If there's anything alive at all, it's a gaga old lady on a life rent in Bournemouth or Santa Barb, but even that's the greatest rarity. Dear old John Buchan blithers away happily about getting behind the façade. First a prognathous Westphalian business man, and then a white-faced little Jew in a bathchair: as a description of reality this is about as accurate as it would be of James Bond and M."

"I particularly like the bathchair."

"Yes, there's no more sinister symbol of the universal spider spinning secret webs."

You've got the cliché: find the person.

The cliché is one of the Communist Party's staunchest old workhorses: 'les nantis'. It is a skilful word, difficult to translate because of overtones. Literally 'those provided with goods', but 'the bosses'; 'the possessors'? More 'the cornerers', 'the plunderers', but these are too crude, too libellous. Arlette's English, though workmanlike, was not subtle enough to find a perfectly innocuous word with as pungent a reek of acquisitive greed.

Strasbourg has its share of multinationals: Swiss supermarkets and Dutch beerbarons; squalid ramifications, bathchairs everywhere: seven-sisterish intrigues as obscure as the butter mountain and the wine lake. It has perhaps more than its share of family firms with sturdy, reassuring Alsacien names. Like all such enclaves, it is a very clannish place, and is as happy to be robbed by two or even three generations of local nantis as by the Margarine Trust. These people have no Wall Street subtleties: France, since the time of Colbert, has been dug in behind a fortress of protectionism, and it's philosophy has always been simple: slap a hundred per cent mark-up on everything. The manufacturer has the same mentality: he would rather sell ten paperclips at ten per cent profit than a hundred at one per cent, and pass his day complaining to the government about unfair German competition. This is why shopping in France is so laborious, and so nasty. Appetite whetted by the high-value German and Swiss currencies next door, Strasbourg's good-old Schmidt and Muller put their prices still further up, and make it the dearest town in France. Arlette who had lived for twenty years in Holland wished forlornly that these two beastly countries would start civilizing one another.

The Place Broglie, pronounced Breuil to make it more élite, is the most elegant bit of the old town: down at the bottom is the operahouse, and the Military Government, with a rather toney Officers' Club. Midway is the Hotel de Ville, an eighteenth century palace of real distinction and genuine beauty. Up at the top is rather lower, not only architecturally: commerce is just low. This end is dominated by the Bank of France, occupying a large and ugly fortress, formerly the mayor's residence; and here, it is said, Rouget de l'Isle first played to an admiring audience a recent composition entitled the Song of the Rhine Army, later tolerably well-known as La Marseillaise. The commercial enterprises around, lent distinction by this privileged proximity, are not as grand as one might think. Monsieur Thibault's leather-shop ('Maroquinerie' is a lot grander than just leather) was the showiest. He had several floors, and a bargain-basement below.

Arlette had a purse, old but much-loved, bought for her by Ruth. As well as having sentimental value, it had a nice shape, was of excellent design, and of good material: in fact, the sort of thing you never can find when you look for it. After many years of violent abuse, it had not given way – being moreover of good workmanship – but its catch had become afflicted by the palsy, and no longer caught, but fell in and out instead. Arthur's mechanical abilities, like hers, were zero: he had looked at it and failed to understand why it should no longer catch.

"Can you fix this?"

The salesgirl turned it round and round, languid and clueless.

"You'd do better to buy a new one, wouldn't you." Not put as a question.

"I like this one." Plainly, that was too difficult. Thought is so exhausting. The solution generally hit upon is Pass it along to someone else.

"You might try upstairs, I suppose." Left bombed-out by this much effort.

Next floor was the Arts of Living; a disembowelling of goats and baby camels whose flesh Arabs, presumably, had eaten. Zebras and ostriches cost a lot more. Several reptiles have become endangered species as a consequence of this racket. Arlette had no particular sympathy for alligators, but they are preferable to the two-footed ones. Nothing for her here: she floated up a further flight to Haute Couture. This began with Personalizing things – your telephone, your shopping list – right down to your meat-grinder if you like. It took in things like elephant-feet umbrella stands along the way. The clients here can neither read nor write, so that desk tops, bureau sets and pen trays can safely be left to the bookbinder, but anything to do with cards, drinks or cigars goes well.

As you go up floor by floor the saleswomen rise in age and in status, but not in energy. The vendeuse looked with loathing at Arlette, who wore no fur nor even skin, and with more at the worn and shabby purse.

"Of course we can repair it, if you wish," taking a card with a gold letterhead out of a drawer. "What name?"

"You mean three weeks' wait, forty francs, and value-added-tax on top?"

"For a new catch, what did you expect?"

"I don't believe it needs anything of the sort."

"It has in any case to go up to the workshop."

"Which is here? Why can't we just ask them?"

"What," asked a man's voice, "is creating all the difficulty?"

"The catch is worn out in all probability and the lady seems to think –" The man snatched the purse impatiently without looking at Arlette, held it under the light and shouted, "Madame Henriette," still without looking up. A stout middle-aged lady came running from somewhere. "Pliers," he said.

The vendeuse arranged objects that were already arranged. The stout lady ran behind a screen, pattered back breathing heavily. The man held his hand out without looking, brought the spring-balanced lamp a little closer, took a deft grip, bent the metal imperceptibly, snapped the catch which now worked perfectly, pushed the lamp impatiently back, held both purse and pliers out to Madame Henriette, who seemed quite accustomed to all this, and said simply, "Here." The stout lady, who had gold hair in curls and a kind face, handed Arlette her purse with a timid smile.

"Thank you very much," said Arlette and left. Was it the young one who answered the old one, 'So am I, Obadiah, so am I.'?

She had not brought the car into central Strasbourg: leaving it outside was less trouble than working it into some misbegotten underground parking. But she took it to go to the Rue Ravel, where Madame Laboisserie was effusive in greeting. Another pack of nantis. She listened to a lot of voluble explanations, told herself that the rich are people too. When they look at you, that is.

17. Plainly police business

When she started 'the office' she had been told to be careful not to get involved with matters concerning the police, and the very first thing she'd gone and done was to do just that. She had been forgiven, since her tangle, further entangled by her own inexperience, had brought kudos to a number of police officers. Her paternal commissaire from PJ had kept a fatherly eye upon her for some months until, satisfied that on the whole she did more good than harm, he had left her, as she now realized, with a neat lesson: do not seek to understand why the police do things; equally, why they do not do other things you might have thought, in your innocence, they ought to be doing. Above all, do not get in their hair and do not call yourself unnecessarily to their attention.

She had become friendly enough with the paternal to ring him up once or twice when oddities appeared that she felt uncertain how to handle. After all, he had told her to do just that. It could happen, too, that one felt vulnerable, even obscurely threatened. Aren't the police supposed to be there to protect people? In the same fashion, the citizen may sometimes feel he needs legal advice. The law is there to remedy inequity, or so she was led to believe as a child. In practice, if you do trot off to legal gentlemen, warmed by the belief that you are experiencing injustices, you will be told that it is a much better idea to endure the lack of equity in most human relations. Just so with the police. If you persist in telling them about the evil person who stole your child's new and expensive bicycle, they will try to suppress yawns and focus their wandering attention, but only within the limits of the same official courtesy which makes a motorbike cop salute you with disciplined smartness before telling you about the speed limit on that patch back there. They'd far rather not see you at all. Don't kid yourself into thinking they'd like to build statistics on bike thefts, and have a file on the frequency of certain places, methods, times-of-day, and so forth.

Thus, though much perturbed by the attack upon poor Xavier, Arlette was going to be wary about prodding cops on the subject. Whatever their reasons were, and Sergeant Subleyras neither knew, nor was any longer in a position to find out (pity, rather, he had resigned: no bad thing to have a friend inside a bureaucracy), they had decided apparently that the matter wasn't interesting. Lock-picking intruder who got disturbed, disliked that, bashed the disturber: a banality. If you don't like that, then a homosexual encounter that turned sour. It'll all be the same by the time your bruises are healed.

The complete lack of logic in all this didn't perturb them at all. This left Arlette high and dry. People ring you up making nasty suggestions? You should hear the things people say to us . . .

So she smiled cheerfully upon Xavier, said she was pursuing one or two little ideas but wasn't sure they'd come to much, and to get his bruises healed; that was the first priority. She sorted out the abortion-seeker. She listened to her tape, made some phonecalls, wrote a couple of letters, dealt with a couple of bores. Her telephone rang.

"Have a nice quiet weekend?" said the soft, hoarse voice. "I'm in no hurry either. Thinking of what game we'll play next, to ginger you up, like." She had put a pocket recorder on the spare ear-piece; she leaned forward and switched it on: this should not alter the sound the way a tapped line did. Fellow didn't want to be recorded. Because of what he says? Or because, somewhere, his voice might be recognized? Voiceprints, Arthur told her, are as individual as fingers. It might not be a waste of time.

"I'd really like to understand, you know. I don't mean your purpose; that seems clear enough. But the meaning – if there is any. Is there some link to anybody I know?" Chuckles.

"Maybe I'll help you just a little bit. Just so as you'll know who you owe it to, when it comes to you. A friend, a good friend, of Henri le Hollandais."

"Still means nothing to me. Your lines are as crossed as everything you do. The man you attacked, I hardly know at all."

"Make music; I like it. You're as clear as glass. I'm up there in the observatory there across the road. I can see and hear everything you get up to. Give me a good laugh." He rang off and left her frowning. Henri le Hollandais sounded like one of those Amsterdam jokers in Piet's funny stories, a century ago. She went back to work.

If she could get hold of the Laboisserie boy – that sounded too like police work; and she was no more anxious to meet Argentine cops than these funnybunny equivalents here at home – what would she say? That all was forgotten and forgiven, and so what? Estelle had gone on about Uncle François, who was Tante Edwige's husband and who would . . . all that was going round and round in circles and the boy would not be the least bit interested. That he should realize he was not a pariah, good. That he should mend his fences, good. That he should realize that throwing his family out of his life was not needed and even actively harmful . . . but his view of the future would not be a good job in Strasbourg provided by Uncle François.

Suddenly a voice was ringing in her inner ear. 'He comes from Holland: his name's Henkie.' Sounding in French more like Onky, which threw one, until one thought that even in Holland people aren't called Onky. Whereas a great many Dutch people are called Henk. It is because of the peculiar Dutch mania for pet or babyname abbreviations. A Wilhelmina becomes instantly a Willy or a Mientje, will never be anything else all her life, and wouldn't even recognize her own real name. The Dutch bicycle champion, Joop Zoetemelk, adopted moreover by the French since he married a French girl and lives here, is known to all as Yop. Tell them his name is Joe and they won't believe you. (Known to Arthur, a great bike fan, as Monsieur Lait-sucré and in moments of enthusiasm as Youpi.)

Henk is short for Hendrik and Hendrik is Henri; not after all some exceedingly obscure fourth-century Irish missionary who spread the gospel in Lithuania.

This crack in the darkness ought to allow further light to spread. What could she recall about Dutch Henkie?

He had died, by falling off a barge into the Rhine perfectly plausibly, off a greasy deck in a bobble of current, while emptying the rubbish overside. She'd gone on holiday – had there been any sequel?

The Commissaire of police had not been anxious for a sequel. Had declared in a voice of bland officialdom that it all seemed perfectly normal to him. Nothing to excite the German river police about, or anybody else.

What else had he had to tell? That Henk was yes, a cook on a river tug; was also a gangster, among other activities a specialist in violence for hire to anybody with an interest in using violence, and too cautious or cowardly to do it himself.

Had very likely killed people but evidence for this did not add up to legal proof.

He had let fall some curious and gratuitous information: Arlette racked her brains. He'd told Henk to be seen no more in France (did a barge on the Rhine count as France, or sort-of extra-territorial?). He'd been rather smiling and content to hear of Henk-overboard. Arlette, not quite sure whether she was saying it jokingly, had said You didn't have him pushed, did you? No, no, no, with roars of laughter, but – what was it? – had he finished the phrase? Wasn't going to raise a manhunt if anybody had? Or was she imagining that?

She turned back pages in her daybook to before the holidays, looked the date up, phoned the invaluable fellow-she-knew on the composition of the local paper, asked him would he look it up.

Answer came that afternoon. It had been a 'Fait Divers'. Happened at pretty near the limit of Alsace, where the Rhine ceases to be French. Body found some days later away down stream. Much lacerated, not to say mutilated. But there was no follow-up to it. Why, should there have been?

Just incidental curiosity.

That somebody had arranged this death was conceivable, since she had herself conceived the idea at that time. People, including the police and Arthur, would of course say that this exemplified her incorrigible, even morbid, taste for melodrama. Hypothesize for a moment if you please.

The somebody, let's say of a tidy and administrative cast of mind, is not wishful for the arrangement to take place in France. Those two handy necessities to the melodramatic mind, the First and Second Murderers, were a bit clumsy as they often are. Say a bit premature. Instead of being well downstream into Germany, the boat puts back into Lauterbourg.

You do realize I hope, my dear woman, that you have absolutely no right whatsoever to imagine anything of the sort.

Simply hypothesizing, gentlemen. I do not suggest that this individual, the woman Davidson, formerly known as woman van der Valk, imagines any such thing. Follow me closely. It is a personage as yet unseen, but quite real, who is imagining things. Observe this logic.

One, this fellow exists, because I don't go about hearing voices. Not Joan of Arc, nor that annoying friend of Arthur's, Mr Gilbert Pinfold, who was not only permanently pissed but putting huge doses of barbiturates on top.

Two, he describes himself as a Friend of Henri-le-Hollandais. And why should he think I have any connection with or interest in HlH? I wasn't even a witness.

Because three, he's the one who imagines things. Like it?

Listen, Arlette dear, let's get it clear: Friend is of an imbecile cast of mind. Friend sees people juxtaposed, and sees a casual connection – witness the attack upon Xavier. You were in companionship, and apparently friendly, with the paternal Commissaire. Arrived at Lauterbourg in his car, you recall? Friend thus, repeating the Xavier pattern, equates your accidental presence at the scene with complicity in it.

And doesn't this mean that Friend knows, or makes at least an informed guess, that the Paternal *did* have complicity in it? Stop in your tracks right there, girl.

Can't you see, you're piling one supposition upon another, and that leads you to far-fetched conclusions. One doesn't mind it being far-fetched, but the conclusion must be utterly false. Just like those silly and tiresome German people who were convinced Arthur was their father. Clutching at any handy straw to shore up the theory they wanted to believe in, they ended by committing themselves irrevocably to its being true. It *had* to be true.

A couple of days ago, Madame, you had a full-scale demonstration of what happens when people fall so deeply in love with a mistake. They make themselves totally ridiculous. You should be able to see that Friend has tumbled into the same trap. Do me a favour, girl: don't make it three in a row.

Whatever this was or this wasn't, decided Arlette, determined not to work herself up, it was plainly police business. By police I don't mean those slobs down the road. Nor ex-Sergeant Subleyras. But Police Judiciaire.

A quandary here. If it was the Paternal it would be a simple matter. Ring him up, say Look, I know nothing and I want to stay that way. But a perfectly casual connection with you has somehow dragged me into the shit. So it's up to you to get me out, okay?

That was a present conditional, meaning she wasn't sure either that she could or would do this, but it was at least possible.

Reality indeed was a past conditional. Not 'would be'; 'would have been'. Had not Sergeant Subleyras informed her that the Paternal was gone, translated to exalted spheres? There was a new one in his place.

Now a divisional commissaire of Police Judiciaire, commanding an important, thickly populated region like Strasbourg – sensitive too, and a listening post, because of the double frontier with Germany and Switzerland, is a complex person, dealing with complex affairs. An iceberg, showing only a tip. This was simply self-evident. One had only to recall Schleyer. Mr Schleyer (one recalled) was the titular head of German industry, the patron of the Patrons, the bosses' boss. Assassinated by the Red Faction, the so-called Baader-Meinhof gang. To be more precise kidnapped in Köln, hidden down in South Germany, transferred when things got too hot to Switzerland, and perhaps France – there had been a confusing pattern of dodge-and-double-back on the three-cornered frontier. But when the body was discovered, it was in Mulhouse, and that is a French town. Coming within the competence of the Regional Service of Police Judiciaire in Strasbourg. Which, in its subsequent prolonged dealings with the Germans and the Swiss, had to show diplomatic skills, tact, nicety of touch.

For a cop, in fact, about the roughest test you could face. It is not just a murder enquiry: it's the political heat you have to take. Prefects, Ministers, even Heads of State are breathing down your neck; you're up to here in all the Secret Service 'parallel police'; with your free hand, if you have one, you're fending off the entire international press. As for your own staff, whose readiness and wakefulness is under severe strain, they do nothing but complain that these goddam Germans have unlimited funds and the very latest, ultrasophisticated, electronic communications and tracking material, while they have to make do, more or less, with a donkey cart and a World War One field telephone.

She put the whole puzzle out of her mind: thinking along these lines wasn't going to get her anywhere at all. Who did she know at the PJ office?

Well, there was Papi, an inspector, meaning medium-grade officer. Experienced, intelligent, tortuous like all these PJ types – but on the whole sympathetic. He should be able to handle a thing like this, or know who could . . . There was also Corinne Klein, a junior inspector who had taught her some of the things that police females are supposed to know about. As a woman, disadvantaged by the machismo mentalities of Criminal Brigades, and a bit too junior.

"Hallo. Papi, please . . . Not in the office? . . . Gone? what d'you mean, gone? Gone where to? . . . oh, lor' . . . well then, Corinne Klein, please, if she's there." Blasted Papi posted, Avignon or somewhere. "Hallo Corinne? – Arlette . . . Middling, and yourself? Look, can you manage a drink? Like to hear how the world goes – when are you off? What about the pub in the Rue de Zürich? Okay, make it then? No, now if you like, I'm free. Okay, ten minutes."

Even meeting the PJ might be tricky. Friend was hanging about. Did he know any of them? Was he really following her about, or was that all a lot of bullshit designed to get her rattled? She wasn't going to get rattled. But she would put her gunbelt on. Her wearing a gun was a thing Corinne's trained eye would not miss, but would not be perturbed by. Arlette had a right to carry a gun. Her permission to do so had come right from this PJ office, and it had been Corinne that had taught her to manage it.

18. The boy who stood on the burning deck

Corinne was waiting for her, and was, moreover, wearing a gun herself. It is not difficult to tell: a tendency to loose, hip-length jackets. Police agents, even the girls, are not mucking about with whore-pistols. The pearl-handled nickelled twenty-two went out with Carmen Sternwood, and the thirty-two not much later. It's all the big calibre now. If you're going to point it at all, it has to impress people. If it's someone who thinks he's the Monster and isn't impressed, the thing has to stop him, even if he's coming at you like a Diesel train. The smallest that will do this is a nine-millimetre calibre, an American 38. The boys have taken to magnums, but these have too much charge for a woman's wrist and forearm, unless she were an East-German swimmer or something. Arlette's was a revolver with a short barrel; no effective range, but both impressive and guaranteed to stop a bear. What Corinne's was, she had never enquired. She was a shortish, stubby girl; the local morphology. Nicely shaped, with a square handsome head, hair cut short – as opposed to those on television, police-girls do not have long hair – and good legs. Arlette was a lot taller, but child-bearing had given her a bigger behind. Corinne indeed had a tiny behind like a frog, enviable when you have to wear a gunbelt. If the beastly thing is to be of any use, it is no good having it in your handbag.

The two women sat in the corner of the pub and had a beer.

Gossip, shop, jokes. They were easy with one another; got on comfortably. They didn't know one another well: nothing heart to heart about them. Corinne knew perfectly that Arlette had asked her for a professional purpose: until it came out, one simply observed the forms.

"So you've a new boss, I hear."

"Indeed we have. Early days yet. Got to watch your step with him. Big contrast."

"What way?"

"Oh the other, you know, looked all austere and ascetic but was fairly easy-going, a good delegator. This one's rather younger, has an affable teddybear manner. Plumpish face and soft-spoken, but cracks the whip. That's fairly normal in a new guy taking over a big department, but you can see it's going to be the authoritarian style, once the getting-to-know-you is done with. What's this memo, who wrote it, where is she, send her up here: what's the meaning of this? Big fitness campaign: no excess waistline tolerated."

"I was on holiday: must have missed the announcement. What's his name?"

"Casabianca. Out of the mafia down in Nice. And he'll stand on the burning deck all right, whence all but he have fled. A small, local fire, he'll say: put it out by myself. Pass me that bucket."

"I'm not sure that he sounds altogether my cup of tea."

Corinne laughed good-humouredly.

"You'll be all right. You stay quiet and nobody'll worry about you. You've good marks. All that stuff Devious Dan invented about giving you a permit was to have a rug to pull if need be. Giving it to let you know he could withdraw it again any time. If it's Casa you're worried about, you can forget it. He's less legalistic than Berger was." If it was – even ever so slightly – patronizing, this was not going to ruffle Arlette. Corinne had saved her life, and that was not pitching it too high, upon an occasion. Professionally, it was true; in the call-of-duty. Nevertheless.

"Tell me, Corinne, did you ever come across mention of someone called Henri le Hollandais?"

"No." Frown: Arlette had no business hearing anything before she did.

"Well, I know nothing about him. He was a fellow who fell off a river boat and got drowned. I happened to be having a drink with Daniel Berger at the time." No need to mention that it had been lunch. Monsieur Berger's paternal ways might have been one of Dan's Devious Ways. "He had a record, baddish was the impression I got. This was before the holidays. There's some idle fellow now who claims to have been his pal, and who rings me up with a heavy menace act. I wouldn't pay any attention to that, naturally, but a perfectly harmless client of mine got punched in the face, pretty spitefully: this idiot seems to have thought he was a friend of mine. And then mentioning this name. As though he felt obliged to conduct a vendetta. Like, I say, it was pure coincidence. I don't know this Onky, as Berger called him, from Prince Bernhard, but if he was some kind of department business, I thought it best that someone ought to know and you were the obvious person," suppressing all thought of Inspector Papi.

"I see. And you've no notion who this joker is?"

"Nor what he wants, except that it might make him feel better to punch my face too. I've a bit of his voice on a recorder. No description – the punch-up was in a dark passage, and he'd unscrewed the corridor bulb. The local boys were called, but they've just poohpoohed it as a break in."

"And you don't want your face punched."

"Well, I'll shell my own peas, but suppose it were to overlap something that is no business of mine?"

"Quite right to tell me. Doesn't mean, of course, that it's going to be business of ours."

"Nor, if it were, would I expect any long confidential disclosures," said Arlette a little snappishly.

"Local joker, your impression?"

"Who can tell? Not with an accent."

"What's Onky?"

"Dutch for Henri. I might be completely mistaken. But there's no other link I could make or think of."

"Oh, well, I'll look it up. Don't make a big thing of it, right?"

"I'm not standing on any burning deck as far as I know. You ought to know me better. I certainly am not trying to strike any big heroic attitudes."

"You're on your way home now?" asked Corinne idly, finishing her beer.

"Still got to buy my supper."

"Tcha, so have I. Keep in touch then, honey. Say hallo to the Prof for me."

"Sure."

She had left the car up at the top of the road, and she felt pretty sure that if anybody followed her she would know about it by now. People ringing up with Hollywoodish mumbles were bluffers, on the whole.

The Rue de Zürich was where she had lived for some years before meeting Arthur, but she did not take a sentimental view of it. Simply a pavement she knew every inch of. If the deck here were to get warm under her feet, she would feel it through her shoes. She did not believe in anything to be frightened of. Felt indeed ashamed of taking her gun, of surrounding herself with hypersensitivity to loiterers. Some petty sneak . . . Nor was she worried about Arthur. He walked home across the university 'campus', but it was still daylight when he did, and he was in the habit of carrying a large stick.

People were going home, and traffic vilely congested. It took her near half an hour to get across town to the district known as the Tivoli, between the concert-hall, called with resounding pomp the Palace of Music and Congress, and the little waterway called the Aar, which serpentines along between gardens and gives this residential area a considerable cachet.

A smallish house, but with a garden in front as well; a rarity in this town. A big cedar tree and a linden gave an enviable quiet and privacy. Nice house in a rustic style common round here: wooden clapboards painted a whitish grey. Unobtrusively divided into two flats, and Mr Thibault's was the top one, and his large and shiny Mercedes stood under the linden. The solid street gate did not give to her hand.

"Like to speak to Monsieur Thibault, if that's convenient."

"And what might you want with Monsieur Thibault?" asked a woman's voice, distorted by the speakbox in the gatepost, but polite enough.

"Oh, I'm not selling encyclopedias." She was aware of observation from a window as she crossed the flagstoned path. But she cut an acceptable figure. Not horrible looking, nice legs, respectably enough dressed to be let in at any door. He hadn't looked at her that morning in the shop, and she did not believe she was recognizable.

The entrance was up steps and through a glassed-in, tiled verandah at the back. Trees there, too, in their autumn foliage, and beyond the placid grey stream with leaves floating on it. The woman who let her in was small, soignée, with curly brown hair cut short, dressed expensively in a woollen frock, who looked at her with curiosity.

"He doesn't know you, does he?"

"No, I'm a stranger to him. Here's my card." Which simply said 'Arlette van der Valk' and nothing else: it didn't have any guns or eyes in the corner.

"He's around somewhere. If you don't mind waiting here a sec., I'll just see."

The inner hallway was pleasant, too, with a good parquet floor and fine-grained oak panelling, but had rather too much leather around. Like Dickens' Mr Venus, Monsieur Thibault lived surrounded by the trophies of his art.

A man appeared in a plum-coloured velvet smoking jacket, who had changed his shirt with the idea of not going out any more that evening.

"Well, Madame. Suppose you tell me to what I owe this honour. Sit down, why don't you," after the quick rake of the eye told him this wasn't Jehovah's Witnesses. There was a long long sofa in what was doubtless buffalo, since its head was on the wall above with eyes and horns pointed at her. He perched on the other end, made a movement with a cigarette box. She said no thanks with her finger, and her voice said "I run, or rather am, an agency, Monsieur Thibault, for trying to help people in trouble of different sorts."

"Really? In Paris?"

"No, here. There's no reason," smiling, "why you should ever have heard of me."

"And I'm in trouble am I?" smiling.

"If you are, you haven't made it my business," they were

getting on merrily now, "and to set your mind quite at ease, I don't try to tout from door to door. So I'll be very brief. You had a burglary at your country cottage, and through no fault of your own, as was made quite clear at the time, a boy got killed." He was knitting the brow slightly, so she glanced upward at the row of heads and horns and added pleasantly, "I see you're a mighty hunter." He decided that it was best treated lightly and said, "Yes, mighty hunter," lightly.

"And equally, through no fault of her own, a simple kind woman, who is a widow, and has not had the easiest of lives, has lost her son."

He took a cigarette and lit it slowly.

"And she'd like some money, I suppose. And you've consented to act as intermediary: is that it?"

"I don't think she wants any money," colourless, "and she hasn't suggested anything of the sort, or indeed anything. What I have thought might be more to the point is that at no cost to yourself you might take her circumstances, which of course you knew nothing of, into consideration. You might make a gesture. I think she'd appreciate it very much if you simply went to see her, and said something of your regret for what had happened. I know that this isn't very easy, since in your position it is natural to feel defensive and stiffened. But it wouldn't cost a great effort. These are not bad people. They have felt embitterment. A boy throwing a brick; it was deplorable, but it happens."

He was listening to her expressionless, and did not interrupt when she paused.

"It would be up to you of course, but it isn't impossible to imagine something you could do that would not be patronizing, nor taken as such if offered. There's another brother I've seen and spoken to, a couple of years older. Quiet and steady, an honest, serious boy, well spoken of by his employer. It's in no sense an amend I'm asking of you: one could envisualize a good turn done this boy, a word said, a hand held out, that could find him perhaps a better job, a step up. And in this way you could, when all is said, efface any lingering traces of bitterness. So there – I thought I'd come to you in simplicity to put it to you. I've no concealed thought or ulterior motive: there's no 'deal' of any sort." He thought, and stabbed the cigarette out slowly.

"I don't choose to proceed in this matter. The boy got what he was looking for, which may be rough justice, but that's his hard luck. It's to be hoped that it serves at least as a lesson to others. There are too many: it's easy to break into unguarded weekend places. Wanton – they're out for kicks after a few beers, and the damage they do is out of all proportion to any punishment they risk, even if they are caught." He stopped himself abruptly. A speech he had made several times, that everybody has already listened to.

"In fact, I don't intend to discuss this. I appreciate that you have not been trying to put pressure on me, which is why I heard you out, but I'll trouble you no further. I can put that better: I'll trouble you not to trouble yourself. That's clear, I think. So if you'll excuse me . . ."

"Before closing the door on me – you close the door on yourself. Why not sleep on it? – it hadn't before entered your mind."

"Make no mistake; it isn't going to now. Good evening to you."

She hadn't expected anything at all. It was neither more nor less than what one would have hoped for.

She drove home the direct way, banging her nose on traffic lights every hundred metres. The stupid way, but she was in the mood to bang her nose on things. Place de Bordeaux, along the boulevards, over the Ill at the Pont de Dordogne and along to the Rue de Verdun. Every light went red as she reached it. She forced herself not to accelerate the car hard, not to play the game of beating the lights, to be the very soul of good-humoured patience.

The Rue de l'Observatoire was dark, now, and she took a wary look around after turning her lights out. No sneaks were going to sneak up on her, not if common prudence could prevent it. She locked the car carefully, senses abristle. Somebody had slammed a car door, at the instant she had herself. She straightened up and got her house keys out so that she would not have to fumble on the step. Suddenly what seemed a large, silent, black shadow loomed up alongside her.

Arlette made a quick step of recoil. She'd been jumped on before in the dark, in this street. She made a tiny squeak between her teeth, something like a kitten when its paw is trodden upon. She had her hand on her gun. The black shadow was that of a man, large in an overcoat and dark hat. It raised the hat in a polite, placid movement and said, "Do not be alarmed." The movement disclosed a plump, baldish visage. The voice was soft and a little hoarse.

She took another step back, drew the gun, held it under her jacket.

"And who are you?" holding her voice down. The man stood still, made a slight formal bow.

"René Casabianca." He smiled very slightly as she got rid of the pistol. "Suppose we go in to your house," he suggested.

The deck had got very hot there under her feet for a second.

19. Les marginaux

He stood back politely to let her enter first. She pressed the switch and the hallway, dark even in broad daylight, flooded with light. These houses have high ceilings. Nobody was going to take those bulbs out without a stepladder. She closed the door and stood against it, in a heavy, cosy silence smelling of dust.

"Do you mind showing me an identity proof?" The overcoat was dark blue. A little early in the year for a winter coat. Perhaps he felt the cold. There is a difference in temperature between Strasbourg and Nice.

"You are prudent. That is quite right."

"Come on up." She walked quietly up the wide shallow stairs, ritually turning out lights on each landing as she lit the flight above. He stood back as she undid the bolt on her own door, put a professional eye on the thick slab of oak – these houses date from the last century – and the top-and-bottom bar inside; nodded.

"You couldn't do any better."

"I don't have any valuables. But I like to sleep sound of a night." She was about to let him through the 'airlock' into the flat beyond: he put his hand gently on her elbow and pointed to the 'office'. Knows his way about, she thought: Corinne, of course. Had done his homework. She was impressed.

"More discreet," he murmured, looking at her big seascape; Toulon harbour, on a grey day. "That's very nice. I should enjoy meeting your husband, but this is just as well between ourselves."

"Sit down then, Commissaire." The confessional-chair was after all comfortable.

"Thanks, I won't take it off." He unbuttoned the coat: sober dark brown suit within.

"Smoke if you feel like it."

"Thanks, I don't."

"Can I get you a drink?"

"Thanks, I never do. Well now. My little Miss Klein . . ."

"That's right. I felt I ought to mention it."

"That was quite correct, and sensible. My predecessor had a good opinion of you, dear lady. I should not dream, of course, of calling his judgment into question. I am glad to see for myself that it was sound. Very well now." He got ready for a formal exposition. Arlette watched, amused at Corinne's description: 'put this fire out by myself': and the realities of this soft-spoken person. It just looked soft.

Would be catquick upon occasion; he was massive but not fat. Large, square face with small intelligent eyes. A southern pallor, not unhealthy. The orotund professional manner and polished phrase of the superior functionary. A good lucid setter-out of points. Buttery, slippery, extremely sly behind the frank open air, the confidential tone.

"I have wasted no time in coming to see you; it is essential that you should understand, that you should not be frightened, and that you should do nothing impetuous. By accident, you have become entwined in a matter of which you know nothing: I shall explain it. Clarity, above all." They are all superior liars, and the moment they speak of clarity they are going to bullshit you, but he did it well. Arlette was mesmerized.

"We knew this person existed, but had failed to identify him. A petty fellow, of no importance. Capable, doubtless, of small annoyances: you, dear lady, furnish us with evidence of this. I rely upon your discretion. If your husband, as a general rule, is in your confidence I see no objection, but let it go no further.

"The deceased Henri, ah, the Hollandais. Folklore name. He was, as you have heard say, a criminal individual. Dabbling in things; all was fish to his net, one might say. Engaged among other things in traffics for which his activities on board boats lent a cloak of legitimacy.

"You need not, I need hardly say, imagine lurid matters. There were no barges with false bottoms stuffed with cocaine. But he made regular trips, could enter or leave a country without causing comment. A courier is useful, staging-posts are useful: there are things to organize, a route to keep greased and smooth. I need not go into detail. Drugs, I think not. Certainly, between Europe and these countries – Iran for one – there is always traffic in narcotics, but professionally these gentry keep things separate. A link may part, but there'll be no run in the stocking. You have a right to an explanation; I content myself by saying a traffic in women. White slavery as it is journalistically spoken of never quite ceases: the emphasis changes. A clutter of cabaret singers and topless dancers and hostess this-or-that: they're aware enough of the fact that this is polite prostitution, but make the mistake of thinking of it as both lucrative and voluntary until they get trapped. Now we can't stop people going where they choose, and we can't warn people who don't want to listen to warnings. We try to put brakes upon it; we try to stop a railroading that is seen to be too brazen and too greedy. Leave it at that.

"Now the Hollandais came to grief: no need to go into that. We may suppose that this individual was his tool, knowing something, probably not much, of his affairs. Would like, very possibly, to step into his shoes. We may suppose that he has not. Why? Because, it is plain, this is not a very bright person. He's a crude, smallsize rogue. He attempts to convince you that his aim is to avenge. Rogues do not devote themselves in honour to avenging the fallen comrade: they leave such notions to Jean-Paul Belmondo. Furthermore why behave so stupidly, why telephone his intentions, why this ridiculous attack upon a man hardly known to you? It is clear, he is feeling you out. If he can frighten you, if he can gain any leverage upon you, he smells a chance of squeezing some money out of you. Absurd? – you aren't rich? – you're a poor choice for a ransom attempt? So he needs small sums, and this fact advertises that he needs money, and plays no important role in the schemes of the Hollandais – or others. He was, no doubt, used for little errands. A few hundred francs at a time. He misses this supplement of income.

"Am I making sense? Then here is the rest. We should like to put him out of circulation. To remove a nuisance, naturally. There is the possibility, too, that he may know something more. Little, and fragmentary; no doubt of that. But we are patient searchers after small missing pieces in cutouts. Fit him in, and a picture may have become clearer. So to conclude: I'd like you to mousetrap this silly little man for me, and your balanced good sense and experience make you an excellent choice. You aren't getting entwined in a PJ operation: disabuse yourself of any such supposition. Rather, I entwine a thread of my own into an operation of yours, help you to bring it to a rapid conclusion, remove a scrap of grit in your eye, and hope that it may be of use to ourselves. Very likely it won't, but it's worth trying. All right?"

"I'm glad myself of help and advice, so what is there to say?"

"Good. Now you need have no apprehension. He attacks somebody nearby, but not close to you. He will not do that, but he'll try to persuade you he will. He'll make more of these phonecalls. We won't tap you, but keep your recorder on. You have a scrap of his voice, I believe."

Arlette reached for the little recorder on the table and unclipped the cassette.

"I thought his voice sounded rather like yours," she said amiably.

Mr Casabianca had a little smile. Like Corinne's, a thought superior, a scrap of condescension, that the police tend to wear in face of someone who has been, is being, is about to be manipulated. With him, something else again. A divisional commissaire can be accounted a subtle sort of fellow. He is more than a high-grade civil servant. He is the legal expert trained to smell the equivocal in a dossier: himself a past master in the art of prevarication, he can put his finger unerringly on a passage of prose that is a thought too smooth. There is complicity in his smile, and a little contempt. 'I know how to protect myself' says this faint hint of a snicker 'but do you? We shall see.'

"We'll have him, in the course of the next day or so." A greasy affability, but the grease is not cheap or rancid. Buttery. "I don't need to give you any prompting. If you were reading from a script, he'd be sly enough to smell that this was mousetrap cheese he was being offered. If you sound a little unsure of yourself, it'll make just the bait he'll reach for. Play him along, hesitate, shuffle and mumble, and while he thinks he has a hook well into you, he'll be the less conscious that it's in his own dumb-bell jaw. You ring young Corinne Klein, and she'll look after it. Mmmm?" Arlette reached out slowly for a cigarette and took her time getting it right way round. Being mousetrapped herself into being cheese . . . it was somehow typical. And if she said she wanted nothing to do with it . . . that would not only be 'a bad mark' but would leave her vulnerable to the Friend. Who might not be everything – nor quite such a fool – as they were suggesting. She was perfectly well aware that the confidential tales of Mr Casabianca were like government statistics: they could be fitted in to anything. At the very least, Arlette could be a silly girl, but she wasn't getting chatted into white slavery.

"I'm not sure," she said, "that I'm either clever enough or stupid enough to be adept at this sort of operation. When there is something I can do, and it renders a service, I'm glad to do it, and I'm glad to place reliance in your help. This man frightens me, because frankly violence does frighten me, and if I'm to be rid of him I need your help, so I'm in no position to refuse you mine. I don't like what you suggest, and if I had any choice I'd refuse it, but you've put it in a way that makes it impossible to say no, so that I'd better swallow it and like it. Well – I'll have to wait upon what my Friend has to suggest."

"That's very sensibly put," said the Commissaire, "so we'll leave it at that. As soon as you hear anything, give us a buzz. Should Klein be out of the office, leave the usual message; to contact you urgently. I'll leave you to get on with your supper," affably. "Don't trouble, dear lady, I can find my way. And should your friend be keeping an eye upon your homecoming, let me tell you that you won't be compromised. I left a man in the car, who has been maintaining an interest in the street outside. Good evening to you, and a bon appetit."

"Likewise." He looked, indeed, like a man who took a keen interest in what was on his plate. She felt uncertain whether or not this would be thought a reassuring trait.

Arthur, in an apron, was tasting soup off a wooden spoon, was interested in the unexpected visitor, grinned a bit and made up an impromptu Dutch rhyme, which stumbled and then collapsed.

She went and put some music on the player: Davidova playing Chopin.

We are the marginals, she thought. The police, very worldly-wise, not to say self-satisfied, puts its gleaming little crumblike eye upon us. Intellectuals, it says with a snigger. Talk a lot, but nowise dangerous. Big mouth, nasty tongue, coarse language about Our President, but not a threat to public order. We will, though, always be watched. Any little opportunity to place a bananaskin in our path will not be missed. And if we should happen to slip on it, they will not be displeased. The man Davidson; he does little harm. Rude about the Gross National Product and the Nation, and the Liberal Society. But sticks to his job on the whole, which is to find ways of abolishing prisons, and that's a forlorn hope, huh? The bonne-femme van der Valk, she does no harm either. Meddlesome mare but all this folk – it carries no weight. You can always distract it with Human Rights in Czechoslovakia. Marginal, all that. But keep an eye on it, simply because it's marginal. If at any moment it becomes a nuisance, then it's nice to have a little something in reserve. A technical infringement, which will be pretext enough should the occasion arise to have it sent back to scrubbing floors, which is where it belongs.

The police, by its nature, wishes heartily that General Franco would arrive, and set the Nation to rights.

20. The New Village

It's a funny place, Neudorf. Arlette had lived several years in Strasbourg without ever setting foot there. There is no reason for going there: it is totally without interest; as a part of the world it is both boring and hideous. If you are going towards Germany it is the inexplicably long and dreary stretch before you reach the river, the Europa Bridge, the frontier posts gay with flags. If you are coming from Germany you wonder impatiently when you will reach Strasbourg. The city was built five kilometres away from the river precisely because the land on this bank is lowlying and marshy, and the Rhine made a habit of flooding it. The problem was solved by a network of canals and harbours, giving a Dutch look to the whole of East Strasbourg and creating an impassable barrier. On the other, southern side of Neudorf the main road to Colmar, now an autoroute, makes equally a frontier. The whole 'quarter' is shaped like a literal quarter of a cake or cheese, with its central pointed end touching Strasbourg – one must cross yet another canal to reach the old city – and its outer perimeter the industrial terrains round the river-harbour. Between these rigid barricades, Neudorf asphyxiates.

It is ridiculously named, being neither new, nor a village. It is small consolation that the neighbouring quarter on the southwest side, the Montagne Verte, is anything but green and even from river level far from being a mountain.

Arthur Davidson was interested in Neudorf because, he said, being a sociologist means, supposedly, that you take an interest in society; a thing remarkably few sociologists do: as a rule they prefer statistics. Working as he did for the Council of Europe, an organization much like the United Nations, having no contact whatever with reality but feeding him with reams and reams of statistics about the consumption of patent medicines (subsection constipation remedies) in, say, Jugoslavia, he had a hunger for real life. This was one reason why Arlette had been urged to take up help-and-counsel work. Another was that the Council, and its incestuous kindred the European Parliament and the Court of Human Rights, is a toney affair, very well paid and with high prestige. It is all housed in the flossy northeastern quarter of Strasbourg; the pleasant wooded and watered district along the river Ill. The personnel naturally lives along here: asked where Neudorf was they'd look puzzled.

It is the most 'working class' district of Strasbourg; the most urban, crowded, populous. And of course the most under-privileged; albeit the largest, the least represented on the city council, with no park or open green space whatsoever, and completely lacking any leisure or cultural amenity. You will look in vain here for any rest or refreshment apart from getting drunk. There are however two cemeteries, an orphanage and an abandoned gasworks.

One interesting development is that up to twenty years ago there were tiny enclaves, almost rural. At the industrial edges along the canals and railway lines was a close huddle of grimy sheds and workshops, but in the middle were cottages and orchards; even a field or two where things grew. As the city has expanded Neudorf has become an inner suburb and these spaces have been seized for a population of petty-bourgeois white-collar flatdwellers. There is no prestige to living here, but that need not stop the rents being high.

Arlette had got to know the place well: it was fertile in her customers. Put Strasbourg in scale to New York and Neudorf would be its Brooklyn. Here one can just glimpse still the palimpsest of a village. How many generations ago was it possible to trace the outlines of the wooded ridges that Washington defended against the redcoats, before falling back across the East River to the Harlem Heights?

Solange Bartholdi was just going out shopping. When she saw Arlette she put her bag down, her apron back on, suggested a cup of coffee.

"Or would you rather a beer? I don't drink it, but the boys . . . Pascal . . . I can see it in your face, what you've come to say. Nice of you. You could have written a little line. If that. Most people would think all right, if there's nothing to say, say nothing, forget it. I'd have understood. You aren't like that. But you needn't, you know." Arlette tried to struggle against this fatalism but her words were lame. No doubt of it, there was nothing useful she could suggest. Against Monsieur Thibault's flat hard-edged words she had found no riposte: there was nothing to say to Solange. Somewhere away at the back of her mind was a wish to say that tunnels had curves imperceptible in the dark. Follow . . . but altogether too many people have used this metaphor: there is no way it can even be a joke any more. It is too saddening. People want to go on believing in a turn, in a patch of darkness paler than the rest, in a crumb of brightness one scarcely dares believe can be light. Something phosphorescent; or an optical illusion. There is no light, nor possibility of any. Go on, and at the end is a rockfall, a caving-in. The air is bad, here: turn around and go back, while you still have strength to put a foot before the other.

"I never really believed there were anything, like. I never said to Pascal I was trying . . . he'd have said, Don't waste your time. Or he'd have had some daft idea of going chucking a grenade or such . . ." The pathetic little kitchen, oil-painted and smelling of cabbage: the dark livingroom with its effort to be gay; flowery wallpaper, the dreadful glossy veneers on furniture, and brass trim that peeled off. She wished so badly there were something to say or to do, and everything she thought of would only serve to make matters worse.

She sat in the car, and looked at the evil street. The world is very evil. This truism – she could hear Arthur's tone, not altogether sarcastic. 'The English Protestant Church dear, in which I was brought up; Hymns Ancient and Modern, number 226, freely after the De Contemptu Mundi, a poem composed by St Bernard of Clairvaux, I'm uncertain of the date, around eleven hundred would it be? – matters little, the Dark Age. Hora novissima, tempora pessima. Ever since, enlightenment has often been thought to be at hand. When it fails, as it always does, Saint Bernard is a person it's good to keep in mind.'

A few streets further, down towards the bottom of the sack, lived Sergeant Subleyras, whom one still saw, inevitably, as a Sergeant. Rather like Mr George in *Bleak House*. Around here Neudorf becomes hilarious. Out of the choked crammed streets one crosses all of a sudden a railway-line (the main line to Munich, to Salzburg, to Vienna) and comes out upon a large grassy field, actually with trees around its edge, stretching right across to the industrial terrain of the Rue de la Rochelle. And surely this would be suitable as the park so badly needed.

Certainly. It is there at all because it is the old Strasbourg airfield and was kept intact (like much else; the Maginot Line is not far away) as Military Terrain. It has been kept as an airfield, for the convenience of the owners of private planes, who benefit, quite naturally, from the protection of those people whom God has placed in Authority over us. Amen.

Subleyras lived just short of this phenomenon, in a block with actually a tree in front of the door. Planes taking off over his head when the wind was in the east diminished, slightly, the pleasures thus enjoyed.

He was looking very civilian, in a darned old highnecked sweater and shapeless trousers, and Mexican sandals. He had the sort of hair that never did look untidy, so unlike her limp straggle or Arthur's drooping English locks: it never even needs combing.

"That's a welcome surprise. Come on in then."

"I brought a bottle of plonk," said Arlette.

"Then come in twice as fast. The children are at school. Janine is at work. I'm painting. You don't mind?"

"Mind . . . what a silly word."

The livingroom had the extreme houseproud tidiness that can be so antipathetic; of places where cleanliness is an end unto itself and self-respect becomes arrogance and intolerance, a caste symbol. She had seen far too many of these in Holland, and they are frequent in France. Objects, like people in these rooms, are dragooned into tame acquiescence. The police are inclined to this kind of living, with a meek little wife scuttling about setting things straight on the mantel, quantities of starched lace curtain, children disciplined with a leather belt, and an off-duty God looking at the television with deep-rooted approval amid a holy silence. Arlette had a horrid feeling that she had mistaken herself utterly in her view of Subleyras. Luckily, before giving way to consternation, she looked at the other end of the room where the redecorating had not yet begun: the walls were full of children's drawings.

"This is very classic – the recently retired gentleman takes up the little domestic chores for which his wife has been clamouring, and which he was always going to do next week." She sat in an armchair. To be sure it was the 'good three-piece suite' and intensely respectable, but not prissy. Dark green corduroy, good quality, well-worn, much-brushed, but the children had never been forbidden to sit on it.

"Oh yes, very classic – when you get the house agent in and prospective buyers, you have the place dollied up smart: more money that way." He was uncorking the bottle: she was just getting an ordinary Prisunic glass. Not something pretending to be cut crystal, and not with little mats under it. "There should be some peanuts somewhere, but we seem to have eaten them all." Nothing stiff in the manner.

"You're selling? Not going to live any more in the lovely New Village? Here by the lyceum, such a Nice Neighbourhood."

"That's right," grinning, "ought to get a fairly good sale. We better, because it's just about the only resource we have. We've been here a good few years, the mortgage is all paid up, so I'm taking pains: repaint, repaper, and make as professional a job as I can."

"What are you going to do?" curiously, raising her glass in answer to his toast, accepting the sort of cigarette one buys for guests when one doesn't smoke oneself. Her eye fell on the bookshelves, full of books carefully dusted and neatly lined up, but very thoroughly read: heavy with technical and professional information, with school books, with what in France are called vulgarizations. Not a pejorative word: means simply a teach-yourself for the interested amateur. Physics, biology, chemistry. Absolutely nothing to be patronizing about. A man who keeps his tools sharp, oiled, and polished.

"Good glass of wine this," recorking the bottle carefully. "No, we're not staying in good old Neudorf. Buy, as cheap as I can, a house in the country, with a bit of space, something for a workshop. Bit of a garden I should hope, some vegetables, some animals. Janine's good with that. The children gain something from that, if they lose something at school." Arlette nodded, agreeing. She had moved into the town, to get a better school for Ruth. But she'd been widowed, and Ruth the only child left at school, and depending a lot on an academic success. With a man, and with younger children, the country every time . . .

"I don't know much. I'm fairly good with my hands, though; I'm strong, I'm healthy. So's Janine. The important thing is – she backs me up, every step. We know it'll be bloody hard. But if one can get past five years without borrowing from the bank . . ."

Arlette was more than interested: sitting up and forgetting about the drink.

"Never, never, never borrow from banks."

"I'm not sure it's good economics, but I'm sure as hell it's good practice. That's my weakness though – book-keeping, business, selling; I know nothing about that. Have to say plenty of prayers. But I've picked up a lot of old iron. I like fixing up these old stoves and cookers. I want to make a bit of a forge. I don't feel too sure of it. But it's all I've got."

Arlette was thinking – but the New Village used to be like this. Small, simple houses. Yard with a pump, a shed for a workshop. Barn for a scrap of hay, a few potatoes, apples, maize hung up to dry, a half dozen chickens and a few rabbits. Space for logs and some rudimentary machinery. No 'farming' in any sense of the word. Simple metallurgy; bit of tinsmithing, electroplating, panel-beating. The French had this in their blood. But could you even do this in the backwoods, any more? You sure as hell couldn't in Neudorf.

21. Professional advice

"I don't want to talk about myself," said Subleyras. "Rather hear what brings you this way. Wasn't just to see how I was making out, was it?"

"A goodish bit, all the same," she answered. "People who'll resign from a job, especially one like yours, and out of idealism yet – they're pretty rare. And start again from scratch. They're interesting, you know."

"Idealism yet – yock. Sounds too starry-eyed for me. Put it negatively rather, say there's plenty people who vomit their jobs, who wouldn't keep them another minute, only can they afford to throw them up? That's rough. I've been here a fewish years. Ground here was real cheap then. These flats didn't cost much. Nobody lived out here except real petty people, like me. Bus conductors, garage hands, gardeners, shoemakers. We bought on a low mortgage, with a government credit, three-four per cent stuff. These last years we could accelerate to pay it off. What's now? – people with big cars and nice suits. Thirty years at twenty per cent, and they got to pay for the lift and the electric central heating. Fellow stuck with that, and with children to bring up, he might have ideals, but he better forget about them quick. Oy, Janine said I mustn't forget to put the pressure cooker on. No, have another glass. I don't want to chase you. And you got that look in your eye, of something you'd like to tell me and are hesitating whether or not. I can listen. You won't take it amiss, if I keep the paint-brush in my hand? – just want to get this panel finished, before the children come."

Arlette unburdened her heart, on the subject of Commissaire Casabianca.

Subleyras kept the serious, concentrated face and unhurried, even gestures of a painter, didn't look at her, didn't interrupt. When he spoke, it was in the same andante tempo.

"Sounds a fairly typical police operation. You do all the work, have all the bother. We needn't say worry, because he's certainly right: this fellow you call the Friend is feeling you out. He doesn't know where you stand, nor how pally with the PJ you might be. So he's moving around real careful, feinting at you. Little bit of intimidation, little bit of tickle your ribs, bit of silence to shake you off balance. Are you a PJ informer or aren't you? He's not sure, and he won't attack you or anything till he is. And you might be good for money. So worry, no: don't be frightened.

"But bother, yes, you've got to wait and let him come to you. And you take the risk – of failure: there's no great physical risk because yes, Casabianca will look after you. He wouldn't go to all this trouble unless he was prepared to: he wants this Friend. How badly I couldn't say. Nor can I say how much clue he's got. He may know the identity, all about him, but looking for a hold, legal hold, use you to mousetrap him."

"He admits as much."

"Yes, but when they use that Honest John act, they're lying. Make no mistake, you do the job: they take the credit.

"Notice – well, you have – how they've got you boxed in. Refuse to do it and you're not a cooperative citizen. What d'you think, they'll say, we give you this licence to work; and a gun and everything? So that you can be helpful, when we see occasion. A PJ cop never passes up a chance to acquire a good indicator. You hear all sorts of unlikely things: never know when some little information comes up useful. Like this drug thing you got into by accident, last year. Handy that was, for them.

"But you aren't a cop. Do what they want, and technically you're illegal, not to speak of a morally and ethically dubious business. They've a comfortable hold on you. They know about your activities, make it clear they're winking at any infractions you may commit; you're in their debt, you're in their pocket. Just what they like."

"You could be a bit prejudiced, couldn't you? When you were on the urban force, the PJ weren't necessarily your closest pals."

"It's a fair point. There's too many goddam police forces in this country and there's a fair degree of suspicion and jealousy between them all right, and a lot of manoeuvring about who gets the credit. You know about it, I reckon; we were urban cops, and in a town this size the Municip is organized to be sort of autonomous, in principle. The gendarmerie is another pair of shoes altogether, paramilitary, comes under Army. The Police Judiciaire is different again; it comes under Interior, has authority over the whole territory, and of course it's élite, or supposed to be. In practice all this overlaps a lot. I didn't like the PJ a whole lot, no. They get away with stuff, and protection, that we'd have got done for. But there's good people in it." He went and turned the pressure cooker down, came and took a sip from his glass.

"What you got to understand about cops – any cops – they aren't law-abiding."

"Fair enough; the law is a ass. No law-enforcement has much to do with law: I learned that with my first husband."

"I'd forgotten. Your first man was a city cop. Teach me to shut my big mouth. But did he fake evidence, or plant it?"

"If he did, he didn't tell me."

"No, of course not. And I don't know how things are in Holland."

"Not much different. Some better, some worse. The police in Amsterdam didn't have a very good reputation, and didn't deserve one."

"We'll leave your man out of it."

"The chances are that he did dodgy things when he had to. To keep up in the job, to be not-too-badly marked – one has to."

"Right. A cop is subordinate to government authority, and that's the whole weakness. What the government wants bent – you bend. You get this governmental way of thinking, which is all special pleading and selective thinking. And servility: all cops are servile. One can get a good commissaire, just as one can get a good minister. They aren't all sinister ruffians, not on the PJ neither. But the best are stuck with the system. Be a good team player, or no promotion."

Subleyras studied his work carefully, standing back to get the light on it; rinsed his brush in the turps, wiped his hands on the paint rag; poured her a third glass she didn't want, but wasn't going to refuse.

"Why did I hesitate so long, about throwing it up? Why come to you, at a moment when I was balanced on a hair? Why, if it was all so bad? First off, it's not all that bad: there's good cops. Second, there's no happiness without limitations, admitting the rule, going by it. Even when you don't like it, don't feel like it. Without the rule it's nothing. Like a marriage. Say I come home, want to make love with my wife. She's tired, she's not in any mood for it; she accepts it and makes like she enjoys it. For me. Happens she can come home, and she's ready for a bit of love. And I say love: just sex isn't any love, and isn't worth a damn, right? And suppose I've been up on some shitty job, and I'm not just tired, but I've got disgusted – a man can, as you probably know. I might have been up to here in whores and transvestites. But I've no right to push her off and say no, Josephine, I'm not in the mood. That's the rule: a woman has to have the same right as a man, or it's no marriage. But the rule there's got to be. All these people slopping over about their liberties just make me sick."

"I heard a woman the other day saying she'd never accept what she called the Violence of marriage. The poor cow."

"Yes: you know what I mean. Rambling though, aren't I? I don't know Casabianca. Not an uncommon type by the sound: all rounded and jolly and reasonable. He's a crook or not, I wouldn't know. But steer clear of him as much as you can. That's advice. You better not listen to it. Professional advice."

"It's good."

"I suppose it's possible," said Arthur, "and in fact one knows it to be possible, though the chance factor is always bigger than one would like, because it's been done. The economics are simple: put every penny you make back into the business. Fine, if you can do without eating for two or three years: it's bound to be that before one begins to haul ahead – but then, if at that moment you haven't the bank on your back . . ."

"You need luck," thought Arlette aloud, "and that's too elusive. Get bronchitis at just the wrong moment or drop a hammer on your toe, and months of labour go for naught. Can one, I mean is there any way of putting luck on your side?"

Arthur got up and went to the fireplace, or where there would have been a fireplace if this had been an English house. He did a lot of thinking in a characteristic attitude, standing with his back to an imaginary fire with his hands in his pockets. An Englishman smoking a pipe needs anyhow a fireplace to tap his pipe out on. He can't do it on his heel because of the carpet, and because of women making faces. An ashtray is altogether bad: the shape is all wrong, the sound unpleasant, and there is risk of breakage. Arthur needed further English chimneypiece accessories; a mantel to lean elbows on, a looking-glass whose frame one sticks memos in, ideally a leather-covered fender to sit on. Arlette had done her best, providing a sort of shallow dish, as though for the dog to eat out of and made to her specification by a puzzled Arab in Marrakesh, and recently a lovely block of sandstone, a remnant of the Citadel in Strasbourg and with a natural hollow on one side made perhaps by rainwater. It weighed about seven kilos and was ideal for tapping pipes on, as though designed by Vauban for that very purpose.

"I don't know," said Arthur, "but you can make a living, however small your talent is, if you've originality. If you do something mechanical like taking photographs or playing the piano, this is pretty difficult. If you've something with infinite variation like a singing voice, it's easier. You have to do something that's recognizably yours at a glance." Should he be in a Club? No: the furniture is too ugly, the conversation far too boring, and there are no women. But the exiled Englishman always does something preposterous, like wearing solar topees. One can see George Orwell, on that frightful hillside in the pouring rain, complaining of Catalans never cleaning their rifle and taking a shit wherever they happened to be standing, finding meticulous, ritual, original ways of performing these chores; unmistakably English from ten kilometres off. While shaving, Arthur could look at all those gold-lettered cards stuck round the edge of the glass, see whose wedding he'd been invited to that day. Whistling to himself 'Variations on a Theme of Haydn', by Johannes Brahms, followed by 'Don't Let's be Beastly to the Germans'.

There is something touching, but above all intensely English, about Noel Coward dying in Jamaica while reading an E. Nesbit book in bed.

Arlette, under perpetual exposure to eccentricity, behaved in ways sometimes coloured by English casts of thought. In Holland she had behaved in unbearably French fashion, complaining about such Dutch addictions as gin, cheap cigars and talking Dutch. In England she went on a good deal about the English addictions to sugar, silly accents and poison-green peas. In France, the unspeakableness of being French claimed her attention. In this way the jingo, the chauvin and the national were held at bay. And a Mediterranean hard-headed soumindedness was enlightened by strange outcrops of fantasy.

22. Bribery and corruption

The day held several things needing time and needing thought but one of them was Xavier, whom she found healed but apathetic, and whom she urged out for a cup of coffee. Nobody seemed to be watching them, following them, or taking any interest at all, and she wondered what was going on in Friend's mind.

"One gets ideas. They don't have to have any value in themselves. They might start one's mind working along a new path, that's all. We can say that you have a multitude of talents, some conspicuous and others perhaps undiscovered, maybe even unsuspected. The most obvious one is the big frustration. There's precious little that you don't know about commerce, and it's ridiculous wasting all this on some idiocy like door-to-door insurance policies. What I'm about to suggest may appear ridiculous too, but just think about it, and it does no harm to explore it. I know a man who is in some ways in much the same situation as you, but who left his position because he found it was wasting his existence. He is about to start something new: it's still in the planning stage. He's virtually single-handed. His wife's in this with him, but she too has to reforge her abilities into something totally new: she's a teacher.

"He's got lots of skills, he's technically inventive and good with his hands, and he's experienced in the ways of the world. But one thing he knows nothing about and it worries him; that's commercial practice, like elementary book-keeping, buy and sell margins, the whole area of how to survive in business. To him it's I buy something, I make it into something else, I sell it again, I make a living from that: he's never done this. He realizes that sounds a bit too simple. He has for instance a horror of borrowing, because that undermines his independence. I can sympathize with that, because I'd feel exactly the same, but at the same moment if I were in commerce I realize I'd make a success of it because I'm a bargainer at heart, whereas he isn't, and that's why he left his job at the age of oh, mid-thirties somewhere. Younger than you. Are you getting my drift?" Xavier's dull eye was beginning to get some life in it.

"Yes."

"Well, it's bound to be a fantastic gamble, and if I'm any judge he has a very good chance of running himself into the ground without an associate who understands business, and with one, I'd say a good chance of doing rather well. And either way, four or five very hard years, but perhaps singularly interesting. Would it be a good idea to go and talk to him?"

"Yes," said Xavier.

Now where, thought Arlette, did that idea come from?

"It's not at all badly thought," said Arthur. "You got it presumably from sheer instinct, but it's in *Little Dorrit*. Daniel Doyce the inventor, who's always getting screwed up by the Patents Office. Dickens doesn't take any pains with him, he remains quite a shadowy sort of minor character, but he's well characterized with a 'plastic engineer's thumb' that feels and understands the shapes and meanings of things. And he joins up with Arthur Clennam, who knows all about commerce, but is otherwise a totally useless drink of water. This might be clever of you. But will a pathetically rigid sort of bourgeois like Xavier, who is a fearful bore, be able to make any headway with a suspicious sort of peasant like Subleyras?"

"Worth trying, I thought," said Arlette.

A little before closing-time she went into the town: once people started to go home, she would find space for the car. At the backs of buildings are little privileged enclaves, where the transport of the Executive class, notoriously incapable of walking twenty-five metres, enjoys immunity from the harassments awaiting anyone with a heavy shopping-bag. There is no question of Corruption of municipal functionaries, but arrangements have been made. Arlette observed an expensive model of Mercedes, very nicely polished and packing lots of power, with regret that the evil eye alone was not strong enough to let all the air out of the tyres. She was only just in time: Monsieur Thibault liked to start for home before the rush-hour built towards universal frustration.

Once he was gone, senior employees started sneaking out, and the back door started getting fixed for the night in a clash of metal panels. Nobody would get in there without setting off a heap of electronic alarms. She went to the little alley towards the Place Broglie, where the salesgirls were leaving. In these dumpy housewives, scurrying out to bestride unlikely steeds – Peugeot mopeds for the most part – it is hard to recognize the haughty black-gowned virgins, who touch up their eyelashes at the perfume counter.

When one thought of it, typical that the woman she was looking for should be the last out. There must be somebody utterly reliable to see that the lights are all out, no taps left running in the ladies' lavatory, before the ritual of the Keys. When Arlette saw a fairly broad behind in a leather raincoat stooped over the floor-lock of the safety grille, she was reassured. Madame Henriette was the hinge on which the place turned, she who does the menial tasks; getting on a stepladder to change burned-out bulbs, scrubbing the carpet where some cow spilled a whole dainty flagon of nail-varnish, fixing the electric typewriter which refuses-to-go-this-morning: bringing the cheques to the bank.

Arlette's notion did not deserve any gaudy coral dawn, was indeed only a crude idea of retribution, grey-green and greasy like the Limpopo River, like Strasbourg in evening rush-hour, but . . . The lady straightened up, stretched with the key to the alarm, put the bunch carefully away in the inside compartment of her handbag. Arlette wondered how she was going to get at them there.

"Madame Henriette."

"Oo, you gave me a start. Oh, good evening madam, did you leave something in the shop?"

"Not exactly. I'd like to talk to you, though." The fat face was kind but puzzled. "Are you in a very great hurry?"

"Hurry . . . not really." It is the incompetent who are always in a very great hurry. "I've menfolk to provide for. But I'm often later than this." Puzzled, but something extra was plainly in the wind, and for taking trouble everyone else is always too *pressé*.

"I'm in a rather awkward situation and I'd like your advice."

"Something to do with the shop?"

"That's it – perhaps we could sit down somewhere," thinking

hard. Pubs would be crowded, teashops were shut – a hotel was the best bet.

"I usually wait for my bus here," irresolute.

"Oh no – I'll drive you home."

"Oh . . . that's kind. I don't bike any more; the traffic's that dangerous." A hotel dark and narrow, formerly sordid, now done up in blue velvet for guests of a perpetually thirsty sort: a languid waiter was hanging about.

"What would you like to drink?"

"Oo – could I have a whisky?" He came with Chivas of course: well, in a good cause.

"I'm going to be very direct," said Arlette. "Your boss – not, you know, the straightest of men."

"Oh yes – I know," with simplicity. "But he pays me my wages, you see."

"No, I'm not complaining about some kind of rip-off," floundering a bit.

"It's best I don't talk about it," with dignity.

"I agree, not something I could expect you to listen to. It's much more serious, I'm afraid."

"Then if I may say so – why come to me? You see, I try not to think about it."

"Me too. Life goes on anyhow. One tends to say, what can one do? But we should do something."

"I know," unhappily. "But one can't walk out. Very likely then I wouldn't have a job at all. And I need it, you see."

"My name is van der Valk. I run a kind of help agency."

"Have I seen your adverts in the paper?" guardedly.

"That's right. It isn't all women who come. Men are ashamed to, but they come too. Mostly though, women. So that I know something about the way women are pushed to the limit – and beyond it."

Henriette's pale eyes were full of that kind of knowledge. She looked at Arlette steadily, but said nothing.

"The woman came to me, whose son got shot. Out at the weekend cottage, breaking in. The thing is, that's not the way she brought him up." A mournful nod, to that. "She's a widow, she's poor, she goes out cleaning, she's never had anything but the rough end. Brought up in a public orphanage, lost her man in a work accident. The boy didn't deserve to lose his life. Totally in the wrong, of course. But he was gunned down."

"I know. It was hushed up, in the paper. It always is . . . But where I am . . . He didn't try to hide it. He said straight out, 'I dare say you've heard; all right, I'll tell you, that's right, and I'd do the same tomorrow, so no quack there in the women's room, you understand?' . . . The whole day I went cold down my back every time he spoke to me. But I've been with him a long time. I've had to shut my eyes tight, sometimes."

"Like about what?" Too hurriedly. The woman shook her head.

"Nothing one can do in a court. She's not looking for money. She wants to clear her name, and how can she? She feels bitter. So I went to see him, hoping at least he'd agree to meet her and say something, to help wipe it out. But he wouldn't budge – refused pointblank to discuss it."

"He always does. Says he's not getting in an argument. Men dig their heels in, when they've done something indefensible."

"I came to you because you know him well."

"To me he'll say things, less guarded, because he doesn't care what I think. What a fool some customer is, how some salesman tried to put it across him. He has contempt for people."

"This stiffened me into revolt. I can't just sit and say it has to be left to Providence."

"He was defending himself," Henriette pointed out, "or his property, which comes to the same thing. And he's tough: I mean to him it was nothing very terrible."

"Of course. And those gangs of boys are frightening. Run away, or let off a gun. I see the point too. But afterwards . . . Wouldn't one think, I've done something awful. There's an excuse to be found, but it's still awful. If you admit that a death is unimportant, then next stop Treblinka. Everyone that seems antisocial, exterminate them. You just saw him as callous and egoist, because you're used to him. But it was criminal, you know."

"I do see."

"And because property, in this vile country, is more thought of than humans, the judge let him go."

"But why come to me?" sadly; angrily.

"It's vengeful, which is all wrong, but I wanted to find out something disgraceful about him, to show him up. And I felt sure you'd know."

"Yes," in a very small voice. "But I couldn't. I owe him loyalty after all."

"When I saw you locking up, I had even a wild idea of pinching your keys."

"You mean you would . . . ? – but you couldn't do that!"

"I think I could, if I screwed myself up to it. I'm convinced there's something to be found, something compromising that he wouldn't want made public. But I couldn't, without getting you into trouble. Without the keys I can't; I wouldn't know how. So I thought of asking you, instead."

"I could never let you have the keys. Even if I pretended I'd lost them. Had my bag snatched or something. I'm trusted with them."

"Yes. I know. But you're not trusted with his little tricks. He doesn't hide them; you said yourself. Out of contempt."

Henriette stared bleakly across the overdecorated, horrid little lobby.

"I'm not going to do anything violent," said Arlette, finishing a dribble of Perrier water tasting faintly of whisky. "I must have something I can prove. I can use it then as leverage on him. I damn well don't have to be strictly law-abiding."

"He has illegal skins," suddenly looking at her.

"What way illegal? – duty not paid or something?"

"Protected species," unhappily.

"You mean panthers?" Arthur Davidson's wishful thinking!

"I don't know about that – though there have been panthers. But alligators, and a sort of long-haired monkey. And sea-otter."

"Sea-otter! Look, we must get hold of one. Or better, a paper, an invoice or something – linking him to it."

"I couldn't do that," horrified.

"Perhaps just the accusation," thinking out loud. "Force him anyhow to get rid of them, to cover up. One small thing he wouldn't make a profit on. It wouldn't point to you. Several other people must know. They must be shipped in – disguised as something else."

"I know who brings them," said Henriette suddenly.

Arlette realized that she must not be too greedy all at once. There was some way. Arthur would know how one could make publicity. And fraud – getting legal proof of fraud. A thing Xavier would know about. And, surely, her friend Sergeant Subleyras . . . one hadn't been on a crime squad for nothing, surely.

"I'll settle up with you, waiter," she said abruptly. While other settlements were pending.

23. Friendly supermarket

The note said 'Don't act scared: just make like normal'. The words were cut out of the local paper, pinned to a narrow strip by an edge of scotch tape. The strip had been folded small to the size of a price ticket, and lay on a tin of tomatoes. It wasn't a price ticket, and this caught Arlette's eye. The tomatoes sat in a supermarket trolley, which she was pushing. The note had been planted in a moment of that special supermarket trance: your habitual brand of paddywhack has vanished and been replaced by another, totally unknown to you and thirty per cent dearer.

French supermarkets divide into those with canned air and those without. On the whole, she preferred the latter. The smell, predominantly synthetic vanilla and cardboard, does have notes of rotted vegetables and cheese as well as wet dog. This is better than no smell: food after all ought to smell of something, reasoned Arlette. On the other hand, the air-conditioned ones have big wide corridors for you and your bier. In the small ones you can die of asphyxia, or buried under a landslide of special-offer, or stabbed by a Bulgarian sword-stick, and you will still get carried along by the inexorable flow towards the checkout, without anybody noticing. It is a splendid setting for one of those antique locked-room mysteries, with the body under the avalanche of empty cartons in the corner: could stay there a week unnoticed. Won't be the smell that draws attention finally, neither. Nero Wolfe would reckon you deserved all you got: these places don't just sell petfood; they sell nothing else.

Backed into a bay surrounded by towering crates of beer, Arlette read the note and threw it away. Necessary gesture of insolence, even if it were a clue for Mr Casabianca. She was frightened, though more of claustrophobia than anything else.

It was a test of her nerve and resolution. Very well, she'd stay perfectly quiet and go along with it.

Sure enough, while she was pointing at cheese, and saying to the girl 'No not that one, That One', another note arrived. This said 'Don't scream, don't panic. Go down to the parking lot and unlock the car door.' This one was handwritten, but by someone who knew that no expert can make much of printing with a ballpoint pen. Her mouth was dry; she took a packet of chewing-gum from the stack by the pay-off. She did have a moment of wanting to grab the cashgirl's bell and ring it frenziedly, but what good would that do? Somebody might leap the barrier and bolt off, but who'd be interested? Not carrying a crate of whisky, was he?

All underground parking lots are grisly. Deep Throat is there behind the pillar, not to speak of tyre-slashers, penis-flashers, and people who will hit you across the face with wrenched-off metal radio-antennas. You can imagine pretty nearly anything, particularly when chewing gum, supposed to promote a flow of saliva, doesn't. A curt graffito on the wall told her the Minister of the Interior Equalled Hitler, which was no news. Nor help. A notice saying Do not Leave your Trolley Here, completed by Climb in it and Go to Sleep, was no better. She packed things into the boot of the Lancia, her neck hair doing horrible primitive defence-reactions. She could see no one, though a perpetual slamming of tinny doors told her people were everywhere. She unlocked the driver's door, got in, rolled the window down, took several deep breaths, spat out the chewing-gum which hadn't helped and tasted disgusting, rolled the window up again, settled herself, flexed her toes, clipped the safety belt, discovered that getting to her gun under her car-coat was difficult enough without, unclipped it again, put the lights on and eased the motor gently into gear. At the last moment she leaned across and unlocked the catch on the off door.

The lights, sweeping across naked concrete and Way Out, showed her nothing. There was nobody, but people occupied stowing cardboard cartons in cars, taking no notice of her. It was just a gag, to shake her nerves.

Just before Out, a sharp right-angle turn slows you before you accelerate up the ramp into something resembling air. As she flicked her lights out somebody opened the door and got in, so neatly she would have admired it. There was nothing to see: one needs one's eyes for the narrow ramp. On the street, when she could swivel a glance sideways there was a gun loosely pointing in her direction on a knee: a soft hoarse voice she recognized said, "Just drive quietly where I tell you."

This scene from a thousand movies steadied her, obscurely comforted her: she felt she was on familiar ground after all. She found her voice.

"I didn't need to unlock the door. I've been wanting to talk to you. You needn't point the thing at me."

"Just keep your eyes on the road." A hand went up and twisted the inside mirror, so that he could see around. They turned a while following his directions, came out on the long quiet stretch of the Quai des Belges. It prolongs into a tree-lined, pleasant section called the Quai du Genéral Picquart, with the canal on one side and comfortable, quiet houses with gardens across the street.

"Pull in under the trees and park." She did so, docile. "Cut the motor and give me the keys. No, don't look at me. Right, now I think you've got a gun. Bring it out slow and let's have it. All right. Nobody following you, no cops. Good. Now if you want to yell or something I'll tip you in the canal. You going to play ball?"

"I have to know what you want."

"We drive a bit further, we can talk. Just in case they got a direction-finder on your car, we change cars. Hop." While he was locking her car she got a look at him, which told her very little. A drab raincoat and a little hat. Dark glasses on a face with no colour and little feature. Anyone, Monsieur Toutlemonde between thirty and forty, drab, tidy, and utterly inconspicuous. He pointed with his chin to where another car stood a few metres along, pointing the way they had come, a medium-size Renault as drab as himself, dark red, neither clean nor dirty. He handed her a key on a tab. "You drive." They went back, over the Pont d'Anvers, turned right at the coal harbour, along towards Neudorf, back over the canal bridge, left at the Rue du Havre, and along the industrial terrain of the Rue de la Rochelle, until at last they turned off to the bank of the Rhine at the ship-lock, where at length he seemed satisfied that they were neither followed nor overheard.

She felt for a cigarette: he took the bag from her, looked in it before giving it back to her.

"Oh, for God's sake," she said impatiently, "stop being dramatic. All this act since the supermarket – come to that, for a week, now. Just tell me what it's all about."

"Been talking to your cop friends?"

"I don't have any cop friends."

"Look, try to cross me up, quickest way to getting acid in your face."

"Oh, this is useless. What can I do to persuade you that I had nothing to do with Henri le Hollandais? I didn't even know who he was. I was with Berger, went along for the ride. I had nothing better to do. He told me nothing. His name. That he was a gangster. So what? It wasn't and isn't any business of mine. You're another, but I don't know you, you do nothing to make me want to know you. Pestering me just makes you conspicuous. It's stupid."

"You're a grass for them. And bait."

"Oh, Bonne Mère. I have to be able to convince you that I don't meddle with police business. You're police business. I don't want to know anything about you."

"What are you getting at?" The voice told her nothing either. Traces of a local accent, but acquired rather than inborn. Just ordinary.

"I'm trying to tell you I work on sufferance. If I didn't, I'd be out of a job: I have to obey the rule."

"So you do what they tell you."

"It doesn't have to include being catspaw for them. What can I do but tell you? I couldn't make you out; you're part of something I don't know. It's some PJ business – I could see that. I went to Casabianca to protect myself. He'd like to mousetrap you; that's his affair: concerns me no further."

"You used to be married, they tell me, to a Dutch cop. You better persuade me but good that you didn't sell the Hollandais out."

"That was ten years ago: it's a piece of my life that's gone. Can't you see, you fool, that you're butting your own nose in trouble? Pester me, and follow me like this, I can't help but lead them to you. Attack me and they'll know who did it. I ask only that you leave me alone. If the car is booby-trapped I know nothing about it. I could have a bug on me right now and not know it," inventing recklessly from television films. "If you could drop a note in my trolley back there, couldn't they put something in my pocket?"

"It wouldn't carry any distance."

"Oh, was that why you dragged me all the way out here? Well, if I'm not back before lunch my husband will be making a hullabaloo, and the first thing he'll call will be cops, and not city cops. Casabianca."

"Prove it. Go on, prove it. Lead a cop anywhere near me, and there'll never be a day you pass without fearing for your skin and your eyesight. I got friends, too."

"You poor ass, it's your own suspicion dragging you down. You're in a dilemma. You can only get out of it by trusting me."

He looked carefully all around. There was a small boy

throwing stones in the water. There was an elderly man, watching rapt a big Swiss motor barge being processed in the ship lock. There were two men in overalls and a bashed-up Renault Four utility which had Service des Voiries written on it. They were sitting smoking. They looked extremely like plainclothes cops, which probably meant they were the Service des Voiries having a smoke and doing nothing: hell, the municipality of a town the size of Strasbourg has a thousand employees at any moment of the day, doing just that.

"I could blast you with your own gun and tip you in the Rhine."

"You could, I suppose, if it were anywhere near worth it, or if I had deserved it. If I have to make the choice, I dare say I'd rather be shot than drowned, like the Hollandais."

There was a silence, during which he took his eyes off the roving activity of the scene outside and focused them on her, even swivelling his body to face her, holding the look so long that for the first time she began to feel real fear. She had felt frightened, yes, but it had been a surface fear. She had been touched by the world of violence, pulled by the coat, as it were, into the toothed gears of the criminal world, where violence exists for violence's sake and no rational argument can protect one. But this had happened before and she had felt strangely unmarked by it.

In her own car, only a twelvemonth ago, she had been kidnapped, held down by force, tied up and gagged – most unpleasantly, with sticking-plaster – threatened, and finally shown a violence that, it had been calculated, was quite enough of a trauma to crush a human being, and a woman at that: the palm of her hand had been cut cruelly and deeply with a razor. She had been left like that, in the middle of the night in the empty car, on a deserted pathway beyond the outskirts of the town. And somehow she had not been nearly as frightened as she should have been.

Arthur had been surprised. He had offered to get rid of the car for her, though it was nearly new, thinking that an experience this traumatic would make it impossible for her to use it.

She had been most indignant. What, my car? It was a wedding present. Never!

To Arlette there was an explanation, and a simple one. 'I came out of a sheltered home,' she told Arthur, 'but much more important I grew up surrounded by love. It was nothing much. My father was a vague, lazy, self-indulgent person, with something of an addiction to burgundy. My mother was a silly woman on the whole: when I was young I thought she had the brains of a hen. But they were always there.' It had been difficult for Arthur to understand. She could very well remember the shock and extreme horror of betrayal, by people she had thought trustworthy, people who should have been trustworthy. Schoolteacher, nun, official. But the refuge of her home had not betrayed her: she had never been deprived of it.

She became so conscious of this, so aware of her immense and unlikely fortune, that trust became the hinge on which her whole life turned; when she married, and it was her turn to carry the responsibility of never betraying the trust reposed in her, she carried it very far, to lengths people found unreasonable. She had resolved from the moment she found herself pregnant that never would a child that comes in saying 'Where's Mama?' be disappointed. The child, she said, that has this total security of never having been betrayed, will grow up able to face anything. It is an impossible ideal, said Arthur. Maybe, she returned: it is a necessity.

She gazed stonily out in front of her through the dirty windscreen, surrounded by the stink of car. These men, whose whole life is one long agony of the fear of betrayal, these men who are the criminals, they are the endproduct of a world in which nobody keeps his word. Starting with our beloved President, whose every utterance is a lie.

"The Hollandais," said her Friend slowly, "was not drowned. He was shot, and thrown in the water." Now it was her turn to face him, mouth stupidly open. "You didn't know that?"

"No."

"Believing kind of a simpleton, aren't you?"

"Yes. I am. That's the only way I can work. Believing what people tell me."

"Won't do you much good."

"No, it gets me into a lot of trouble. But it does me this much good. Sometimes people start believing me."

He drove her back to the Quai des Belges; dropped her outside the Foreign Legion barrack. It was a couple of hundred metres short of where her car was parked. As the Renault gathered speed he tossed her her keys. Even if she had wanted to, it would have been useless taking the number: the plates would be fake, anyhow.

Friend . . . Well, perhaps. She didn't know what his definition of friendship was. Perhaps Henri le Hollandais had been a Friend, and a friend too, maybe. The friendship in the milieu, the underworld, between people who have done time together; there's a lot of folklore about this. Maybe it exists, thought Arlette. It could be something to be envied by a lot of people who have never done time, and never will, but to whom friendship is something your neighbourhood supermarket feels for you.

24. Abidance by law

She got home late and flustered; dinner was a patched-up performance. Arthur did not ask where she had been, nor what she-thought-she-had-been-doing. If he did, when a meal was both late and uneatable, as sometimes happened, it was a rhetorical expression. It did not mean Where Have You Been? It meant Hasn't your intelligence and experience yet made you aware that giving your man a vile meal rebounds in his making himself as disagreeable as may be for it may be several hours? . . .

Arthur had learned about the trust. A man who had suffered much betrayal throughout his life, and whose difficulties sprang, quite often, from an irrational belief in the virtues of intelligence. Arlette snorted with bottomless contempt for all this so-called intelligence. 'Homo sapiens,' she had said cuttingly, before they were married, 'who invented this imbecile expression? Knowledge . . . if sapientia had ever led to any wisdom, mankind wouldn't be in the hole it is today.' 'Dog who hasn't the brains of a peahen,' she had concluded more recently, 'knows a lot more about how to live than man does. Good old boy, yes I do love you, oh get your horrible claws off my stockings, you vile beast.'

Apart from more vulgar attractions, Arthur knew very well, he had seen quite mindlessly that this was a trustworthy woman.

There was a payment to be made. From odd scraps of conversation, reminiscence and examples of a wry, sour humour, he had noticed that life with Piet van der Valk had not always been domestic bliss on either side. On his side, the good Inspector had had a naughty feebleness for young girls who were not as innocent as they made out: and Arlette had a very shrewd, French hard-headed judgment of people. And especially young girls. On her side, she had a sexual jealousy that could quite simply and literally be murderous. Old Piet had been kept in line now and then by a healthy respect for his own skin. A consideration kept in the forefront of cops' minds. Especially those on homicide squads. A whore, as the Book of Proverbs says succinctly, is a deep ditch; And a strange woman is a narrow pit. She also lieth in wait as for a prey, And increaseth the transgressors among men.

Arlette had a special way of saying 'Getting sentimental about young girls'. Arthur, battered and sometimes pathetic English sociologist in middle age, and often sadly muddle-headed with it, was a wary soul.

When Arthur went out after supper, saying vaguely 'I don't suppose I'll be very late', she did not suppose he had an appointment somewhere to go and commit adultery. Simply, one is in the mood occasionally for solitude. If there were a lecture or a learned conference, as sometimes happened, though he was just as likely to say he had far too much work, and then sit enrapt watching John Wayne, he would probably have said so. But it wasn't a thing to which she proposed to give thought. She had lots to give thought to; on the whole too much. So better on the whole to enjoy this lovely solitude, which was rare enough to be a treat. Instead of thinking one could Do-something-to-one's-face, adopt a horizontal attitude, and listen perhaps to Teresa Berganza singing Carmen? Which would be Enjoyment: there was all too little of that.

It must have been about a quarter to nine when enjoyment was abruptly bruised by a sharp ring at the doorbell. She decided to pay no attention but the ring was repeated and it was no good anyhow: the shrill note clashed jarringly with Don José. She pressed the button that lifted the needle, the button releasing the front door; peeked through the judas in the landing door: wasn't letting just anyone in this time of night.

A boy stood on the landing. Rather wet; must be raining out. Otherwise unremarkable: the wet made lank dark hair darker and lanker and a black leather jerkin made a sallow face sallower, oblique dark eyes, a bit Slav, like ripe olives. A boy's jaw needing a shave. The face twitched nervously while waiting for an answer; a hand came up and wiped wet off the nose. She didn't know the face, but there was something familiar about it. She opened the door. Under the arm of the leather jerkin was a roughly wrapped parcel. A messenger boy of some sort. Parcel about the shape and size of gramophone records. If it were a present, it was welcome. The boy's trousers were sopping : been on a bike.

"Uh – you're Missis van der Valk? Well – uh, I've got a present for you."

"That's nice." Not heavy, too limp to be records. "You got rather wet, I'm afraid. Wait just a sec.," with an idea of giving him a tip. He cleared his throat.

"I'm uh, Pascal Bartholdi." Ah, the familiar look was a look of Mum.

"I wondered why I thought I might know you," smiling. Nicely mannered, quiet boy, but why was he so nervous, sniffling and twitching there? "But what's the present?" smiling, wanting to put him at his ease. She fumbled in her purse, "Here, you must have a drink on me."

"I don't want a drink. I wanted you to have this. African thing. I seen them on television." Seeing her perplexity, he made an effort. "Big spotted cat." Stabbing with his finger, searching furiously for the word. "It's not allowed, it's not allowed." She was unwrapping the brown paper. It was doubled over in a plastic sleeve. It was an unmistakable ocelot.

"Oh my God." Saul on the Damascus road got knocked arse over tip into the ditch and got up with an appalling ache in the back of his neck. Fearful smell of scorching hair: hers prickled horridly. Now in classical times the word 'horrid' – Arthur's voice being didactic – means bristling: wild boars and such when met unexpectedly. Quite so: ocelots. They galloped very suddenly at startled fawns, extremely horrid.

"Come in, Pascal. You can't stay like that. And we're both going to have a drink," in a dozy haze, switching on the little fan heater. "Where – where did you get this?"

"I knocked it off," shrugging. Classical thundering Jove tossing grenades at her like a goddam pétanque-player. She knew the whole story already. She had to verify, each detail was a new shellburst. Exploding boules, great fun. Classical Jove, very hot player. Standing there with one in his hand, weighing up the situation. Je tire ou je pointe? Shoot, or lay one up?

"Where?"

"In the bastard's shop, where else? I thought of busting the place up. Found this and thought that smarter." Pointe: it curved lazily up, plonked dully, rolled just a scrap, to within an inch of the jack.

"When?"

"Just now, of course." Tire: towering up high, vertically down with a thunderous crack upon her skull, sending it scooting off – out of play, but definitely. "Was going to bring it home. Thought then, you'd know better than us, how to bring it home to the bastard."

"Pascal, drink this. Sit down there; the thing will warm you, it blows hot air, you mustn't catch a chill. You awful ass, the police will suspect you first thing."

"Don't see why. I was real careful. Wasn't difficult, just took a bit of nerve, like. A mate of mine was in there a few days back delivering stuff, told me where I could hole up for half an hour."

"Tell me carefully. Tell me every single little detail, every phase of it."

If there was any tiny remote chance, she had to get a safety net under this boy, who would otherwise plummet straight down into the bubbling quaking asphalt lake, red-hot: see Dante, Trinidad geography of, etcetera. And a safety net under herself? Wasn't she plummeting down there with him? What would Henriette think – say! – when she heard of this? That nice kind Madame van der Valk had chatted her up nicely . . .

"What time was it you got in? How did you get in?" And how did he get out?

" 'Bout half-past five. Frigged about a bit in that basement, till none of those women were looking, nipped through into the junkroom at the back. Nobody there. Found a good hidey-hole behind the dustbins, lots of old boxes and paper trash, curled up under there, stank a bit, but no problem. Nothing to do but keep quiet half an hour, ol' biddy locked up, 'n' had the place to myself. Dead easy."

"Weren't you supposed to be at work?"

"Was a bit slackish, so I said around five I got a bit of a bellyache, can I get off earlyish, boss was easy about it."

"Oh dear, you see they'll certainly check everything you did with your time. You must go straight, and try to fabricate – do you know what I mean?"

"Sure, I can fix that with mates of mine."

"And all evening – and when you go to bed, try and – don't be obtrusive about it, but put the cat out or something, to be seen so that neighbours can say they saw you. Have an absolutely simple story and stick to it no matter what, nothing complicated, but tell it over and over again and never vary anything. I only hope I can – what about the alarms?"

"What about them? No trouble once you're inside. Lot of electronic muck that's tricky, but there's bound to be a cable for power. I found the switchboard, broke open the junction box, it's only wire and a lead seal, follow the cable, pull the plug on the sod, whole thing's dead from there on." She had been watching Henriette turn the keys, and the boy had been inside.

And the boy had walked out at the back, somewhere between eight and eight-thirty, bland as custard. The rolling metal door, like that of a garage, was no difficulty from inside once the alarm was switched off. A hasp coming down to a staple driven into the concrete floor, secured by a simple padlock which he'd broken with the crowbar kept in the stockroom for opening crates with.

It all looked like a quick and nasty termination to Arlette van der Valk's career as helper and adviser. Even if she managed to keep the boy out of it, and that, she swore, would be her dying contribution to poor Solange Bartholdi – breaking, entering and burglary in the night hours would fetch seven years and she wouldn't be surprised, even with Paul Friedmann defending – she herself was a gone goose, hanging by a thread. And that thread was Henriette.

Arthur was drenched too. He had his panoply, a Burberry coat supposed to be rainproof, an American hat, a stick. He had been for a good long walk all by himself in the rain. A nice time he'd have, proving an alibi.

Eight-thirty, not a bad time for a burglary. If anyone did see you leaving it wasn't late, they'd think you popped back because you'd forgotten your glasses, or to turn the thermostat down. But nobody would. They'd all be eating, or watching the television news – both together, in France. There are people on the streets, but thinking of the pub, the football game, the evening cinema; somewhere they're in a hurry to get to and not staring round them. As for the police, it eats too; peacefully digesting a heavy, probably unhealthy meal. Crime? Come back in an hour; what d'you think this is then – the firebrigade? With much picking of teeth and noisy sucking: sell anything nowadays and call it ham, they do.

As for Commissaire Casabianca, he was not watching this

house. The PJ had better things to do. The boy had come on a bike. There'd been no one in the hall.

The ocelot skin lay on the table. She shivered looking at it. Arthur looked at it, did not shiver, paced about like the panther, in a cold English fury.

"Bit too much elegant negligence. No business of mine what you do upon lawful occasions. I mean lawful, nothing to do with too many pink gins in the wardroom or dropping the sextant overboard. You can be as eccentric as you please, join the Rosicrucians or the Freemasons, join the Foreign Legion for all it bothers me. But abidance by the goddam law . . . You poor imbecile: the town swarms with cops and boy are they sensitive to any breath of scandal. They want the European Parliament in this town, and they hold their breath for fear of anyone acting the idiot. Cop slapped that Danish deputy who was being noisy in a nightclub, and his ass got posted to Tahiti so fast it charred. Austrian Foreign Minister got mugged by those two funnies who claimed he tried a homosexual pick-up – delayed and stifled out of sight. Dutch Minister got pissed and heaved massive ashtray through hotel's enormous window – oh sorry, just a bit of innocent horseplay. People are just waiting for a real scandal, like Giscard pocketing diamonds from that nigger gangster. And this is the moment you choose to knock over a black-market fur dealer."

25. Hocus-pocus

"Tomorrow morning," Arthur had recovered his patient voice, "this man finds his shop broken open and a secret cupboard rifled. That would only rate three lines in the local paper. But he's going to make an infernal fuss. You thought that because he had a burglary before and shot a boy, he'd be ashamed and intimidated? Now he's hit where it really hurts; he'll lash out with all he's got – money, and influence, plenty of both. There'll be a full-scale police enquiry. They won't just say 'oh dear' and forget about it, like poor old Xavier getting bashed. They'll work on it.

"When they do, your Madame Chose is the first person they come to. You went the rounds as usual before locking up? You then locked up – demonstrate your routine. And while going through the routine you were accosted, and your attention distracted by a woman with a tale of wanting your sympathy: ain't that interesting. Hypothesis, you bent this woman to take her eyes off her keys for a sec., long enough for your accomplice to slip in. The judge of instruction will like this hypothesis."

"Preposterous," said Arlette, white but firm. "How would I do such a silly thing that would point so obviously to myself as well as to her?"

"They'll worry about that? All they want is a motivation and a plausible story that can't be disproved, and they've got both."

"Then I go to jail," said Arlette defiantly. "I won't let that boy be hammered. If he got ideas of that sort, it was my fault through loose talk to his mother. I got the silly ideas. I was ready to do something quite criminally irresponsible, and it was that woman Henriette, who with simple commonsense fidelity showed me how foolish I was. So I pay the price."

"And I," said Arthur soberly, "too. You think there's any job for me here after this? Or anywhere else, in a university? I can go and catch butterflies in Paraguay, beside good Doctor Mengele."

"I did it, and I won't back down, and I'll make it absolutely clear that I was alone, and that Doctor Davidson had no knowledge whatsoever, either before or afterwards, of what was in my mind."

"My poor silly girl. Is that all that being married means to me – to protect myself?"

"Then what are we to do?"

"We must get help from somewhere to cover this. If that

can't be managed – well . . . we can get both our bags packed for Argentina, my poppet."

"I can eat crow," slowly, "to Corinne Klein. Trust to God and Casabianca. I'd have to turn the Friend over, and I'd made my mind up not to. In fact promised him not to. And if I do . . . either way I'm finished in this job . . . But rather than have you penalized . . . I don't deserve anyhow to continue in work of this sort. I haven't maintained my own principles."

"Casabianca," flatly, "will not cover up for you. He has enough on his plate, what with that drugs plant that didn't come off, and the Turks that were beaten up by some of his slightly over-zealous subordinates. The Friend isn't important enough to him. The police isn't about to do anything, but protect its own sweet self. But I'm not sure that I haven't a better idea . . . Sergeant Subleyras."

"Oh no," hopelessly.

"Kindly shut up," said Arthur. "You've caused damage enough for one night." Arlette, subdued, went to the lavatory. When she got back, she heard Arthur's voice, saying, "Not something to talk about on the phone . . . All right."

"What did he say?" hoping against hopelessness.

"That he'd be right over," short in every sense.

"Like a doctor. Come quick, I've an awful pain. Very well, I'll be right over. But is it a genuine or a false angina?"

"Exactly like a doctor," flat, without humour.

Time passed, nearly a quarter of an hour of it.

She could hear explanations in the hall. The two men had not met before; would they get on together? Subleyras placid as usual; Subleyras appearing, in the worndown clothes he kept for at-home.

"I considered shaving, but decided you were in a hurry."

"A drink," said Arthur, "and a brief outline of a most unpromising set of circumstances."

"Both. But while you'll tell it much better, Madame will tell it much more revealingly." Doctor is Here.

Humiliating or not a nice surprise: at the end of the brief outline Subleyras laughed. Not the loud English guffaw (in Arthur so disconcerting), nor the coarse Dutch humour (Piet van der Valk's first reaction to most unexpected happenings – to give him time to think). Simply, a big spontaneous laugh.

"As Robin Hood you're a fuckup." But nicely; so kindly that she was instantly overcome with tears. "No, don't cry. You've done in fact quite well. But a Robin has to be a technician. Now you were watching while both the back and front doors were shut. Describe this process. As slowly and as accurately as you can recall. Every detail."

"*Bon*," when she had finished. "Technically speaking, this is feasible." The ridiculous sense of relief. The surgeon has looked at the X-rays. The thing isn't inoperable. "As for your notions of subverting the Lady of the Keys . . . let me explain myself. I think your dotty notion there might to some extent be my fault. If I hadn't come worrying you about my excess of scruple, like the man who resigned from the C.I.A., I think this idea might not have entered your head."

There was a small hard grain of truth in this.

"And you know, Madame – "

"Arlette."

"All right, you know my name is Charley, it's in your little book. You did me a good turn. You showed me that it isn't what one does, but what one is. Twelve years I've thought I was a cop; I've found I was mistaken. Not too old, I hope, to do something else. I am still, while the habit lasts, a good police technician. I know most of what there is to know about security locks. More vital is the time factor. Boiling it down, we need to convey the notion first that this job was done a different way, second that it was done a great deal later; say in the middle of the night. You see? – that's the only way we can get you all off the hook – your Madame Henriette, yourself, and this boy of yours: smart boy that, I'd like to meet him.

"It'll take a while still," looking at his watch, "speaking as a person who knows as well the little mechanisms of police patrols. If we then make a thoroughly convincing affair of breaking the front door – then there's never been any question of keys, or of an inside job, and no suspicion can possibly fall upon this woman. She will realize though that you or your friends are behind this break. Will she give you away? I think that because you trusted her, and you respected her honour about the job she was trusted with, she'll pay you back. I think she won't say a word. But you're in her hands. And I'm in yours. If they bring this home to you – and you give me away . . . an ex-cop breaking parole: wouldn't Mother be pleased!"

"My whole life," said Arlette, "is built on trust."

"Kid," said Subleyras, "you're white as a sheet. You'll do. I'd like to take you with me, but it's necessary, just in case the point arises, that you stay in this house, and that you be able to prove it. With if need be, a respectable witness."

"That's what I told the Bartholdi boy," answered Arlette, with an effort at a grin.

"Good, then I've got to go home and pick up a couple of tools."

"I'd better tell you – it's just possible there's somebody watching this house – nothing to do with this," hastily. A garbled stammer about the Friend, to which Subleyras listened with a faint fixed smile.

"You do complicate existence," he said patiently. "Might sound priggish – I'd say you acted sensibly and rightly. If I were you, I wouldn't worry. If there's anyone hanging round I'd smell them – I looked when I came. Casabianca's got no immediate interest; as well for you!" She felt herself blushing stupidly. "What you can do while I'm away is rout ol' Xavier out – he'll be a useful addition."

"You met him then?" stupidly.

"I did indeed," grinning.

The 'tools' made a striking contrast. One was simply a massive cold chisel with an unusually long shaft. "More leverage that way," said Subleyras, becoming less sergeant-like by the second. The other was a flimsy plastic pistolgrip, battery-powered, like those sold to housewives for liquidizing soup or whipping egg whites.

"Like one of those indecent vibrators?"

"You mean a clit-tickler," suggested Arthur.

"Really!"

"Hallo Xavier," said Subleyras tactfully.

"What can it be for?"

"Skeleton keys," with patience, "went out with Inspector Lestrade and this is a picklock, as supplied to the C.I.A. You clip in a little thingy according to the type of lock and you wiggle it. Rather like drilling teeth and about as fascinating."

"Why does it vibrate?"

"Woman's question," said Arthur. "Because locks are complicated inside, dear child."

"You can't even open a condensed milk can, so you can stop being male and technical," crushingly.

"Can I drive the Getaway Car?" asked Xavier, enjoying it.

"If you don't mind ten minutes' walk first. You're going to be lookout, and you Arthur are the other, up the other end. There'll be about five minutes of totally undramatic fiddle about two hours from now, while the night shift cops are enjoying their coffee break."

"Here's some grub," said Arlette, "and what am I, apart from cook, and Imbecile of the Year?"

"You stop pitying yourself and imagining things – and you meditate upon your sins. Because if we were pinched on this job . . . don't worry, we won't be."

"But I realize."

"I think you do, and that you won't pull a gag like this in a hurry again – stop it now, girl. If you didn't trust me, and I you, what would be the point of either of us existing?"

"Yes – that more or less is what I was trying to make Friend understand. What people like Casabianca never will understand. Not being able to trust people is what made the Minister kill himself."

"If we've two hours to kill," remarked Arthur lighting his pipe, "conversation will get more and more like that on the departure platform of the Gare de Lyon. We must give ourselves something to concentrate upon. Extremely banal though the suggestion is, mine is that we play cards."

Subleyras played cards the way one does when in the habit of night shifts. Arthur slowly, with a professional concentration of memory and observation, and the English love of a dotty gamble at rather long odds. Xavier – which nobody had expected – brilliantly; uncanny at guessing what card was in which hand.

"Janey," said Subleyras, disconcerted, "you ought to be in Las Vegas."

Arlette, who hated cards, relapsed into a female role of supplying drinks. She had to ransack her cupboards – there wasn't any whisky left.

26. ¡Que se las arregle!

While the men were all away – Leathergating – Arlette was at last losing herself in an extremely intricate and beautiful piece by Bartók. She had established a bit of an alibi by taking Truedog on his DST act (Surveillance of the Territory) of the Observatory railings. She had to hang around a long time before meeting anyone on the same errand, because of being Belated, but met at last the gentleman in the Rue de l'Université, with the nice labrador whose manners put Dog (first growling then cringing against her leg) to such shame. She was getting hooked on Bartók when the telephone rang. It is supposed to be a harmless thing, the telephone.

The wrench was dreadful. She put both hands to her stomach and pressed hard with her fingertips. Then she had to get up to stop the pick-up, with time to get frightened again. The phone in the silence was like a pneumatic drill.

"Yes."

"Oh. I've been trying to get hold of you all day." Rubbish: in a thin, complaining voice. Voice of that deadly cow, Estelle Laboisserie. Of all people . . . True, she had left her office phone on record, hadn't lifted the tape, and heaven knew what was on it. But she loathed anybody who rang out of office time. Doctors have to answer phones, and successful criminal lawyers, and Ministers. But those are all awful people. She also hated people who interrupted music. And most she detested Estelle Laboisserie – skinny bitch – and Ghislaine – fat spotty bitch – and Thing who rang-up-from-Australia (also in the middle of the night): oh, the entire tribe. Alas, she had a promise to keep.

Said "Hold the line," breathed deeply through her nose, said, "Yes madame."

"All day," repeated the whiney voice, that of a spoilt child.

"I've been working all day. In fact I'm still working now. So what was it all about?"

"But – as we agreed: the travel agency has everything fixed for you. Plane, hotel reservation, the tickets have to be picked up, the bookings have to be confirmed, we've gone to a great deal of trouble and very considerable expense and – "

"Look, try and understand that it's on this account that I still find myself at work past midnight." A white lie, and a counterthrust too good to miss.

"Well I didn't know that . . ."

"Listen, I'm waiting at this moment for an item of news which will clear up an affair and greatly relieve my mind." True; true. "And I'll ring you as early as may be in the morning to confirm. I hope I shan't need to put the booking back."

"Oh . . . well then . . . as long as I know. As long as it's settled, you see, we're, we've been so anxious, getting worse day by day and we – "

"I've said it already and can only repeat: I can't give any guarantees. I'll do my honest best by whatever means I can discover or invent – you'll have to be content with that. Sorry if I appear edgy, but I'm very tired."

"If it's a question of money – "

"I have to be perfectly honest: I realize it's a lot of money and you're probably throwing it away. If you wish to withdraw, I shall understand. I'll make no claim on you for such time as I have given."

"No, no – that's not our attitude at all. Uh – er – hold the line." Bangs and splutters, sounds of expostulation, and the voice of the girl Ghislaine.

"Please, Mrs Davidson, please, please do go. I know my brother's in awful trouble and we're all quite sure you can help. Please don't say no."

"My dear girl, I'm not saying no. I'll go, and tomorrow if possible."

"Oh good, good, thank you – here's my mother back."

"So you'll ring me first thing? That's agreed?"

"Promised."

"Fine."

She'd gone and dished herself up now! Found herself shaking a little, as much with rage as anything. People . . . Wanted a drink and there wasn't any whisky. Frigged about among bottles, found some Spanish brandy, by Arthur called Good Old Oval-Osborne.

How did they 'know' the boy was in 'awful trouble'? It sounded as though the Consulate in Buenos Aires was not letting its right hand know what its left hand was getting up to; characteristic governmental hypocrisy and effrontery, officially termed Diplomacy.

Oh, que se las arreglan! Sort it out for yourselves! And put another exclamation-mark in front of that, a Spanish one upsidedown!

But you've given your promise and can't go back on it. You can't break things off.

Like Bartók: if interrupted it can't go back and begin again. You are whole, and you keep your word, or you're nothing: you'd be exactly the same as the men you despise, who break their word, are ashamed to say so, send their wives to make excuses for them.

She poured herself some more Osborne: whatever shape this was, it wasn't square, but watch it, girl, you're getting sloshed. She put Bartók back on the shelf, hunted for other kinds of Percussion and Celeste; came up with the Benny Goodman Quartet, a death-defying act off the high edge of the clarinet's register, exactly what was needed. Gene Krupa is far too noisy and emotional – compared to, oh, say Ray Bauduc, he was a lousy drummer. But by the time they reach 'Avalon' nothing matters any more, and we all go off the edge of the known world together. Avalon is the Island of the Blest. I wish, I wish that I were there . . .

You can't play the Benny Goodman Quartet at one in the morning, even in an old and solidly built house, without the sound well down, or you'd have the neighbours on your head; and she wasn't that sloshed. She heard the car coming discreetly down the street and stopping on tiptoe outside. Feather-footed through the plashy fen passes the questing vole: too sloshed to know where that piece of deathless prose comes from. It did occur to her, though, that if she needed another alibi witness, then Estelle Laboisserie would have served some purpose.

From Evelyn Waugh, said Arthur. *Scoop* and this is most appropriate. Not sloshed but about to get so. He and Xavier were like small boys whose football team has just scored, and who must dance.

Charley was not exuberant, but not ashamed of himself.

"Clean job," he said. "No, nothing, thanks. I'll get off home if I may. A funny thing; when I was on duty, and it could be tricky sometimes, Janine slept like a rose. And now I'm a civilian, she won't sleep till I'm in. Call on me any time, but not for things like this."

"You call on me any time and for anything," said Arlette going downstairs with him. "I'd like to meet Janine too. I'm glad you met Xavier."

"He's a clever fellow. He'll be quite invaluable. Goodnight." She didn't give him a kiss, even one of drunken bonhomie: not her style. But she would have liked to, as he sailed away unfazed as the Duke of Wellington after a damned close-run thing.

Xavier, who had a sense of tact, left as well.

"Must be up early in the morning. Busy a-forging things. Wasn't of any great use, but glad to be, of whatever. Well – sleep tight."

Arthur was staring at the Osborne bottle, now at low tide.

"All those bulls on hilltops," he muttered. "Oh, there you are! You can give thanks, and your idiot boy with you, because both of you have saved your ass. Boy, was I frightened! I wouldn't be a gangster for a million. But the scary stuff on movies, the Hitchcock thing . . . nothing happened at all. I think we could have loaded a furniture van and nobody would have blinked."

"But what did he do? Begin at the beginning."

"He said in the car, got to bust the front, so nobody would gather that the boy had been inside."

"Yes, I gathered that."

"But how to bust the front without setting alarms off was what I couldn't gather – I mean the alarm was supposed to be on. I stood open-mouthed. Charley marches straight up to that box where they keep the transformer or the relay, or whatever it's called. Don't be dim – Electricité de France. Mostly a sort of concrete hut with a steel door and a terrifying warning about High Tension. Charley puts the crowbar in, the door went pop and he pulled the main switch: plunges the entire subsector into darkness. You see – no more juice: alarm kaput. E.D.F. have of course a technician on night duty, but he takes his time. Charley across the square, crowbar into the floor lock of the grille!"

"But were there no people?"

"I was so scared of the cops that I wanted to make a fake call, send them all out to some monstrous disaster out in the Wantzenau, but Charley wasn't having that: immoral! People pass of course – Place Broglie, sort of public. So I was up one end with a nasty cough if anyone came pottering, and Xavier down on the corner with a sneezing fit. Only three people came, and as Charley predicted they hurried on past, because whatever you're up to they don't want their consciences disturbed. What he was most afraid of was a drunk, who might be volubly pally or else quarrelsome, and noisy either way, but we were spared that. He was inside the grille by then, and working on the glass door like an F.B.I. bagman. Only took three minutes all told, though it seemed like half an hour. Main police shop only a hundred metres away: I was steamed up. He went in alone."

"What did he do there?"

"Nothing! – what was there to do? The cable on the switchboard inside was pulled already. That would look all right; in case, you see, the juice outside was turned back on quicker than expected. It did go on too: people must have been phoning right and left. And I imagine E.D.F. called the cops to say come and look where naughty vandals – autonomists probably or antinuclear demonstrators – have bust our good junction box – but we didn't stop to see. Charley had bust the back – from the outside you can't see or get any leverage, but inside it's just a big padlock on a hasp – and we were away. Left the car across the river, not to get tangled in any one-way streets. And the crowbar which is an incriminating thing to be carrying about at night, he simply chucked in the river right under the windows of the Préfecture! Where I dare say there was a flap, with all their lights out. Ploop and the whole Place Broglie gone black," laughing childishly, heartily. "Floodlights outside the Hotel de Ville and the Préfecture – all the Son et Lumière on the blink. Exactly like the lovely bit in the *Wind in the Willows* – pistol for the Rat, pistol for the Mole, pistol for the Badger!"

"And now?"

"Now – that man is a nasty sort of personage, and if we light a fire under him he has only himself to blame. Xavier wants to create a huge scandal: lot of crude retribution, but I see his point and yours too. Strike a blow for your Madame Bartholdi. Send letters of denunciation to the Palace of Justice, the Service des Douanes, the Fiscal Fraud Inspector. Even if the fellow destroys all invoices and stuff, there'll be the panther skin to hang on him. If we'd had an aerosol we'd have written on the door; Compliments from the Friends of the Baby Seals, up your pipe signed Brigitte Bardot, who'll be delighted.

"Oh yes," with drunken relish, "cat right in among pigeons and you'll see feathers fly."

"You will. I won't."

"You won't? Why won't you?"

"Because," said Arlette, "I'm off to Buenos Aires."

27. Me las arreglé

"Oh God," said Arthur, "more odtaa."

"But you hadn't forgotten?"

"No, no – but I was hoping it wouldn't happen."

"So was I. Then while you were away, I got a greatly agitated phone call. And then I had time to think."

"You shouldn't try to think when you're in a distraught state; all wound up as you are."

"I'm no longer in the least wound up. This," said Arlette, "had a very flattening, not to say sobering, effect."

"Which – your stupidities just past? Or the prospect of further stupidities still to come?"

"Please," with unusual meekness, "let's go to bed now: I'm very tired."

It was one of Strasbourg's worst mornings: dry but chilly, with a fusty dirty cover of grey cloud, no wind, a smell of chemicals: a gritty, sunken-eyed, alkaseltzerish sort of morning. Arthur's face, freshly shaved, was tight and papery. Her own face simply didn't bear looking at; her hair was limp and lifeless. Even the headline 'A Daring Break-in' on the regional page of the local newspaper failed to stir her: she just felt dull. She slipped out and made her telephone call. Arthur was still in sombre meditation when she came back, moving a spoon round and round in some cold coffee.

"I've plenty of time to pack. But not for any train – midday plane to Paris and that dreary shuttle between two airports."

He drank the coffee and said, "Oh God, I put sugar in twice."

"My poor boy," she said kissing his hair.

He pulled himself together then, turned round and put his arms round her.

"No – if you've got to, you've got to. It's just that I can't imagine what good it's likely to do."

"None very likely – indeed almost certainly. But I have to try. I have made a mess of everything, all round."

"That's not true, you know."

"One fails so much. God send something a little better. The irony is that these are people in whom I have no interest. I can't even bring myself to feel much sympathy. Perhaps that's just as well. I am more detached about it all."

"It's not a very nice place, you know, to go to."

"I know nothing at all about it."

"That's just it – you know nothing at all about it."

"Sabré," said Arlette, "me las arreglar." I will know how to sort it out. Se Débrouiller is the verb that gave the System D to France, and conjugating it, in all its tenses, was one of her gifts. Arthur held her by the hips and gave her a hug.

"I've no doubt," he said, "you will."

"It's only for a few days. I count on three at most. Add travel time and expect me back then at the latest."

"I'll drive you to the airport. What time's your take-off?"

"A big kiss."

"A big kiss. And make sure you eat properly. By the way, I stole your toothpaste." Airport conversations are all the same.

"I shall eat all the things you don't like. Cauliflower! On second thoughts, no; I'd have to eat it five days running. Look after yourself, my girl."

"Last call for Paris please. Now boarding," said the obnoxious loudspeaker girl.

"There's nothing you've forgotten?" asked Arthur with the special imbecility proper to these occasions.

"Any more Paris passengers?" screamed a stewardess with odious French shrillness.

"Fuck you," muttered Arthur, and with a memory of a long-ago comedian, "No not you, Mother, sit down. 'Bye."

Arlette dragged out desolately. Nothing in the world is nastier than airports.

The early-morning Paris plane is squashed full of businessmen relatively subdued by the crack-of-dawn awakening; haggard and quiet and shuffling furtively through their papers which they know by heart already: all frightened of the day in front of them, of the sack, of a heart-attack, of forgetting their lines. The mid-morning plane is better: less of a crowd and they are all excessively jolly, drinking up a good appetite and looking forward to a company-paid lunch. It is the best time of day for the poor wretches. Surely the figures will show something better than that miserable one and a quarter per cent.

Arlette did not share in the euphoria, but fell mercifully asleep, awakened only by a loud bump at Orly. Bus. Spectacularly vile view of Paris through dirty windows. Passengers all dead, poisoned by that toasted-cheese sandwich that is the Paris airport's special gift to gastronomy.

Roissy, now known as Charlie-Airport and it is not a change for the better, opens its maw and processes you. Treblinka railway-siding, with its gay paint, little trees, enthusiastic posters of happy families setting forth for happy hols, is nothing to it. Come on lads and lassies, Arbeit Macht Frei. Buy scarves, umbrellas, Scotch cameras and Japanese whisky. Arlette sat there and longed for someone to come and give her a fatal injection.

But once – at last – aboard Aerolineas' spanking treasure-loaded galleon, spirits rose. Nowhere else for them to go. De abajo, arriba, which is Spanish very roughly for up-up-and-away. There was no space in front or behind, but by God's infinite mercy there was space to the side for the junk she had – very little – and the junk the girls brought – a great deal. She organized herself – se las arregló – and began to feel comfortable. She was not in the least an Experienced Traveller, but did know the basics of airlines, which are after all relatively simple: never eat the food; never try to call the girls; support it patiently when they come unbidden; never, never try to go to the lavatory. She got hold of a mask and some pillows, curled up and slept. Missed, mercifully, breakfast in the middle of the afternoon, exciting views of Dakar, The Movie, virtually all of the aloft part.

She woke vastly refreshed. A couple of hours to go, but that would give her time to start speaking Spanish. A girl passed by and beamed at her: one passenger who had not given any trouble. Would she like some coffee? A drink? She had a couple of stiff jolts of those weird things with names like Pampero or Rawhide and containing passion-fruit-juice. The girls instantly looked much nicer; even the passengers became tolerable. By a succession of extraordinary Lotto-wins the lavatory was free, clean, and tidy: she repaired herself lavishly and made a hearty lunch of gambas and espárragos and pollo, all tasting exactly the same, but she didn't mind a bit.

If the first discovery made about Argentina is that the wine at five francs is as good as the French equivalent at twenty dollars, one is on the right track. Further proof: the pleasure of watching all the other passengers rushing for the lavatory in the hour before touchdown and frustrating one another very greatly. And Buenos Aires Airport is dirtier than Roissy, but there is no way it could be nastier. It also smells a great deal better. She was not even shaken by contact with officialdom. She was, by all means, a tourist. She was by no means a member of the Communist Party or indeed any other. To the best of her knowledge she was uncontaminated by cholera, typhoid, yellow fever or foot-and-mouth disease: her Documentación was simply fine. And it was a lovely day.

It was time to gather her wits and find out what she did know about Argentina. Which was very little, but it would have to do.

I am in the Southern Hemisphere, where I have never been. I crossed thus the Equator, but still in Roissy air, so that was all *mierda de toro*. The thing to remember is the seasons are back to front: Christmas is summer, so this is now late spring and very nice too. It rains quite a lot, but I 'ave the umbrella and I 'ave the raincoat, so that's all right. I 'ave further strong flat shoes; good because I'm going to do a lot of walking. It is a very large city indeed, but there is the metro, and I'm on expenses, there is the taxi. I will walk as much as I possibly can, but will not murder the feet. There is nothing here in the least strange or disconcerting. You might as well be at home. This is not just a much larger, much prettier Marseille, or even Barcelona: it has, obviously, dimensions you see but do not understand: it suffices to know they are there. A peculiar flung-together impression. Add Barcelona and Marseille and Genoa: then forget all about the Mediterranean and throw in Hamburg. Add, lavishly, that pretty strong stuff distilled from cactus-juice. And passion-fruit juice.

With much politeness and efficiency and carrying-her-bag, the taxi left her at her hotel. A short trip, but he had certainly gone around a long way. She did not care. The hotel was like every hotel she had ever stayed in in Paris: an antiquated décor and a lift best avoided; a superb staircase with much lavish ironwork to the balustrades, stucco to the ceilings and faded but impressive velvet. Many huge spotty looking-glasses, and curly rococo tables with people's breakfast trays on them. Mysterious doors with screens in front of them. Rooms being redecorated, with the plasterer sitting on the rolled-up carpet drinking beer. Complicated cutglass chandeliers being mended by nobody, with a lot of disembowelled wiring hanging down. A very pleasant large room, high-ceilinged, with shabby faded furniture, a new bed replacing the old horror with a valley in the middle. The Spanish pageboy, called grimly in French a chasseur, is called in Spanish a buttons. She overtipped *los botones* largely: he grinned at her and from the superiority of eleven years old said, 'You want anything, I'm your man'.

Very nice. A telephone that didn't work and a bathroom that did, with massive nineteenth-century plumbing in bronze coexisting with twentieth-century ditto in shiny black plastic and peeling chrome.

The doorplates and handles were in the same thick, luxuriously figured bronze, and concealed solid old-fashioned locks with a night latch. Good, she wasn't going to get murdered in her bed, nor raped neither by no big hairy macho cabrio. And as for the street . . . and as for all these winding passages too, full of curtained doorways, massive pieces of man-high furniture, and dud electric-light bulbs . . . One could hear hair-raising tales of assault just about anywhere on the American continent. There was enough truth in these to make a woman by herself take a precaution or two, and Arlette reckoned herself a careful girl. One of the things she had learned from Corinne Klein, who had given her self-protection lessons, was that the scene in which the slightly-built virgin tosses the huge inflamed goat airily through the landscape fails to work except with singularly timid and fumbling goats.

Arlette unpacked. In the bowels of her suitcase was a small box of manicure things, metallic objects which do not set airport security-checks a-tweeter. In with the scissors and files was a knife, an ordinary folding pocket-knife but the best there is, a hand-made Laguiole with a brass and ivory grip and a long narrow blade of razor steel. When opened it has an excellent balance. The bag she had brought was likewise a solid affair; the oblong type with a flap coming all the way down. Under this flap was stitched a loop, and the open knife lodged in this loop. The bag carries on your left side, under the arm. It slides easily to the front and the right hand makes the same movement as a cross-draw from a shoulder holster. Experience has shown that if the most professional and evil-minded of goats takes you in an armlock you lose consciousness very fast, but you have plenty of time to get at your knife. On the occasions when you are not wearing your gun in its hip holster, when for instance you are wearing a frock, the knife is as good or better. It has both edge and point. Either will take a goat's mind off the object in view, for any length of time up to permanency.

When she sallied out, feeling chipper, the crooked corners and shadowy alcoves of all these damn passages were not alarming.

Hotels will often try and sell you the kind of cigarettes advertised in glossy magazines. They have also dinky little street maps with cute little drawings of the more grandiose monuments. Arlette went down the street until she met a cigar shop, and went in. Here she met a gossipy, friendly person, and the usual conversation ensued. Oho, and aha, una Francesa, without doubt a Parisiensa? No no, dear man, de Mediterráneo, de cerca de Toulon, all right if you want it so de cerca de Marsella. Yes, all extremely bonita and hermosa and how about some Argentine cigarettes? Oh they're blonde tobacco? Don't like blonde cigarettes, make me cough, wuff wuff. That's right, brown ones, like French ones if you insist, but want local ones, something like Cuban or Colombian ones.

This cast a slight chill. Cuba I seem to have heard of: where is Colombia, isn't that some banana place with earthquakes? You had better be clear about this: in the South American continent, only Argentina exists. Brazil exists, or so it is said, but those are blacks. And don't speak Spanish. Not like us. Now a rubia from the Mediterranean, that is like us.

A bountiful friendship was flowing by this time. Arlette secured small nice cigarillos, and went off with her ears ringing. She had learned that Porteño, and there's nothing more patriotically Porteño than people in cigarshops, bore only a vague resemblance to her kind of schoolgirl Spanish.

There was also this damn street map. It was the other kind, which is big enough to be readable, but a great deal too big to do anything with on street-corners, except to be blown away in a high wind. She bought a large straw shopping-bag to keep it in, and had a drink to get her breath back.

One never sees anything of large cities, for one only sees when walking, and while one can walk, one gets nowhere much. The distances are very distant, sure, but much worse is the concept of grandeur that squashes human beings. This lack of proportion is very boring. As Thomas Beecham said of the Sydney Harbour Bridge, it is far too large and should instantly be knocked down; this applies to everywhere. Crossing the Champs Elysées becomes a chore akin in strenuousness to swimming the Channel: it is now too much of a bore to go and see what is on the other side. Walking down Piccadilly is the stupidest thing you can do, because all you come to is Hyde Park Corner.

The modern world has also removed perspective, as costing too much. Some very large buildings are extremely beautiful, like the Louvre, which is why the City of Paris has arranged that you should no longer see it. Saint Peter's is visible, just, because nobody has quite dared yet knock down the Bernini colonnades. The converse is also true: the huge and magnificent perspective down the Mall shows you – alas – Buckingham Palace, which is unmistakably Barclay's Bank. The difference between visible and invisible cities is the difference between Venice and Rome.

With a considerable expenditure of energy Arlette discovered the metro, and eventually the Chancellery of the French Embassy, greatly fortified against hostile natives and guarded by gorillas, for fear that an Argentinian ayatollah should declare all the paperwork to be Espionage.

As in all chancelleries, in all embassies, there were elegant young women, and elegant young men, with the universal family look of incapacity. With a succession of these physically and mentally feeble persons there was a succession of long arguments.

She wanted the Consulate. No she did not. Yes she did; no she didn't. She must be warned with the utmost emphasis against all ill-judged and tactless approaches to the Authorities. Now who was she, anyhow, apart from plainly being an excessively tiresome person?

After a while she fought her way into an inner office, where there was an Attaché. Now would she please explain herself clearly? An Embassy Official? Next best thing: a highly-placed Consular Official. Who was he? If he had wished that known, doubtless he would have made the necessary approaches himself.

After mulling this over for a long time, and remaining flummoxed, and finding her immovably obstinate to both threat and blandishment, the Attaché went and got the Counsellor, an elderly diplomat of a long thin sort, with bilious eyes and stiff grey hair in a long brosse that made him longer and thinner than ever, but being Counsellor had much experience and some brains, and even some traces of humour.

"Let me tell you this, Madame. Anybody searching for missing persons in this city, in case you hadn't heard, is about as welcome as Fidel Castro, and just about as conspicuous, and we can't do anything about that. En cada tierra su uso, or roughly, other land, other manners."

"To which my cleaning woman would reply, Dame dinero y no me consejos, give me the money and not so much advice. Seriously, this isn't a political matter, or I don't believe it to be so. If it is, it's a French affair, which is why I respect my principal's desire for anonymity. All I want is the right address, which you certainly know."

"You realize that the Embassy will take no responsibility whatever for you, and is not to be held liable for any scrape you get into? Nor can you mention any names belonging here. Do that and they'll check it out, and then heaven help you."

"If I didn't know this, I wouldn't have come in the first place."

"As long as you do: the trouble we got into over those awful nuns . . ."

"A quien madruga, Dios le ayuda." Those who get up early, God helps.

"That had better be true. Very well, there's a Captain Barton who might conceivably see his way to straightening you out. They do, occasionally, upon no logic that anybody has ever been able to discover. No I won't write it down: do that for yourself. The address is that of the police Kommandatur."

"In, no doubt, the Prinz Albrechtstrasse."

"Don't make jokes like that around here. I can tell you, they don't go down at all well. If, furthermore, you have invented this tale of a consular official, it is my duty to warn you that you may not feel inclined for any further joking."

"You mean like telling a traffic cop I'm the Senator's cousin and I'll have the badge off the bastard? That would indeed be childish, here."

"So my fairly considerable experience of human beings inclines me to judge. Or you wouldn't have got in here. You would do better, you know, to tell me who it is. If it's as you say, he'll be in our book. There is – then – a possibility that we might be able to help you."

She shook her head.

"I promised," she said.

"Well well; I can respect that. I can also respect your confidence."

"There would have been people in Paris equally well placed. He chose not to confide in them. People who had been at school with him. I wasn't going to argue with him about it."

"Maybe I see his point," muttered the Counsellor. "Well, I'll press you no further. You handle your own responsibilities."

Quite, thought Arlette. Including the having nothing to do with the occasionally-amiable Captain Barton, who knows the telephone number of the French Embassy, and gets invited to their parties.

She now felt very tired, and took a taxi home. These days that the jet doubles, the artificial stimulus of Speed, one has to pay for them. She had an unexpectedly amiable, and flirtatious taxi-driver. But not the male goat. A family man. Affectionate to his wife. It is not enough, to be affectionate towards your wife.

She had a shower, and a brief kip. And went and had dinner in the hotel restaurant. She'd had worse meals. There was nothing even remotely Argentinian about it, save the spelling on the menu. It all tasted exactly like the equivalent in New Delhi and Melbourne. But she didn't care. She only wanted calories. She studied the torn-apart pieces of her street map, and would have picked the brains of her head-waiter if he had had any.

28. ¡Pa que aprenda!

She went out after supper, for a breath of fresh air, or to walk the dog, or whatever it is called. And what were these buenos aires they went on about? – place was as smelly as Strasbourg and with a good deal less excuse. Trade Winds? – or no, not perhaps trade winds; she didn't know what they were called, but there ought to be healthful sea breezes.

Better though at night, and a clear night, and blazing moreover with stars: such stars as she had heard of and never seen, and now was the moment. She didn't know really where she was, but was clear that it was a long way south. South!

Once on a marvellous winter night in the Vosges, with the whole heaven crackling and snapping, Piet had tried to explain the principle of celestial navigation, and failed utterly. She had never got beyond the stage of the child being taken in the garden by its father, and there is the Bear, quite right, not the least like a bear; a saucepan. And Orion. And the Dog Star.

And now she was truly, truly South, and none of these things were there any more, helpful guides to navigation. She could be anywhere, and probably somewhere like Toronto. But no! because there by gum was the Southern Cross.

Arthur Davidson, who was not a university professor, did not lecture. He was, however, a deft enough lecturer and last winter had been called upon to address the Literary and Historical Society, and had chosen one of his favourites, or rather two: Rudyard Kipling, and Phony Attitudes.

With a good piece of rhetoric you can make people do anything. Repeat a slogan like Delenda est Carthago and nobody bothers whether it makes any sense. Kipling invented a superbly cadenced line about the Long Trail, our own trail, the out trail, and made a whole generation burst out blubbering. 'The old lost stars wheel back, dear lass, and the Southern Cross rides high', and everyone thought, 'Oh yes, that's right, India'. Whereas of course Kipling's India is twenty degrees north latitude and his one sight of all this had been on a boat going to Australia, but luckily none of the English knew North Latitude from Greenwich Mean Time.

Arlette missed Arthur badly, felt sadly alone in this horrible South, and wondered, not for the first time, what the hell she was doing there.

Entering, bright and early next morning, one of these large official buildings mentally ticketed as 'that stinking pink palazzo', she was stopped by the concierge and a spirited dialogue in kitchen Spanish ensued.

"I wish to see the general."

"What general?"

"The commanding general."

"Commanding what?"

"The department."

"Oh, the Commander."

"That's right." Saying, 'Tell him it's Don Juan' was tempting, but would not help matters.

"On what subject?"

"A personal subject."

'With what object?"

"With the object of explaining myself to the Commander."

"You have a complaint?"

"No."

"You have been badly treated?"

"No."

"You are *estranjera*? You are not domiciled here?"

"No."

"You make this complaint on behalf of another person?"

"I have no complaint."

"How is it then that you wish to see the Commander?"

"The things that I say will be of interest to the Commander."

"That is easy to say."

"It can however be proved to the satisfaction of the Commander."

"The Commander is not here."

"He works, however, here."

"Where else?"

"Then I shall wait for his arrival."

"You may have to wait long."

"Not so."

"How so, not so?"

"Because the Commander works hard and has much conscience."

"It is necessary to make an appointment."

"Then we shall make one."

"It is obligatory to fill in certain forms."

"You shall be very kind and help me in this task."

"You have the documentación?"

Half an hour later they were quite close friends.

"Your request is being dealt with."

"Most kind. I should like the favour of a glass of water."

"There is no water."

"What do you do when you have thirst?"

"In the service of the State it is necessary to control oneself."

"It happens from time to time that one is thirsty."

"One drinks a cup of coffee, upon payment."

"Then may I have some coffee? But I should prefer water."

"There is the machine. For those who pay, there is coffee. There is also coca-cola."

"I dislike coca-cola. But I should like the pleasure of offering you a cup of coffee."

"That is polite. I shall accept. That is more money than the machine admits."

"It will serve to buy flowers, to put upon your desk."

"There is water. But it is reserved for the personnel of the administration."

"I do not wish to infringe the regulations of the administration. But I have hope that the Commander will allow me to drink water."

"I will take the responsibility upon myself. But you observe; it is imprudent to set a precedent. If all the public entered here to demand water . . ."

"That is very true."

Half an hour later.

"Mount the stairway. Arrive at the third gallery. Room 332. Knock and demand permission. The Commander has been informed of your request."

"There is the elevator?"

"There is the elevator, but it is reserved for the mutilated and the infirm. One must not waste the resources of the State."

"That is very true."

Room 332 was small, and contained a table and a middle-aged personage. His cap was on the table, and bore a captain's insignia. She never learned whether this was Captain Barton, but on the whole she doubted it. This person was less diplomatic.

"State your business."

"I would like to see the Commander."

"That won't do, you know."

"Captain, it is my pleasure to meet you, and my misfortune that I can only state my business to the General."

"I am his aide. You understand, one does not enter here as into a mill to buy flour."

"I understand."

"You may rely upon my discretion."

"I am convinced of it. I am unhappily obliged to see the General."

"One word – no."

"I am a very patient person."

"And you will find the door behind you."

"And utterly harmless. But quite interesting."

"And obstinate. And you try my patience."

"It causes me pain," humbly.

"You're a journalist."

"No."

"Your documentación. All of it." Humbly, she produced her identity papers.

"Perhaps you would not object to giving me your handbag."

"I have nothing to hide."

He opened the handbag, discovered the Laguiole knife, and raised his eyebrows. He spread papers out across his desk. Driving licences and the like.

"I speak no French. I can read it."

"It is my regret that my Spanish is primitive."

"What's this for?" It was her card, signed by the former PJ Commissaire in Strasbourg, stating his knowledge of her activities. Unofficial, but useful. She always carried it.

"I have a small bureau, for advice and where possible help to those in perplexity or misery."

"It says," returning to other papers, "here that you are a housewife."

"That is true, and I am proud of it."

"Good! But people who meddle in the affairs of others are not necessarily welcome, wherever they go."

"I am so well aware of this, Captain, that I refuse to meddle in any affairs of this country."

"Good." He pressed a bellpush and shuffled the papers in a heap. A clerk came in and stood.

"Take a look at these under the lamp, and tell me whether they are genuine." He lit a cigarette, without offering her one. "And you think that we can help you?"

"It is a very simple matter that brings me here. I have no connection with the press. Or with any other body, official or unofficial. I am just me."

"And what is your viewpoint, upon our administration?"

"Captain, if I manage to do the job I came for I shall be paid, I hope, a fee. So far I have been given an advance upon my expenses, of travel here, and a day or so's stay. But I am certainly not going to be paid by anyone to hold viewpoints concerning any administration. Yours, or mine."

"And you refuse to explain yourself to me."

"That would be a foolish error. I have to say that a confidence was revealed to me, which I have not the right to break. For the same reason, I have nothing to say to the Embassy here, or the Consulate. I promised, you see."

The clerk came back, laid her little heap of paper on the desk, said nothing, and went out again. The captain knocked ash off his cigarette and seemed to meditate.

"Señora, without wishing to be insulting – are you aware that you are ridiculous?"

"Oh yes," said Arlette. "All honest people are ridiculous."

He gave a short laugh, half cough. He picked up his telephone, and pressed buttons on it.

"I will give you your wish. You may regret my doing so."

"But one does what one has to."

"That is true. Señora Walther? I have a customer for you." He put the phone down. There was a silence. He pointed to the handbag. "That stays here." She nodded.

Señora Walther was a small, thin woman. She had coarse

black hair with grey threads in it, a slight moustache, steel-rimmed spectacles.

"Will you accompany me, please?" she said politely.

They went to the end of the passage, where there was a large double-folding door of heavy tropical hardwood, much scuffed and scratched. Inside there was a very large room. Arlette looked around in surprise. Nobody lived in it, nor did it look used for anything. There was a lot of marble, and gilt. There was a huge chandelier. There were immense pier looking-glasses, and a large sunburst clock saying a quarter to three, with cherubs holding it up. There were stiff Empire chairs ranged along the walls, and an ornate Savonnerie carpet in the middle, like all the rest faded and spotted.

"Strip to the skin, please," said Señora Walther in her polite monotone.

One does what one has to do. Arlette said nothing, avoided making a face, and undressed. Each thing she took off she handed to Señora Walther standing there for this purpose, who looked at things and laid them neatly on faded grey-green satin.

"Lift your arms, please. Turn around. Straddle your legs. Face me please, again." Arlette caught sight of herself in the big mirror and could not stop making a face at it. The little woman smiled, very slightly. "You may dress. I am sorry. It is the rule."

"Arms?"

"More likely, tape recorders. Anything at all." She waited till Arlette was dressed, and said, "Please sit down. And wait for me." She went through the set of double-doors at the far side. Arlette sat on an Empire chair which afforded no comfort, and rearranged her hair with her fingers.

The little woman came back, held the door, and said, "Please." She closed the door behind Arlette and was no more seen.

She was in a room the same size as the one she had left, en suite with it, with three big windows looking out upon a courtyard, a formal garden and a fountain. The room was furnished as a comfortable private office, with leather sofas, bookshelves, a big desk set to catch the best of the light. A big man was standing, moving with the rapidity and quietness of many big men. He had a pipe between his teeth and was wearing an English tweed hacking-jacket. High forehead, higher by being a bit bald in front, healthily tanned. Bright blue eyes, set far apart. Pleasant expression. Looked, on the whole, like a retired footballer, who is now training the under-fifteens; schoolmasterly, severe look under the smiling, easy exterior.

Maybe Commissaire Maigret looked like this, but his office was not as large. On the desk was one of those angled plaques of clear plastic, with black lettering. It said 'Colonel Oswaldo Suarez Palmer'.

"Good morning, Colonel Palmer."

He smiled with the strong teeth that held the pipe, and said pleasantly,

"*¡Pa que aprenda!*" Expression translatable by, "That'll teach you!'

"Yes, I see."

"Your Spanish I hear is very good. You might prefer to talk English?" in an English virtually unaccented: if anything, Cambridge University. She might have guessed Sandhurst, if she'd ever heard of it. English like Arthur's.

"It's true," gratefully, "I've just about exhausted my Spanish."

"Very well. You've asked to see me. Here I am. I must beg of you not to waste my time or your own. You have not, hitherto, been succinct. Be so now."

"And this young man – does he engage in political activities?"

"I hope for his sake that he doesn't."

"That is succinct. And you call a spade a spade. So few people do so. I do, myself. You've heard of me. I'm the police chief, for the city. Ah, you think, the Chief Executioner. Nice fellow, big clean office. Goes down in the cellar, and Tortures people."

"I have no information about this."

"No, but you've read all about Amnesty International. Splendid people. Very necessary. They don't of course know everything. So let's not frig about. I have an English name, but I am not English. Look at this." At the edge of the huge desk was an enormous globe. He switched on the lamp inside it, spun it, stopped it, took a desk pointer and tapped it.

"You see all this? Northern hemisphere. North America, Europe, Asia, Soviets, China, Japan. India. Great bulk of Africa. All the resources. All the history, all the economic progress, all the manpower. Now down here. Southern hemisphere. What's there? Nothing. Small tail end of Africa. Scrawny little scrag end of America. Australia. New Zealand. Piffling, huh? All empty, no population, nothing. Look at Argentina. Five times the size of France, population less than one half, and France is the emptiest country in Central Europe. Why? Because this was an unimportant little place. In the colonial time, not even a vice-royalty, B.A. was founded a century after Lima, after Quito, after Ascencion – obscure provincial governorship.

"Now it has perhaps struck you that the northern hemisphere, after all these centuries of power and empire, is in something of a decline. Indeed in very considerable trouble. Rivalries, political, economic, the lot. And then at last people start casting an eye down here, saying Hey, that's a pissy little corner, nothing but cows and sheep, but perhaps strategically important, if we get there before the others. Everybody with that idea, and not just Russians, not just Americans. Japanese, Germans. French too sleepy and selfsatisfied, if you'll forgive. English too complacent and lazy. Yack about the Lycée Français or the Islas Malvinas, yoy. But the United States – they would be mighty interested. So all these people who get off the bus here, what are they after? It's my job to know, and it's a tough job, and it's not always a nice job. And these people, sometimes they aren't nice, either.

"We've got everything: space, food, minerals, water, electricity. Compare that to the other land masses in the hemisphere. Something like seven-tenths of Australia is desert. Southern Africa, magnificent land, but they can't get over the conflict between owners and occupiers.

"So that we are very greatly privileged. But we're too poor, too feeble to handle it. And they arrive, with arms outstretched, to help us. Kind of them!"

Arlette thought that perhaps he did protest too much, but kept her mouth shut. She was here to learn, to conjugate the verb '*aprender*' – very well.

"However," ripping his glasses off as though he hated them and throwing them on the blotter, "let's see if we can throw a loop over this problem of yours. Christian name?"

"Gilles."

"Gilles," writing on a small piece of paper with neat small handwriting, "and you've a photograph? Good," stapling it all together, "and a heroin rap in Paris. Let us see what we know," pressing a buzzer. A girl secretary came in through the door on the far side: he handed her the paper and said, "Any form?" exactly like the Scotland Yard Inspector of Arlette's imagination.

"Let nobody impose upon you," taking the glasses off again and staring at her with the bright blue eyes, "I'm here to keep the young plants free of weeds. All the trash of the northern hemisphere gets vomited up here, from antiquated English colonialism to every barbarity ever born of industrial slums." There must be something about the southern hemisphere, thought Arlette, that makes them sound like John Buchan characters. The wildly skidding wheels of her imagination threw her up the phrase from Ray Chandler, 'breezy as a Britisher just in from a tiger-hunt'. His phone buzzed. The computer had come up with the O, because he said "No? Very well," and put it down again. He relit his pipe, said, "Not within my scope. Concerns the intendencia." He thought, and said, "There used – it's thirty years ago, when I was a pipsqueak sub-lieutenant on a course in England – to be two comedians. Radford and Wayne, they had a sort of elderly civil servant act, very funny. At one moment they were respectively the Ministers for Foreign Affairs and the Home Office, and were dealing with people who had Seceded From the Crown. One says to the other 'Aliens; that's your department' and the other replies 'No no, they're undesirable aliens, that's your department'. The Governor might be able to help you: I'll give you a chitty." This old-fashioned expression, reminding her of Arthur, made her giggle. Colonel Palmer caught the giggle, and was pleased with it. Gave a touch to his picture of an extremely efficient Brigadier, of a crack commando outfit, putting up with no nonsense from Basil Seal. They were not so much Buchan as Evelyn Waugh characters. Colonel Palmer belonged in Bellamy's Club.

He had been busy with his buzzer again; there was another girl secretary, with a shorthand pad.

"Take a letter. General Maurizio Renard. The lady who will identify herself by presentation of this note has approached me in a matter upon which I have at present no relevant word. You may be able to suggest to her some suitable course. Yours with respect. Give it me for signature, envelope for bearer; the lady here.

"I'm sending you to the top," said Colonel Palmer with a schoolboyish sort of amusement. "It will be interesting what you make of General Renard. Or what General Renard makes of you – let us hope it isn't hamburger," with a gleam of teeth.

The girl came in with a sheet of heavily embossed paper. He looked at it, put 'Palmer' in the small neat writing, and handed it to be slipped in the long stiff envelope.

"I am greatly in your debt, Colonel."

"Honoured to be of service, Madame," standing up formally, and then dropping the formality suddenly. "It's nothing – amused me, the way you talked yourself in. Don't forget what I've told you," warning forefinger. And changing lightning-quick back to Bellamy's Club, "Off you go, girl, twitch your mantle blue." This was a password which to her great good fortune she recognized. Yet another debt owed to Arthur, who often said the same thing. The gentlemen known to Colonel Palmer, and of course the ladies too, not of course that they are allowed into Bellamy's, have all learned Milton's *Lycidas* in school.

"Is General Renard wood, or pasture?"

"Hohoho. You'll find out. Ask him!" The girl had waited, to show her politely out, the way she had come.

"You can find your road, Señora?"

"He aprendido," said Arlette, meaning it.

She walked quickly. Con mala persona el remedio – mucha

tierra en medio. Put as much distance as you can between yourself and a bad person. But was he a bad person? It is also said: the devil stands at the foot of the cross.

She felt extremely tired, which she put down to acute hunger.

29. De la sartén, en las brasas

An easy one in English, sartén being a frying pan, and brasas being coals-of-fire. She had leisure to fabricate culinary metaphors, because she had been so hungry that she overate. Restaurants in governmental quarters as always tend to alternate between grand and very expensive places smelling of silence, panelled wood, and corpse-like head-waiters, and scruffy places where the help eats, smelling of fish and frying-fat: nothing in between, and the lorn lady didn't fancy either much; uncomfortable all on her ownio.

She had great good fortune: turning corners to get away quick from the stinking pink palazzo, she fell upon a sort of spaghetti joint where she felt quite at home: porteno-napolitana accents, illegible menu with things like lionfish and roast lungs: everything nice and dirty and lashings of extremely good wine. Being rather drunk after clams, she had to eat the roast lung too – at least she didn't know what it was: something asado with lots of salad. They thought her accent killingly funny and kept pressing her to eat more. She resisted both potato and cake and could still walk, she was glad to find out. Nothing but a tiny fishy and a salad tonight, and yoghurt for breakfast. If, that is, I'm not in jail.

The new palazzo was in a terrible Teutonic style, reminding her strongly of the Rhinepalace back at home on the Place de la République. The corridors were dark and Dracula-haunted, the concierge had black teeth and had had blood and raw garlic for lunch. But her grand letter earned her instant consideration: she was brought up only one flight of stairs and inserted in a little waitingroom made inside a large landing, a version of her own, in the Rue de l'Observatoire, but much grander, with moquette, and tweedy chairs, and a lovely lavatory where she brushed her teeth.

Waiting for her was a very polite young man, with a nice suit and rather long hair, who guided her. All the vast gloomy rusticated stonework had been covered in blonde wood, very pretty. The furniture was modern, fresh, clean. The police sneers at things like the Governorship of the Province as vaguely 'Intendencia', but this was higher altogether in the social scale. Where gloomy daylight struggled through neo-gothic stained-glass, there were large bright chromium lamps in great numbers. Almost a Dutch look: courtesy of Philips in Eindhoven. Nobody pounced upon her and stripped her to the skin, although the nice young man looked willing to try in a polite sort of way.

General Renard got up.

"Ah, la rubia francesa, who can quote Milton." He kissed her hand. A glowing reputation had apparently preceded her. Perhaps she'd been Polaroided, too, without a stitch on through that awful great mirror, but here they were going to be chic about it.

General Renard spoke French, with a slight Castilian accent. Not Sandhurst, more Spahi, one could see him in that lovely cape. In any case velly cavallery. Uniform, cut by Lanvin. On his bare desk, a good still-life composed of cap, stick, and gloves. He sat on a hard chair, quiet, upright. Nothing foxy about him, though his hair, which was going greyish, was still reddish, and he had remarkable red-brown eyes. He appeared to be contemplating her with pleasure. He also appeared to be a thought reader.

"Also Lanvin," he said.

"It's my very best suit: I wanted to look nice. But only off the peg, I'm afraid."

"The bag with the knife is an especially nice touch." Whatever the police was, its telephone wagged a tongue.

"There's hardly anything left to know about me," complained Arlette.

"Yes," he assented, "I also know what you want. We shall see, about that."

"Will you help me, General?"

"I am the Governor: that is to say my responsibility is for the several million people inhabiting this province, the most populous, as you are aware, in the country. Yes; in the circumstances I will help you, if as is after all quite probable your young man is here. But it will take a little time. We don't remake the world in a day. Whatever you may believe to the contrary, we do not attempt to have policemen and soldiers breathing down everyone's necks. This is not Eastern Germany. People come – and go – as they please. They read – and say – what they please. Colonel Palmer has a very up-to-date computer. We can, if we so desire, construct an atomic weapon. I do not so desire. I do not believe this to be the future of this country." He suddenly did his thought-reading act again. "You are thinking how boring, how primitive they all are, and all apologizing for their beastly behaviour, as though that made it any more excusable. Well well; in many ways, perhaps in most, we are anything between fifty and a hundred years behind the times. This, as you will perhaps learn, is not altogether the disadvantage the technicians would have us believe." Hm, this was a brighter person than Colonel Oswaldo Suarez Palmer.

Afterwards she was to say 'But what possessed me?'; to ask herself even, for a dotty moment, whether anything had possessed her, some hallucinogenic plant; needing excuses for having been so talkative, and so indiscreet. Fatally so?

Perhaps she had been drunk? She'd had a good deal of natural, undoctored, excellent local wine: even if this was enough to make one reckless, it was no excuse. She had been brought up on stuff like this; could be forgiven for feeling at home, making herself at home: no more.

Vanity? General Renard had encouraged her in as many words to make herself at home. Plainly he liked women and enjoyed her company. Just as she enjoyed the local air, the flavour of this magnificent country. Charming, courteous, intelligent, witty; it wasn't often that one was so privileged by the company kept. Much better company than Colonel Palmer.

Speaking French had something to do with it. However well one comes to handle a language there is something about the native tongue, the paths found for expression – the jokes, the absurd puns. She was after all a Frenchwoman from the south, born into and steeped in the Latin world, the world of maleness, of 'Sois belle et tais-toi'. Twenty years of Piet van der Valk had taught her the absurdity and futility of this world. She understood it; knew that she could never quite escape from it (the way Ruth had, her – adopted – daughter), never quite find total equilibrium. When one is born a serf, one will never altogether shake off serf mentality.

Thus – flattery: she had felt flattered at being listened to, and even to some extent understood by a general, an important general, whose power in the land was great. Power in the land; you said it.

Remaking the world; that was where it had begun.

"The confusion in this benighted land," said General Renard. "Are we using the tools and thoughts of 1980 – or as generally seems by our rate of progress, those of 1880?

"Is the one any better than the other? – mm, we've managed to stamp out smallpox while discovering chemical warfare and biological manipulation. Is electric torture more hygienic than the whip? If sixteenth-century Russia looks awfully familiar, especially to Russians, the Inquisition seems to be flourishing, and not just here. What would Ben Franklin have to say about Mr Zbig?" It had started her off. Renaissance? What Renaissance? The fate of female children in sixth-century B.C. Attica . . .

"I generally have some tea about this time; will you join me?" A goddam teaparty . . .

"So you don't really think that Argentina has anything to learn from the rest of the world."

"I emphatically do not: find me one place where the poor are not oppressed by the rich." And Indians; she'd blithered a lot about Indians: the being in America, no doubt. The

General was entertained – now the Don Juan books; did she feel able to take those seriously? The Castaneda boy was South American, as she doubtless knew; must have made a lot of money.

A literary teaparty, in the sixth arrondissement: they always talk there about a lot of money somebody's made.

She couldn't see anything very difficult about ol' Juan's ideas. All very turgidly and confusedly expressed perhaps, but what would one expect of a young fellow filled with anthropological rubbish by the University of California? – no wonder old Juan had so to laugh. Those girls he trained had no trouble understanding things. Going on about their wombs in a very primitive fashion, but that was to be expected. She herself came from Provence; was there all that much difference to the province of Somora? Both ruined by that disastrous Roman Empire. She'd been filled up too with a lot of rubbish at school: Aix was just as bad as the U. of Cal. But then, of course, she was a woman and had therefore more sense.

Oh dear, she'd gone on chatting like Molly Bloom on the pot.

It must have been the woman stuff that shocked General Renard.

That was what she had failed to take sufficiently into account. Army officers were so easily shocked: they were so dreadfully inexperienced. Women were good, meaning reluctant wives; good mothers, meaning indulgent to the boys and teaching them that a woman is a dreadful, cursed, revolting object: losing no opportunity of reminding the females that they are responsible for all men's frailties, and are Here to be Punished. She knew those wives, the sallow faces pinched around the mouth and nostrils, the candlegrease complexion, saying the rosary interminably in their long white nighties as penance for their sins of the flesh. Olivewood rosary, heirloom, blessed by the last Pope but four.

All other women, including herself, were Whores. Utterly shocking to generals who had always led such sheltered, protected lives stamping out whoredom in Aldershot.

She had shot off her stupid mouth. As Arthur always told

her never to do, and Commissaire Casabianca, and Sergeant Subleyras and oh, everyone. She got so impatient with the silly blind asses.

And what would her cleaning-woman say now? She'd shake her head, and go cluckcluck with her tongue, and say el rio pasado, el santo olvidado. River once passed, you forgot the saint who brought you over . . .

Ask any of the Generals where she'd gone wrong they'd smile, tight and distant, and say it was not enough to be good. No basta ser bueno – sino parecerlo. One had also to appear good.

How much time had passed? A day – two. Nice and restful, so good for the nerves. No illtreatment. Just complete silence. And total indifference. A limbo. Neither a Carmel nor a Home for Fallen Women (it had features of both; she'd have settled for either) but a place of nothing, a nowhere. She'd asked for it . . . Arthur would never find out. Poor Arthur, who had uncomplainingly accepted something so flagrantly against his better judgment.

She had been just barely out on the street, blinking a little in the sunlight after the stained-glass, muted, filtered feel of General Renard's Palace, standing on the pavement enjoying it, wondering whether after all she might not try for an opera ticket at the Colon for that evening. *Turandot* after all is quite something. It might even be well done: there were lots of extremely outstanding Argentinian musicians one had scarcely or never heard of, in Europe.

A man had come up to her: heavyset, a baldish tanned skull, large yellow teeth, a big wide grey tweed jacket with patch pockets – why did she remember those? The jacket looked much too heavy for this warm weather. He had been perfectly quiet, showed her the palm of his half-open hand with some sort of badge in the hollow, and said "Please accompany" in a low neutral voice. He had turned without looking at her again. The youngish one, whose face she had never properly looked at, had given her a tiny, gentle prod in the back to indicate "follow". She had followed, not thinking to yell or run or do anything – what use would it be? The young one opened the back door of a car parked at the pavement, got in wordlessly beside her; the old one got behind the wheel, settled himself heavily, started the motor, drove a few blocks at a slow, unhurried pace, turned a few corners, nothing much, just enough to lose her totally. Came out on a dreary grey street of dusty concrete, turned in behind a faceless, meaningless block of the same, into a sort of small parking lot. Out, and in at a door, a passage with grey vinyl tiles. She remembered they had been freshly mopped, and smelt of wet mop and disinfectant. The place was clean, and very silent. A grey door, a small grey-painted room, a metal table and chair, and another of the same where she was bid sit.

She had recovered, by then, enough to start the 'What is it', the 'But why', the 'Please tell me the meaning'. He had said nothing, done nothing, but put his thick yellow finger to his mouth in a Sssh gesture, sat down. Rummaged in her shopping bag, held his hand out wordlessly for her handbag, rummaged in that. Paid no attention to the knife, taken her identification, written her name at the head of a roneo'd form. There seemed plenty of spaces for entries on it but he left them blank, signed at the bottom, turned the form round, signalled with the yellow finger for her to take the pen and write her own name. There was something Indian in his face. Indians were great believers in silence. White people always talked too much.

"What is it you want me to sign?" she asked, not able to concentrate upon the blurry, pale grey letters.

"Just receipt," he said patiently. "Personal property." He took the shopping bag, put the handbag in it open, pointed at her watch, ear-rings, wedding ring: she had no other jewellery. He signalled her to stand up, patted her empty pockets, pointed at her shoes: she took them off and he put them in the bag. "Come," he said.

Bemused, she followed down the passage, round a corner. Wall to wall, floor to ceiling was a strong steel grille on hinges. He unlocked this with a bunch of keys he took from a pocket. Along the passage was a sort of landing, an open space with a table and a chair, at which a man in uniform sat reading a comic, who barely glanced up and nodded vaguely. Three or four doors opened off the landing.

The second passage was a classic cell-block of some eight or ten doorways, of which she noticed nothing but that it seemed clean, and was quiet. Her guide took her down to the end, chose the last but one, unlocked it, switched the light on, motioned her in, switched the light out, relocked: she heard his footsteps die away, and a jangle of keys at the far end. There was complete silence.

She examined herself for traces of shock: she felt none. There had been no brutality, no blows, no harsh words. A startlement, at being abruptly separated from the world – this was akin to falling off a bicycle. A bruise or two, in this instance to the ego. She was startled at the suddenness, the arbitrariness – the simplicity. Startled at her own helplessness; at her passivity. At her own lack of protest – but should she have demanded a lawyer, a doctor, a consular official? – to what end? There was a Constitution, guaranteeing rights and liberties to the subject, but she felt quite sure there was an emergency law of some sort, enabling authority to hold whoever they fancied, for unspecified time, upon unspecified grounds. In any case her eyes had been open, she had been warned, she had nobody to protest to. She did not know a single soul here. Had not the Counsellor at the Embassy told her in as many words that he would not intervene?

She could consider herself absolved from her promise to M. Laboisserie – whatever this was, it was force majeure. But what good would that do?

There was nothing with which they could charge her that international law would accept. But they didn't have to charge her. They didn't give a damn.

When she did not come home, and no news of her was heard, Arthur would act. It was as well not to think about this, because hopelessness could well be added to helplessness. Meantime, her situation could be a great deal worse: this in itself was ground for hope. She applied herself to stop standing there like a ninny.

The cell-block was clean and quiet, and seemed newish. It

was lofty and there was a small window of thick glass high up on the corridor side. Through this filtered a dim daylight, adequate now that her eyes were used to it. Low down was a grating that admitted air; at the top was a ventilator. The temperature was mild, dry, warmish. This could not be called cruel and unusual punishment. There was no smell, beyond that already noted, faint, of disinfectant. If this was a police station it was well kept. As far as she could make out, there were no bugs or other nasty animals. Just her.

There was little of anything. There was a low concrete block of approximately the dimensions of a bed. Next to the door was a lavatory with no seat. It was clean; she sat on it. The concrete of the floor was smooth, and only slightly dusty. She saw no point in wearing her stockings out, and took them off. There was nothing uncomfortable about bare feet. The walls were painted a medium grey, and recently. They seemed free of scratches or inscriptions. Had she wanted to scratch something she had nothing to scratch with, bar her fingernail.

The block was absolutely silent. Was there anybody in it? She listened, heard nothing. She thought of calling 'Is there anyone there?' and decided against it. If there were, she would learn in good time.

There seemed to be no rule against lying down, and it would be less uncomfortable than sitting on the lavatory. She folded her jacket carefully, with her stockings inside it, to serve as a pillow. She took off her skirt, spread it under her so that it would not get unsightly creases, while keeping her skin off the concrete. In the mild spring temperature, she was not chilled in her cotton vest and knickers. She put her arms down alongside her body, breathed deeply. Nobody turned on bright lights, nobody came and tortured her, nobody came near her. The sensible thing seemed to be to go to sleep, so she did.

She was wakened, perhaps an hour later, by the snap of the peephole in the door and the sudden noise of the lavatory being flushed. Of course – controlled by a tap in the passage. She was left undisturbed. She had wondered why they had left her stockings, but there was no hook or holdfast for her to hang herself, supposing she had wished to. The ventilator grating was too high.

An hour or so later, as far as she could judge, a guard unlocked her door. Youngish, silent, indifferent. He beckoned her out, brought her to the end of the passage, unlocked the door. There was an exercise yard of high grey walls: nothing to see. He handed her a pair of huaracho slippers, worn greasy and much too large, motioned her to walk up and down and take exercise. Hygiene was respected. He paid no attention to her underclothes. He stayed by the door, smoking a cigarette. When he finished it, he killed the butt on his shoe and put it in his pocket. The officer in charge of this jail kept it tidy. He wore what looked an ordinary police uniform, and his trousers were pressed. He had not bothered putting his cap on. After as she judged twenty minutes, he beckoned her in. Twilight seemed to be beginning. He said nothing, put her back in her cell, left her. The walking up and down had done her good. Outside, one or two faint sounds reached her, but seeming far away. A car hooting, a child yelling.

It was beginning to grow dark when he came again. This time he turned the light on in her cell, opened a slide in the door, set up a little folding bracket on the outside. On this he put a plate with some brown beans, a peeled raw onion, a small piece of cheese, a kind of cornpone of roughly-ground maize, and a cup of water. The plate and cup were plain brown enamelled metal, slightly chipped.

"Thank you," she said. He said nothing, but looked at her with no hostility. The beans were tasteless, almost saltless, and she was glad of the onion. The cornpone was good. The water tasted slightly chlorinated. When he came back, he nodded with approval at her eating her food. He let her out. At the top of the passage was a sink with a coldwater tap, and a mop with stiff bristles, and she could do her washing up. He stood there while she worked in her underclothes, but made no effort to touch her. She was grateful for this.

The next time it was another guard; presumably the night shift. Elderly with grey hair, and his cap on. He brought her a light, thin straw mattress, a hard little pillow, a sort of sleeping-bag made of a coarse sheet doubled over and stitched up the side. He watched her through the peephole while she made her bed up and got into it. He turned the light out then, and left her to sleep, in the stillness. From what seemed very far away she could hear a radio playing. Perhaps it was his. There seemed nobody else there in the jail.

In the Lubianka, she remembered having read, one had to sleep with hands outside the blanket. Nobody bothered her here.

He called her in the morning, at dawn. It was rather nice. He opened her door, and beckoned her to bring her bedclothes. Nobody had spoken to her since she had been here. He unlocked the door to the landing and brought her through. There was a cupboard, where she could stack her things on a slatted shelf with a number. She got a broom, and a dustpan and brush. She might sweep her cell out, and the passage. A mop then, and a bucket. He measured a little disinfectant from a tin, and she could fill the bucket at the tap. She mopped inside the lavatory, and he nodded approval. When she had finished the passage, she rinsed the mop and wrung it out, rinsed the bucket and stood it upside down, and she actually got a smile. This police force was as carefully housewifely as in Holland.

Then she was allowed to wash. One of the doors off the landing led to a washplace, with six washbasins and two showers. He opened a cupboard and gave her a piece of gritty soap and a threadbare towel.

"May I have a shower, please?"

"*Si.*" First and only word spoken.

She was frightened because there was no curtain in front of the shower and she was torn between the decencies and wanting dreadfully to wash. But he seemed to understand: he went out, and locked her in. There was only cold water, so she just had to set her teeth. When he came back in she was very shivery and blue, wrapped in the damp towel with her hands crossed in front of her breasts. But to her infinite relief, he brought her overnight case with him. They had packed her a frock, underthings, a toothbrush, even her comb. She could even pin her hair up. He took the case away from her when she brought it back.

"May I wash my other underthings out?"

"*Si.*" It was nice to have a frock on; gave her back some self-respect. She looked for somewhere to hang her wet things. He pointed to the radiator. He was sitting at his table, reading the paper.

On a little electric hotplate, standing on a shelf, was an enamelled metal coffeepot. He went and got her cup from the cupboard, poured her a cup of coffee, and gave her two hard rolls from a paper bag. She was allowed to carry this back to her cell. He had taken her suit and stockings away.

The coffee was thin and bitter, with no milk or sugar, but hot. The rolls were stale. She ate everything.

She stayed locked in, with nothing to do, until a third guard, a broad, chunky one with a boxer's face and a sour expression, came and let her out for 'exercise'. This one did not stay with her. He locked her into the yard and left her there half an hour or more. The sun was shining strongly, but the walls of the yard were too high for it to have penetrated the whole way. There was a hot sunny strip and a cool shady strip, and she alternated the two. She did simple gymnastics with an idea of keeping her blood circulating and her body straight.

Some time around midday the sour one brought her dinner: boiled corn, with some scraps of mutton stew, a piece of bread, a cup of water. In the evening came the young one, with the beans as before and the cheese. Instead of the onion, there was a peeled raw carrot. Well, it was sensible. Whoever had laid down the rules of hygiene had said prisoners needed a fresh vegetable. She preferred the onion, but doubtless it would be there again tomorrow. Perhaps on Sundays there would be an apple. She remembered in another world a woman who had overeaten and promised herself nothing but yoghurt. Well, she had had her piece of cheese. There is nothing in the least unhealthy, she told herself, about this food. I can keep strong, unconstipated, alert. I get an hour outside. What more do I want?

30. Don Juan's advice to the widow

She had done nothing but sleep, so far. There was no complaint she could make about that. A busy time she had had of it, an odtaa time: rest was what she needed. When the 'old' guard woke her at five in the morning she felt fine. Everything happened exactly as it had the day before and this was reassuring. A routine, already. She mopped, this morning, the shower out and 'the office', for which he allowed her a second cup of coffee, and even offered her a cigarette. She refused that, but it was nice of him.

What would happen though, when the shift changed? She would not always be able to count on the delicacy with which he left her alone while she was washing. It was even, she guessed, against the rule. There was at least one more cell-block, whose door was kept shut all the time she was in the office. She saw no other prisoner, but was this by design, or simply good fortune? It seemed likely, even probable, that others would be put in her own block, even were it kept for women. It would be nice to see another woman, if only at the exercise period: would it be allowed? It seemed inevitable that the regulation would be stiffened up. If they kept to the normal turnover of a three-eight shift, the 'young one' would be the next on nights. He had seen her in her underthings and his young indifferent eyes had not changed – but if he used his power to supervise her washing time . . . Suppose this were all done deliberately, to break down her independence and her personality. A few days in solitary, as part of a brainwashing technique. Suppose it were more than a few days . . .

That morning, she had her first taste of what might be in store. Oh, it was nothing; no more than a little 'coup de cafard', a momentary depression, a giddiness that was not to be called anything as serious as vertigo. But showing the way the wind was blowing . . .

She had lain down, the way she was teaching herself, very light, crisp and dry and light as a dead leaf, slowly stretching and loosening one muscle after another into a liquid looseness that would be as weighty and shapeless as one drop of oil after another, stretching her toes and squeezing her insteps, clenching and uncurling her hands, stiffening her neck, arching her back, letting it all go until the drops ran together and made a still calm pool over which flew dragonflies, swallows, a kingfisher . . .

She fell asleep. She had slept quiet and dreamless until this moment, on her front, as draggingly still and comfortable as a dog in the shade . . .

She dreamed. She was here, here in Buenos Aires, at a gala night at the Colon Opera House. She knew, somehow, that this was long ago. Perhaps before the war? Of course, because to her joy Erich Kleiber was going to conduct. He had not yet come on: the theatre was not even full yet, the orchestra was tuning. Kleiber had come here from Berlin, where he was the Chief. Goering had offered him a fantastic contract to stay on, with a huge salary; all in Swiss francs . . . 'Very well' Erich had said, pleasantly, 'I have a free hand of course, with my programmes? Good, the next concert will be entirely Mendelssohn.' Good God, man, said the Reichsmarschall, you can't do that . . . 'No? But in that case – there is a world elsewhere.'

A world elsewhere. Here, here in Buenos Aires. Kleiber had loved it here, loved the criollo style of the Argentinian musicians. Now we are going to do some German music.

It was going to be a lovely evening. She was there in the very centre, in the President's own box, as the President's personal guest. There, up in the enormous dome, was the great chandelier sparkling. When Erich left, at the end of the war, to go back to his beloved Berlin, he pointed up at it and said to the musicians 'Remember. I'll always be up there, looking down at you; listening. And when I'm dead, too . . .'

She was in a very splendid taffeta frock, cut very low, with a necklace and diamond bracelets, her hair specially done, as

President Alvaes' own special guest. He was another great Kleiber fan. If any of the Buenos Aires high society arrived late, as was their detestable custom, he had developed a terrible, killing technique of staring hatingly at them through huge big-game-hunting binoculars.

Oh why didn't Erich hurry up? The musicians were ready. And it was going to be the best of all; it was going to be *Fidelio*.

Something was very wrong. She was up there in the chandelier, and it was cold, and the satin frock pressed tight and cold upon her skin, and the bracelets were too tight, they were hurting her wrists. And she had done something very wrong, she didn't know what it was. She was up there in the chandelier, and the President was staring at her disapprovingly – hatingly – through his terrifying binoculars. Was she dead . . . ?

Bouh: beastly nightmare. You must start again, my girl. Start everything again from the start. She turned on her back, breathed very deeply, unwound everything. The concrete was not cold. It was cool, pleasantly cool.

She was in Paris, sitting at a terrace of some café. They still had the nice old wicker chairs, the marble-topped belle-époque tables with the intricately patterned cast-iron legs. She was waiting for her drink. Lazily she turned the pages of *Le Monde*. Aha, what was this – of interest to whoever lived in Strasbourg . . . 'An illegal traffic exposed' – from our correspondent. 'Raided by the local ecologists' – this sounded entertaining. 'Madame van der Linden, judge of instruction in Strasbourg, yesterday notified Monsieur William Thibault, well-known dealer in furs and leathers in this city, of his inculpation for infringement of the laws in force against all handling in the skins of protected species . . .' Goody, goody: let's hope he now gets pegged for about ten other charges that will bite rather harder. She was herself a protected species, more properly called an endangered species, because protection . . . She was her favourite, the most beautiful of them all, the lynx, the 'Star' – terribly endangered alas, for we are dreadfully vulnerable. We do not have real fear of human beings. Those damned stupid, backward, ignorant peasants with their incurable prejudices. A lynx, they think, slaughters deer . . . There is something very wrong. We live in the forest, in the great forest that used in happier days to cover all of Northern Europe. Before they chopped it all down to build the Invincible Armada. But there is still plenty of forest – why am I in this burning-bare desert? There are Indians, Indians all around me. They make intensely cunning traps, that collapse in upon themselves, that are made of sharply pointed piercing sticks. Whichever way I jump . . .

Another horrible nightmare. She had gone to sleep on her back, it was her own fault.

You must get up. Pace a while. This is a very small cell, and not equipped for pacing. In fact just three metres from the door to the back wall. Four paces; five if I make very small ones. Do not, please, get yourself claustrophobic about these three metres: they are plenty.

Now why had she been dreaming about the desert? And it had been the Arizona desert. Where she had never as much as set foot and of which she knew extremely little. In fact, thinking hard, nothing. Not so very long ago, on television, *Rio Bravo* by Howard Hawks – John Wayne to be sure, but was that the Arizona desert? Mixed up with Arthur being funny about Leslie Howard and Bette Davis, bad beyond belief, in *Petrified Forest*, and an unshaved Bogart with his shotgun across his knees.

But now she had it, and really that explained it all. The 'Don Juan' books, with which Arthur had been considerably taken. Upon her much less impression had been made: 'you are much too French' said Arthur. Not, in other words, with a romantic imagination, like him.

Several things could not be denied. Live in the deserts of Arizona or New Mexico, and Don Juan will begin to make a great deal of sense. Come to that, live anywhere and he has some remarkably sound counsel. Especially, perhaps, to someone in my position, not very keen on this pacing lark, and even less keen on lying down again and having more nightmares. This is not the place to have a coup-de-cafard. Find your spot, ol' Juan would have recommended; sit loose and comfortable on the floor with your back against the wall. If you are not yourself cramped, you have no need to feel cramped.

Have no self-importance. You are full of crappy weaknesses and conceits. Very true indeed. What else? Keep your death constantly present. Mm, that should not be too difficult. Live, said who was it? – someone Spanish?: Saint John de la Cruz? – as though you were going to die tomorrow. Pray, as though you were going to live forever.

Do not have any personal history. Right: these circumstances seem especially well designed for ridding myself of every scrap of personal history.

Keep to no routines. All this bullshit about well, it's midday: it's therefore time to eat. That, here, will be much more difficult, but there are other things that will be easy.

Just go to work, Arlette, on having no self-importance. These guards for instance. There is no point at all in saying 'I like such-a-one': 'I dislike such-a-one because of his nasty boxer's face' – all that is the purest rubbish.

Be a lynx.

They came for her, on the evening of the third day. It might have been about six. The young guard was on. He had put her out for her airing, but she had not had her evening meal. She had been doing Juan-things: 'seeing'; 'stopping-the-world'; 'being-a-warrior'; 'acquiring knowledge'. Jingle, went the keys. Supper, already? – that had gone quick. But instead of putting up the little shelf outside the sliding guichet, he opened the door, said nothing – as usual – but made a slight impatient gesture with his hand, summoning her. Maybe he'd forgotten, and was putting her out for more hygienic yard-work. Maybe she'd forgotten, and hadn't been out at all, that afternoon. She felt sure she had – but perhaps the Juan-technique was more potent than she knew.

But no – back up the corridor, through into 'the office'. A man was waiting for her there. Plain clothes, elderly, smallish, Indian face. Maybe it was Don Juan.

He looked her up and down, nothing nasty; not quite 'cop' either. Without hostility: with a kind of curiosity. He produced the keys to the grille.

"You can come with me."

"Don't I need shoes or anything?"

"No need." He brought her back up the passage and into one of the functional grey rooms she had been in when she came. She did not know whether it was the same. It was absurd to feel anxiety at being taken to the outside. But – where was the next stop? As before, she was bid sit on a stool in front of the table behind which the Indian-looking man installed himself with an air of authority. There was no means of telling what authority he had: he was in shirt sleeves, with an open collar. He had a small, flat leather writing-case, too small to be called a briefcase. From this he drew what she recognized as her *documentación* from her own handbag; the miscellany of passport, cheque book, card-holder, and a stiff-covered black notebook filled with close black handwriting of which she could make nothing upsidedown, even if she had tried. He left her sitting while he consulted this, turning over several pages.

There was another man sitting in the corner, with nothing to say, but he had bright blackish eyes behind glasses with thick dark rims. Well-dressed, this one, in a rich, nicely-cut suit of a bluish-brown colour, a cream shirt, a silk tie with little diamonds, white hands with the nails cut square. Blue-black hair longish, wavy, nicely parted. Agate cufflinks and a square gold wristwatch – he looked too wealthy for either a cop or a government functionary, and she could make nothing of him.

The man at the table had laid down his pen, taken off his glasses, and lit a cigar.

"You have been here three days." It was not quite clear whether this was a statement or a question, so she said nothing.

"Do you consider it as a punishment?" A trick question, plainly, but what was the trick?

"If I have done anything that seems to deserve punishment, I suppose one could call it that," stumbling in Spanish over difficult conditional tenses.

"If it is a punishment, is that an injustice?"

"I don't know. Quisiera – I'd like you to tell me."

"Would you regard it as severe punishment?"

"Well, I was deprived of my liberty, suddenly, with no warning."

"Yes? Go on."

"I feel that some explanation is due to me."

"Yes? You need not feel afraid, to speak out."

"I could make the point that there was no due process, but you know all that already."

"Further?"

"I haven't been ill-treated in any way."

"You mean, physically molested?"

"In no way."

"You asked audience of Colonel Palmer."

"That is correct. I explained my purpose to him."

"Do you expect Colonel Palmer to intervene on your behalf?"

"No. Why should he? I don't expect him to intervene against me, either. As far as I know, he isn't interested in me either way."

"Perhaps the French Embassy?"

"I don't know anyone in the French Embassy. I am French of course, but that doesn't mean much."

"Or General Renard?"

"I scarcely know General Renard. He was kind enough to receive me. We talked for a little."

"You are being given an opportunity to explain yourself. Have you nothing to say? I will take note of your observations; they will be conveyed to the authorities."

"I'd like to be let out, of course, to go about my business. If my business is impossible, I'd like to be told so. Because then plainly I'm wasting my time, and the money of those who asked me to come here."

"No more?"

"That seems to cover it, I think."

"Most people would be eager to make protest, to show indignation, to make vociferous complaint."

"I can't see much point in that. I'm not in the least an important person. I can't see that you'd be interested much, probably."

"You do not ask who I am."

"I have to suppose that your job is to take an interest in strangers, especially those who seem eccentric or unusual."

"Are you the one or the other?"

"Not at all, but I suppose that most visitors don't think of going to ask interviews from important people like Colonel Palmer."

"That will do."

He got up, gathered his things, went through a communicating door to another office, where she could hear a typewriter clacking.

The other man had said nothing at all. He spoke now in a soft-voiced Spanish, without the Porteño accent.

"I am a doctor, Señora. I should like, if you have no objection, to give you a brief simple examination."

"I have no objection."

"Very good. Your health is normal? You have no unusual symptom? You have no chronic or seasonal disability, such as your usual doctor would be aware of? You follow no regular course of treatment? You have been in a hospital or clinic within the last three years? That is all very satisfactory. May I listen to you?" stooping to his bag on the floor, which she had not noticed. "Take your blood pressure? So. As usual, breathe quietly and regularly."

"It is finished. It is for no special purpose. I shall make a little report—like this—" slipping out a memo pad and uncapping a pen, "for the authority, if desired. Stating that upon cursory examination your physical health appears to me good, and that according to my observations your psychological condition is equally sound and balanced. You have a reservation to make?"

"None." He signed his name and tore the sheet off. He gave her a very slight, quiet smile.

'You would like to make your home in Argentina?" he asked politely.

"I haven't seen much of it yet. I should like to be rather better placed to do so."

"We shall hope for that," with formal courtesy.

She had not seen the Indian-man come in. He was standing there looking at her, lizard-face saying nothing. He held a few sheets of typescript.

"This is a summary of the questions put to you and the answers given. Further a brief statement, to the effect that you make no claim upon the help of the State, in accomplishing the purposes of your visit, which is set forth there, in that paragraph. The State, likewise, places no obstacle in your path – there – but takes no responsibility for the success or otherwise of your enterprise – there. Initial the copies and sign them, please. It is useless to ask me whether or no your attempt can be crowned with success: I do not know. Good. That is in order. If the physician has no more to ask you," collecting the other piece of paper, "I shall reaccompany you."

Arlette had thought, innocently, that she would be let go now. No such thing. She was brought back to her cell and wordlessly locked up in it. It is never any use asking Spaniards when such or such a thing is due to happen. Much the same, apparently, hereabouts.

31. How to keep the city in peace

It was, roughly, the middle of the night. How near the middle she could not tell: she had been deeply asleep and not dreaming. The old guard had awakened her by making a soft whistling noise that penetrated gradually. Her cell door stood open, but with his usual kindness he had not switched the harsh cell light on. She saw him in silhouette, from the corridor light. She felt like a Hopi Indian, Emerging into the Fourth World from those hollow reeds in which they had been preserved from the flood that had engulfed the Third World. The silhouette she saw was very likely the god, Masaw. He is the Guardian of the Fourth World.

She crept out of her warm nest, in her vest and knickers, and stood tousled and sleepy on the floor. "Come," he said.

In the office stood a young man in his late twenties, good-looking and very smart in the uniform of a naval officer, with a lock of hair that fell forward on his forehead, like James Bond. He had his lips pursed in a tiny soundless whistle and a permanent half-smiling expression. On one of the metal-tube chairs he had arranged her Lanvin suit, and he was busy with it, shaking out creases and brushing with a clothes-brush. He looked at her with a quizzical kind of expression and said, "This will do very nicely. I beg your pardon; Lynch, Lieutenant Miguel Lynch. Have you stockings, Señora? And her shoes," to the old guard. "Look, I suggest you have just a quick wash, comb your hair you know. Don't put on much make-up. Just enough, you know, to look pleasant." He stood, watching her, while she woke herself up with cold water. He handed her a comb when she was ready for it; as she wanted pins for her hair he had each one ready. He was obviously used to girls, dressing. His half smile did not vary: he handed her her bra, her stockings, her skirt, jacket, shoes. He gave her shoulder a last flip with the clothes-brush where there was a hair, and a scrap of fluff, and said, "There; you look very nice," almost with gallantry. "You don't need a bag. Don't smoke; the General doesn't like it. Let's go, shall we?" She followed, without speaking, without thinking.

In the street he had a Mercedes car, black and shiny and official-looking, with a driver in plainclothes who wasn't Juan Manuel Fangio but looked, anyway from the back, not unlike. The car had white venetian blinds, and these were down. From inside she could see nothing of the streets, but the ride was not long. They got out at a large building, at a side door: it conveyed nothing to her.

At the door was a soldier with a submachine-gun, who saluted smartly: Lieutenant Lynch was a familiar figure. He led her up flights of bare-sounding wooden stairs.

"After eight, the lifts are cut off to save power." They popped through a service door on to a carpeted passage.

"Nourri dans le sérail vous en connaissez les détours."

"That's right," with his ever-ready smile.

There was another sentry in the passage. They went through an anteroom, through a splendid ministerial office there for show – or press conferences – and what looked to be the aides-de-camp's room beyond. Lynch stopped at an inconspicuous door like that of a dressingroom or cloakroom, signed her to pause, slipped through it without knocking.

Arlette felt she was past caring. Plainly another general, or was it an admiral – there were presumably dozens of them, or what was the word 'junta' about? Some goddam secret-police chief, for whom Palmer was only a front, very likely, commanding some bleak penal settlement in the Land of Fire to which she was presumably destined.

Lynch held the door open for her, and slid out deftly. A biggish room, barish. An officer sat writing at a plain wooden table. He did not raise his head, but said with colourless courtesy, "Sit down then, Señora." He was reading down a typed report, annotating in the margin. The walls held shelving, and the shelving was full of files. The window was covered with a venetian blind. The desk lamp was an ordinary metal bureau lamp, the ceiling fixture standard office issue. This must be some secretarial filter, a staff captain commanding paperwork.

He scribbled his initials, pushed the file to one side, raised his head, and Arlette recognized the Chief of State.

Remarkable people have remarkable heads. It is to be presumed that even if you were whipped out of your jail cell in the middle of the night – decidedly confused and perturbed and feeling none too bright – you would still recognize the extraordinary beauty of such a face as Chou en Lai or Sadat. You do not need to be a sculptor. Of most others you would probably say that you needed more time to improve the acquaintance. Arlette was never able to say whether or no General Valentin de Linares was a remarkable person, a mediocre one, or what. She was not given the time for more than the most conventional of masks, the sad, sallow and saturnine visage of ten thousand Spanish army officers. One would be inclined, after, to add caricatural features that were not there at all (like a gold crucifix on a neck-chain and an Errol Flynn moustache), simply because the convention requires them.

He lost no time.

"I have interested myself in the business which, as you told General Renard, brought you here." He did not look like Philip the Second, but had certainly some of the habits of the Prudent King.

"I have had, not without some trouble, this young man identified and interrogated." Mm. What had happened to her in the last three days was unremarked upon. "I do not wish that any person seeking refuge here – and make no mistake, it is a shore of refuge – should be persecuted. Such a person, the purity of whose motives could be shown, has the right to freedom from interference by outside interests."

These were very tedious, very boring remarks, thought Arlette. He looked suddenly at her.

"You gave Colonel Palmer an account of your business. You entertained General Renard with aspects of your personality. Tell me something of your ideas." At this moment Arlette did not think him a mediocre personage, but that might have been sheer vanity.

"I think that men and women ought to be equal," she said. When, after all, would she get another such opportunity? "And I don't mean the sort of crude feminism that abounds everywhere. I believe that no man, however gifted, is complete without a woman. It is a secret. One does not write the biography of Madame de Gaulle or Hendrickje Stoffels. Conversely, without a man, and I mean one man, a woman is not entirely sterile, but I do not believe she'll ever amount to anything much."

The General's eyebrows had gone up a bit, but he smiled without condescension.

"You are not satisfied with the tale of Eve and the apple?"

"Hardly. It sounds to me a tale invented by men, who have always been adept at getting tales believed."

"You are not satisfied with Christianity? You would prefer, perhaps, an Earth Mother?"

"God forbid. A man as a fertilization principle, what a barbaric notion. I hope to die in my faith, just like you. I admit to being a bit heterodox, that's all. A world run by men, General, has not done us very much good, so far. Or even further, since we're plainly in the last stages of decadence." At that he nodded. "We might have just a ghost of a chance still. In the family, but not as it has been, either male- or female-dominated. That is not marriage which is only a union of the flesh, said Saint Somebody. I want a king and a queen upon the throne, and no more popes or ayatollahs."

"It will be difficult to achieve," said the general, seriously.

"Very. I've not got a lot of hope, but it's the only one we have."

"And if it fails?"

"Then the end of the world is very close upon us."

"When I think of it, as I do very frequently, I agree."

"The Indians say, with atomic bombs. Conventionally likely. It doesn't matter much. We have tortured and abused the world we were given: the earth will revenge itself, and the air, and the sea."

"As you say, it does not matter much. But have you thought, of the Last Judgment?" Philip the Second, the Prudent King, thought much of the Last Judgment. "Christ, as he told us, will come again but in majesty, to judge the living and the dead."

"I think he'll spend some time – whatever time means – showing us the incredible obstinacy and stupidity with which we disregard most of what he said the first time, and the imbecility with which we misunderstood the rest."

"He was, however, a man."

"He could hardly be a hermaphrodite."

"Why then, according to your reasoning, did he not marry and found a family?"

"Oh come, General! Our Father who art in heaven!"

"He called himself however the Son of Man." The General seemed quite to enjoy a spot of theology at this hour of the night.

"It's awkward," agreed Arlette, "to marry off a Blessed Trinity. You'll agree though it wouldn't have done, to leave earthly descendants, and go popping off into heaven and just leaving them."

"Your view of matters does not lack merit," said the General, "but I fear that earlier and more rigidly orthodox times would have given you short shrift."

"Oh yes – burned as a witch. It could still happen. France becomes more and more intolerant of anything outside the party line. Will you tell me the difference, General, between Fascism and Communism?"

"Exactly. There isn't any."

"It is left to women, I think, to discover an alternative."

"I am going to bear in mind," said the General, "what you have told me. I must not lose sight of the matter that brought you here," politely, picking up a piece of paper. "We have sifted the matter, with some thoroughness. Weight and measure, you know, is what maintains the town in peace." Is that what you call it, putting me for three days out of circulation? A troublesome woman. A Spanish phrase: *Peso y medida mantienen en paz la villa.* Well. But keep quiet, woman. This isn't the Last Judgment.

"The young man's account of himself is not very satisfactory. I propose to have him put on the plane. Pederasts!" with gloom; "I should like to put them all on a plane."

"But where to? To contaminate Antarctica, and doubtless corrupt the penguins?" He paid no attention to her frivolities, which was as well.

"In your company," finishing and initialling the annotation.

"I am not welcome, in Argentina?"

"You will be, and I hope to be there, to welcome you. Your ideas are a little heterodox: we are, as you are aware, a backward country. We make progress. It is an interminable labour, with interminable details."

"General, General – that's not what is needed. We must have a totally new design."

"I am aware of that," he said sadly, "but I fear that for a

grand design, none of us is man enough. Until," he added, "Christ comes again."

"We will have tried to do our best."

"I try not to forget the parable of the talents." He held out a hand, fine-boned. "*Au revoir*, Madame."

"General, I'm sorry, but you forget that I'm still in jail."

"That can very easily be remedied," ringing the bell. "Miguel," holding out the paper to Lieutenant Lynch, "will you take pains to see that this lady is made comfortable."

It was curious, and to be sure amusing, to see how the head night porter of the grandest hotel in Buenos Aires offered dignified capitulation under honourable terms – rather when you came to think of it like Marshal Pétain – to Lieutenant Lynch.

"This lady is the guest of the government. A good room. You are, I daresay, very full. But you will find one."

"Of course."

"Her luggage will be sent."

"I will have the buttons – I will look after it myself."

"Some nice fruit. We have some good local champagne."

"To be sure."

"I am afraid it is rather late. La señora will not wish to be disturbed in the morning."

"I have made a note."

"I'll ring you, with details of your flight and so on. And I'll have a car sent." It had turned into an Arabian night.

"Thank you," said Arlette timidly.

"A *very* nice room," said the desk-general with unction. His uniform was a great deal grander than that of General Valentin de Linares and he had ribbons upon his impressive breast. He had a splendid head of thick silvery hair, and Arlette felt that with a minimum of encouragement he would tell about his War against Bolshevism on the Russian front.

"I am rather hungry," she said.

"The floor-waiter," – mozo is a low word, not at all applicable – "will make himself a pleasure to serve Madame without delay."

She was brought up into a tower from which, like Rapunzel, she let down her hair. There was a grand glittering view of the harbour and from here at least no smell. The River Plate, which really is a frightful sewer, was from here midnight-blue velvet, and smelled like Schiaparelli. The airconditioning worked by pressing a button. The window opened by pressing a button. The curtains drew by pressing a button. She made foam for herself in the bath; she washed her hair in Formula Carita. The Argentine champagne promoted reckless fantasies. She made a large hearty meal.

Strange to be picking up where she had left off – with overeating. Strange that one's single taste of Buenos Aires nightlife should be sterilized and solitary, exactly like one's taste of Buenos Aires jails. This was really very funny. Would Lieutenant Lynch, who had made honourable amends, perceive just how appropriate it was? And if the jail had been cockroach-infested and vile, would it have made any difference?

Whether you got put in jail, or put in the St Regis Tower, you were disposed of. Both were ways of maintaining the city in peace.

32. Que tiene capa, escapa

"Jesus," said the young man reverentially, "you seem to have a pretty good graft." He wouldn't stay reverential long: in fact he was already shifting on his seat, staring vengeful at the back of the cops who had brought him and had gone to turn his passport over to the marechaussée at the immigration desk, who were putting a lot of ominous rubber stamps in it. Nobody had asked for Arlette's passport.

The airline girls did not quite know what to make of it either. She had been brought by an official car, and they hadn't needed much telling to treat her with consideration. Her booking had been changed to first-class at no extra charge, and they knew what that meant. Whereas this boy wasn't just an undesirable alien being deported, but looked it, which is much worse. His jeans smelt, and he scratched from time to time. And here he was in first-class, even if only as courtesy to the lady, and plainly under her wing.

Arlette, who was nearest to the jeans, was thinking she'd have to wash her hair again, and with 'Marie-Rose' at that. Did it exist still, that sinister bottle with a picture of a nice lady scrubbing a horrid little boy and 'See how they run' printed underneath? She hadn't seen 'Marie-Rose' since she was a little girl at the village school, but ever since long hair came back in, the dear lady was doing a roaring trade.

The boy at first was extremely aggressive.

"I don't want to know what you did or how you did it. Typical bourgeois interference."

"Your family – "

"Fuck my family."

So she kept her mouth shut.

A few hundred kilometres, a few thousand – one didn't go counting them – mellowed him slightly. Drinks helped.

"I don't usually drink. But since it's all free . . . Not bad either, for airline stuff. They want to make a good impression, you see . . ."

"Oh I see."

"You can still get good stuff cheap, if you know where to look. You'll have seen nothing but a few tourist traps. Nothing."

"No, alas."

It got better.

"You know, they are pretty good. I don't know whether you believe all that bullshit about the maricónes. I'm not, myself, pederast, in case you hadn't realized."

"I had, in fact."

"Not that I have to apologize, either way. Police of course do what they want, use the flimsiest pretext or invent one if they can't find one handy. Anything'll do. When it pleases them – to suck up to you with your fucking embassy connections – all those people who were at Normal-Sup with my ever-goddammed papa."

"You are mistaken, as I hope to show you before we reach Paris."

"You don't know it, but there's nothing nicer than an old queen; nothing kinder, more considerate, more unselfish. Just simply kind."

"I do know as it happens."

"I wasn't shacked up with them, you know. Just sheer charity. Like Mother Theresa."

"Really? Eat," she said.

"Yes, I haven't had a square meal since . . . Lousy jail. Boy, do I stink!"

"You do rather, yes."

"It stinks a bit more. But Argentina is exactly like France. Come to that, if you'd ever been clapped in Les Baumettes you'd know a French jail isn't any bunch of violets neither. There is though some attempt at hygiene."

"Yes."

"But on the whole – no difference whatever. Exactly the same fascist crowd. I could tell you a few things, you know, about the French government."

"Gilles – tu sais? – you're preaching to the converted." He still wasn't listening to anything but his own voice.

"I might be able to work up a piece of this. Flog it maybe to the *Nouvel Observateur*. You know the sort of thing – eye-witness stuff from B.A. equivalent of the Santé prison. They all have these wonderful names – like the one in Rome – 'Regina Coeli' – the queen of heaven."

"Until you get to England, and find yourself in Wormwood Scrubs."

"No kidding!"

"I promise you faithfully. But don't – English prison food has you constipated rock-solid inside forty-eight hours. You'd pray for those beans, back in B.A." There was a silence.

"You know about those beans?"

"Oddly enough, I do." But the young find it very difficult to believe that anybody knows anything but themselves.

"America, France, Russia. Sing a song they don't want to hear and they'll clap you in jail just the same. What the hell do they go on about Argentina for?"

But he began looking at her, which was a good sign. This elderly dowdy female – well, perhaps that was a slight exaggeration – what did she know?

"You're not going to tell me you've been in this English jug."

"No. But my husband has."

"Inside?"

"No – prison visitor."

"Oh – a do-gooder."

"That's right," losing patience, "stupid, meddlesome, invincibly ignorant; exactly, in fact, like myself."

"Look – all right; I'm sorry. But don't expect me to sit here overwhelmed with gratitude. I was perfectly well off where I was."

"Yes," said Arlette. "Perhaps. People disappear. They get assassinated on the street. That happens everywhere."

"What d'you know about it?" contemptuously.

"My own husband got shot on the street, that's what I know about it."

"I said I was sorry," deflated.

"People likewise get put arbitrarily in jail, for no reason at all; simply as an administrative convenience – or perhaps to lessen their vanity a little. And this too happens all over the world – on a larger scale in some places than others. And certainly, whatever happens in Argentina is no worse than what happens in Czechoslovakia. If you want to see the world, go there next." There was silence. The plane began its descent. "Lovely Roissy," said Arlette.

She had one more bad moment, which she feared might be an odtaa moment – passing the immigration barrier at the airport. France, land of refuge. Her own passport was handed back without being looked at. The boy's was kept some moments and studied with attention.

"Well," said the boy flippantly, "I leave you here, in the big bad city."

"Come on back with me, Gilles."

"Makes a difference to you, huh? You'll get paid."

"Oh, I consider myself paid. But it will make a difference to you. Your family is an intense annoyance and irritation to you, I realize. But there's not much asked of you. That you should not be lost to them. You don't have to stay, in an atmosphere that makes you sick. You don't have to fight so hard against them either. The same as with the people in Buenos Aires – accept the different sorts of love offered you. Do it for your sister." Unexpectedly enough, he offered no further argument.

She phoned home. To hear Arthur's voice, unfussed and matter-of-fact, was something extraordinary.

"And how was Argentina?" deliberately casual. "Oh go on, stupid, the light's green," to the unwitting driver in front of him.

"It was a very specialized, sterilized slice of Argentina. I really saw very little of it."

"That was one success anyhow." The awkward, self-conscious reunion between the brother and the sister had been spontaneous and touching. "And the adventures in the skin trade, which amount to a whole saga by now – success beyond your wildest dreams."

"I don't want to hear yet. Let me get home, and realize I'm at home. Because I'll be very glad indeed to get home." Successes; failures: what difference was there? Was not the boy perfectly happy there in Argentina? Tomorrow he would be quarrelling with his family. Whatever the saga, would it bring back Solange Bartholdi's son, or do anything at all for her remaining son? Did it help Jacky Karstens' children, learning who their father wasn't? Did it help her, to know or to guess that the police had tipped Henri le Hollandais into the Rhine?

She had done nothing for Sergeant Subleyras. He would have made his own mind up whatever she did. And Xavier . . . God alone knew.

Aunque se hunda el mundo. Although the world collapses . . . After us the deluge: every single generation had always said it. Always the world goes on, whether one hopes or despairs.

She had learned a lot of sententious Spanish phrases, that was all.

Tomorrow there would be more people, more weird letters, confused gabbles on the tape.

One would have to try to do better, that was all.

Arthur listened to her tale. Well, tale . . . Selected pieces of tale, suitably censored for an innocent male audience. He said nothing for a while, though he made a good many faces. Stop making faces! she wanted to say. General Valentin de Linares – by way of being a friend of mine – does not make faces.

"Women!" he said at last, in the deepest of deep bass voices.

"Yes."

"You know, to coin a phrase, there are things in this story fit to frighten the French."

"Yes."

"You actually succeeded in meeting all these generals, and talking to them."

"Well, there was quite a lot of argument with janitors. And, of course, I did get put in jail."

"Why?"

"I don't know. As a sort of administrative convenience? Or as a sort of test. I never will know."

"Appalling."

"I don't know. I got what I went for. At least it wasn't a lot of double-talk, just putting me off. They were accessible, polite, intelligent. The further up one got, the less pious platitudes one encountered. Compare that with the way things would happen in any European country."

"Except that there, one wouldn't get put in jail."

"Maybe not. Maybe something else, nastier still, might happen. Or more likely, nothing at all would happen. Just a great cloud of anaesthetising gas. Isn't that what's wrong with us here? There's an immense amount of talk, but nothing ever happens."

"Yes girl, but good heavens . . . Dreadful place. As the man said, would you like to make your home there?"

"I don't know."

"Have you even read that Amnesty report? Ten thousand people have simply vanished."

"Yes, it's deplorable."

"It's worse than that, it's quite unanswerable."

"Then why d'you want me to try answering it?"

"Women . . ." said Arthur.

It was the cleaning woman, sententious soul, who summed things up. Arlette crawled blearily out of bed, came looking for coffee: there wasn't any.

"I'll make you some fresh. Where have you been then, these last days?"

"Argentina."

"Argentina! But that's said to be a terrible place."

"It was that terrible plane really. Upsets all one's normal rhythms."

"They assassinate people. It was in the paper."

"I suppose it is awful. I don't know, really. Everywhere is awful. We have to begin again everywhere."

"Take my word for it." The expert! "They machine-gun people in the street."

"Do they really?" vaguely, hunting for a teaspoon.

"Dreadful! Now I can remember the Republic, back in Thirty-five . . ." This flow of reminiscence had to be stopped.

"Well, I came back, safe, anyhow, I went on a job, you know, and I even managed to get it done."

"Ah," ominously. "Que tiene capa, escapa!"

"One sees a new place, and one tries to learn. One goes on learning, but I've no idea what."

"Eh oui," said dear old Inocencia, with much solemn gravity, "I'll tell you. One learns that life is hard, what, and as my dear father used to say, that women are expensive."

"What on earth am I to cook for dinner?" asked Arlette.

Nicolas Freeling was born in London and raised in France and England. After his military service in World War II, he traveled extensively throughout Europe, working as a professional cook in a number of hotels and restaurants. His first book, *Love in Amsterdam,* was published in 1961. Since then, he has written seventeen novels and two non-fiction works. His most recent books have been *The Night Lords,* the fourth Henri Castang novel, and *The Widow,* the first in a series about the Widow van der Valk. Mr. Freeling was awarded a Golden Dagger by the Crime Writers in 1963, the Grand Prix de Roman Policier in 1965, and the Edgar Allan Poe Award of the Mystery Writers Association in 1966.

Mr. Freeling lives in France with his wife and their five children.

DATE DUE

SEP 1 1981			
SEP 15 1981			
AUG 8 '83			